Praise for *New York Times* bestselling author Vicki Lewis Thompson

"Vicki Lewis Thompson is one of those rare, gifted writers with the ability to touch her readers' hearts and their funny bones."
—#1 *New York Times* bestselling author Debbie Macomber

"Ms. Thompson does a wonderful job of blending the erotic with romance that is sometimes tender, sometimes funny and always exciting."
—Diana Risso, *Romance Reviews Today*

Praise for *USA TODAY* bestselling author Catherine Mann

"Catherine Mann delivers a powerful, passionate read not to be missed!"
—*New York Times* bestselling author Lori Foster

"Catherine Mann certainly knows how to reach your heart through her characters."
—*Fresh Fiction Reviews*
on *Honorable Intentions*

Praise for *USA TODAY* bestselling author Kathie DeNosky

"[Kathie] DeNosky traces the steps of a marital breakdown with delicacy and understanding."
—*RT Book Reviews*
on *His Marriage to Remember*

"DeNosky's keen touch with family drama and enduring love makes for a great read."
—*RT Book Reviews*
on *Expecting the Rancher's Heir*

VICKI LEWIS THOMPSON

New York Times bestselling author Vicki Lewis Thompson's love affair with cowboys started with the Lone Ranger, continued through Maverick and took a turn south of the border with Zorro. She views cowboys as the Western version of knights in shining armor—rugged men who value honor, honesty and hard work. Fortunately for her, she lives in the Arizona desert, where broad-shouldered, lean-hipped cowboys abound. Blessed with such an abundance of inspiration, she only hopes that she can do them justice. Visit her website at www.vickilewisthompson.com.

CATHERINE MANN

USA TODAY bestselling author and RITA® Award winner Catherine Mann lives in the Florida panhandle with her flyboy husband, their four children, three dogs and one cat (who thinks he's a dog). The Mann family has fostered more than fifty puppies and special needs dogs for their local Humane Society, where Catherine serves on the Board of Directors. More information on Catherine Mann, her work and her adventures in pet fostering can be found online at her website, catherinemann.com, on Facebook (Catherine-MannAuthor) and Twitter (CatherineMann1).

KATHIE DeNOSKY

lives in her native southern Illinois on the land her family settled in 1839. She writes highly sensual stories with a generous amount of humor; her books have appeared on the *USA TODAY* bestseller list and received numerous awards, including two National Readers' Choice Awards. Kathie enjoys going to rodeos, traveling to research settings for her books and listening to country music. Readers may contact her by emailing kathie@kathiedenosky.com. They can also visit her website, www.kathiedenosky.com, or find her on Facebook.

Rescuing Christmas

New York Times **Bestselling Author**

Vicki Lewis Thompson

USA TODAY **Bestselling Authors**

Catherine Mann & Kathie DeNosky

HARLEQUIN®

entertain, enrich, inspire™

ISBN-13: 978-0-373-83768-7

RESCUING CHRISTMAS

Copyright © 2012 by Harlequin Books S.A.

The publisher acknowledges the copyright holders of the individual works as follows:

HOLIDAY HAVEN
Copyright © 2012 by Vicki Lewis Thompson

HOME FOR CHRISTMAS
Copyright © 2012 by Catherine Mann

A PUPPY FOR WILL
Copyright © 2012 by Kathie DeNosky

Recycling programs for this product may not exist in your area.

This edition published by arrangement with Harlequin Books S.A.

For questions and comments about the quality of this book, please contact us at CustomerService@Harlequin.com.

® and TM are trademarks of Harlequin Enterprises Limited or its corporate affiliates. Trademarks indicated with ® are registered in the United States Patent and Trademark Office, the Canadian Trade Marks Office and in other countries.

www.Harlequin.com

Printed in U.S.A.

CONTENTS

Thanks to my animal-loving anthology mates,
Kathie DeNosky and Catherine Mann,
for making this project so rewarding.

Thanks, also, to the hardworking volunteers at
shelters all over the world, as we look forward
to a time of no more homeless pets.

HOLIDAY HAVEN

New York Times Bestselling Author
Vicki Lewis Thompson

CHAPTER ONE

ON MOST DAYS, BEN RHODES enjoyed his job as a cameraman for KFOR, the Tacoma, Washington, TV station that proclaimed *We're here FOR you!* But shooting the six o'clock morning news on this first Monday in December promised to be more fun than usual. They were doing a public service announcement for The Haven, a no-kill animal shelter—and its extremely attractive director, Tansy Dexter. Plus she'd brought dogs.

With her mop of curly black hair, unrehearsed smile and laughing blue eyes, Tansy was a cameraman's dream. She easily outshone the stylized perfection of the KFOR news anchors. But even if she hadn't upstaged them, her canine buddies would have.

She'd walked into the studio carrying a too-cute beige-and-brown shih tzu with button eyes, a red bow on its collar and a face that would melt the hardest heart. Close behind, a little blue-haired lady in a red jogging suit held the leash of a cream-colored Irish wolfhound the size of a small pony. The wolfhound sported a larger red bow on its collar.

The dogs were a brilliant choice. By bringing two such different breeds, Tansy had demonstrated a keen understanding of visual drama.

Anchorwoman Lisa Dunbar moved out from behind the Channel 10 news desk and over to the studio set where they'd be shooting the segment. The set featured three dark green easy chairs, a five-foot artificial Christmas tree and a dark wood coffee table topped with a small red poinsettia. Lisa took the center chair.

While Tansy was being fitted with a mike, she talked soothingly to the small dog. After that she was directed to the chair on Lisa's right, and the grandmother type, who had no mike, was settled on the left. The regal wolfhound claimed a sizeable chunk of real estate on the floor. Head up, he kept a close watch on Tansy.

Station manager Paul Huntington had a soft spot for The Haven because his family had adopted their beloved golden retriever, Sadie, from there a year ago. He'd instructed Ben and the other two cameramen to get as many adorable doggie shots as possible to convince viewers to donate or adopt. Ben planned to follow Paul's directions, but Tansy was so expressive that she'd probably generate as much support as the dogs. In his opinion, faces like hers justified the invention of cameras.

Then again, maybe he was biased. He'd spent so many years training his lens on carefully made-up women like Lisa that Tansy was a refreshing change. Dressed in jeans, sneakers and a blue sweatshirt with the shelter's logo on the front, she seemed genuine and approachable.

Lisa, blonde and elegant in a gray silk suit and a Christmas-red blouse, was the more classically beautiful of the two. But she was also addicted to the spotlight. He wondered if she'd ever competed with animals for center stage. In his experience, the animals won every time.

When everyone was seated, Lisa responded to a cue from the station's director and looked into the camera with practiced ease as she introduced Tansy. "She's brought some friends along," Lisa added. "One of her many dedicated volunteers, Rose Parker, and a dynamic doggie duo." She turned to Tansy. "I hope both these doggies are available for adoption, because I just got a signal from our director that the phones are lighting up."

"They're available, Lisa." Tansy's smile was effortless. "This little guy is Ewok. He's four years old and mostly shih tzu, but we think he might have some cocker spaniel in him, too."

Lisa beamed at the small dog. "What a perfect name. He looks just like those creatures in *Star Wars*. How're you doing, Ewok?"

The little dog stood on Tansy's lap and wriggled happily as he focused his dark button eyes on Lisa.

"Oh, he wants to come to me!"

Tansy laughed. "He might, at that. He loves people. But I'd better keep him over here. Your suit looks expensive."

"I'm sure it could survive a few paw prints."

"Let's wait until he's adjusted to his surroundings."

Lisa managed a tight smile. "That's fine. He's so adorable I'm sure he'll have a home before we wrap up this segment. I'm tempted, myself."

"Ewok could have been adopted a dozen times since he came in, but we're determined he won't leave the shelter without his pal over there, Wookie."

Lisa glanced at the wolfhound. "Ah, I get it. Ewok and Wookie. George Lucas would be thrilled. What's their story?"

"They grew up together and now they're inseparable," Tansy said. "To place them in different homes would really stress them out."

Now Ben understood why the dogs had been brought

in together and why Wookie's attention was firmly on Tansy. She was holding his best pal.

Their story was touching, even to Ben, but he'd decided long ago that adopting a dog or cat was asking for heartache.

"Goodness, that's a challenge," Lisa said. "My little condo wouldn't hold Wookie, I'm afraid."

"He doesn't need as much indoor space as you think."

Lisa chuckled. "No more than a MINI Cooper, at any rate." She turned back to Tansy and Ewok. "I'll put a bug in Santa's ear to give Ewok and Wookie a new home for Christmas."

"Great. And while you're at it, please tell Santa we have plenty of other loving dogs and cats looking for homes."

"Absolutely! We'll be featuring pictures of your cuties right up through Christmas Eve to promote The Haven's Home for the Holidays campaign. Can you fill us in on the details?"

"You bet." Tansy quickly outlined her plan to place as many animals as possible in homes just for the holidays so they wouldn't have to spend the festive season at the shelter. "It's like giving them a Christmas break," she said.

"What a wonderful idea," Lisa said. "I'm sure the residents of Tacoma will respond, especially because it also gives them a chance to try out a pet before making that forever commitment."

"Exactly. But if people can't take an animal over the holidays, I hope they'll consider donating to our Christmas fund-raising campaign."

"Your press release said you're raising money for a special project?" Lisa said.

"We are! We recently removed sixty cats from a

hoarding situation. We couldn't accommodate them in our Kitty Condo, which is our free-roaming cat facility, so they're temporarily being housed in a portable building on loan from a generous donor. So we desperately need to build a second Kitty Condo for our new furry friends." As Tansy became more animated in describing the proposed facility, Ewok put his paws on her chest and began licking her face.

Laughing, she tried to coax him back down onto her lap as she continued. "We're hoping that by Christmas Eve… Ewok, now stop!"

But the little dog was determined to give her kisses, and it was great television. Directions came through Ben's earphones to keep his camera on Tansy. He was only too happy to oblige.

"We hope we'll have the money we need to… Ewok, honestly!" Tansy dissolved into laughter again.

Watching her through the lens of his camera, Ben was fascinated. He'd been intrigued when she'd entered the studio, but her amused struggle with the affectionate little dog captivated him so completely that he forgot the time, forgot the studio, forgot everything but the joyful woman captured in his camera lens.

She was love personified, and a longing to have even a tiny bit directed at him stole the air from his lungs. But he'd learned the hard way to beware that telltale ache. Love was great when you had it, but when it disappeared, the pain brought you to your knees. He'd paid a high price to learn that lesson and wasn't about to forget it.

"Let me have him so you can talk." Leaving her chair, Lisa swooped in and gathered Ewok in her arms.

More instructions came through Ben's earphones. "Follow the dog."

He panned from a rather startled Tansy to a smug Lisa. An outsider might view Lisa's move as an attempt to be helpful. But after observing her since she was hired eighteen months ago, Ben recognized her bid to retake center stage. By holding Ewok, she had it.

"Such a cute little doggie!" She hugged and nuzzled him as if hoping he'd start to lick her, too. Instead Ewok squirmed, obviously wanting to escape. "Go on, Tansy," Lisa said. "I have this sweetie under control."

Ben didn't think so. He widened the shot to include Tansy as Lisa continued to maul the dog.

Tansy gave Ewok a worried glance before clearing her throat. "The bottom line is that we're asking the residents of Tacoma to open their hearts, their homes and their wallets so the animals can have a special holiday and an even better New Year. And we appreciate KFOR's support. The station's always been good to The Haven, but helping promote our holiday campaign goes above and beyond."

"And we're happy to do it." Lisa hugged the shih tzu tight. "After all, we're here FOR…" She paused and her eyes grew wide. With a shriek, she tossed Ewok from her lap onto the coffee table.

"Cut! Cue the commercial!" The command came through Ben's earphones a second after he'd already stopped filming.

Tansy made a grab for Ewok, but the spooked dog dashed across the large coffee table, knocking over the poinsettia and spilling dirt everywhere. Jumping out of her chair, Lisa gestured to the dark stain on her silk skirt. "The little bastard peed on me!"

God, it was hard not to laugh, but Ben loved his job, so he controlled the impulse. Still, Lisa had deserved it. Tansy had tried to save her, but she hadn't listened.

"Ewok!" Tansy dashed after the tiny dog, darting through a maze of camera trolleys and cables.

Ben took off his headset so he could help. By pure coincidence the little bundle of fur ran past him. He made a grab and connected with a warm body. Holding Ewok against his chest, he tried to calm the frightened dog.

"Thank you." Tansy stood in front of him, her blue eyes no longer laughing. "Sometimes he gets overexcited and lets loose. I think that's the cocker spaniel in him. Wookie's usually a steadying influence, but with all the people, and the lights, and the noise…"

And the idiot woman squeezing the breath out of him. But Ben was too much of a professional to say that about a colleague. "Bringing them in together was a brilliant idea, though." He handed Ewok to her. "I hope you find a home for them."

"So do I." She stroked the quivering dog with a gentle touch. He whined and reached up to lick her face again. "It's okay, Ewok. You're fine now. We'll go get Wookie and you'll feel better."

"Adopting them out as a pair is the right thing to do," Ben said. "Stick to your guns on that."

"Don't worry. I intend to." She glanced up and her gaze held his. "You're an animal lover, I can tell." She didn't voice her next thought, but it was there in her eyes. Would *he* take the dogs?

He pretended he hadn't understood her silent question. He did love animals…from a distance. So many people took on pets with a breezy nonchalance, as if loving creatures with a short lifespan was an easy choice that had no consequences. He knew from experience that wasn't true. He wasn't about to explain all that to her, though, so he said nothing.

She blinked as if confused by his silence. "In any event, thanks for capturing Ewok. It's not good for him to race around in a panic."

"It's not good for any of us to race around in a panic." He smiled because looking at her made him want to do that. He swore she had flecks of sunshine in those blue eyes of hers. In Tacoma, where it rained a lot, sunshine in any form was a valuable commodity.

"Guess not." She continued to gaze at him intently. "Have we met before? You look so familiar."

"We haven't met. I would have remembered."

"On the air in five!" called the director.

Ben replaced his headset. "Sorry. Gotta go. Weather's next."

"Right. Thanks again." She hurried away, taking the sunshine with her.

Ben concentrated on filming the weather report and did his best to forget about Tansy Dexter. He preferred his relationships light and breezy—easy come, easy go. And his instincts told him Tansy would expect much more than that.

Judging from the passionate way she spoke up for the animals, her emotions ran deep, deeper than he cared to go. He was glad that people like Tansy existed in the world, but he couldn't follow her chosen path, and she would never understand his decision not to adopt.

She was the kind of woman who would get past his defenses, demand that he drop his guard and become vulnerable again.

There was no way he would risk that.

TANSY'S SUBURBAN HAD been retrofitted for hauling animals. After she and Rose loaded Wookie and Ewok into the back, they hurried around to the front of the vehicle and climbed in, their breath fogging the air. Tansy dug out the keys and coaxed the balky engine to life before switching the heater to high. The cold rain tapping on the windshield could easily turn to snow by nightfall.

Rose rubbed her hands together and held them against her wind-reddened cheeks. "That was interesting."

"It wasn't Ewok's fault." Tansy's anger resurfaced as she left the station's parking lot. "I had to be nice, especially since Paul's running promos from now until Christmas, but I could have throttled that woman."

"She almost throttled Ewok," Rose said. "Good thing she didn't pursue the idea of adopting these two."

"Yeah, that would have been awkward. You and I know she'd only have been doing it as a publicity stunt, but Paul might not have seen it that way. He's a nice guy, and I'd rather not lose his goodwill by refusing to give his publicity-crazed anchorwoman Ewok and Wookie."

"Speaking of nice guys, that cameraman was helpful."

"He was." Tansy's pulse beat a little faster thinking about his sexy brown eyes.

"And gorgeous."

Tansy glanced over at Rose and grinned. "You noticed that, did you?"

"I may be old enough to be his grandmother, but that doesn't mean I can't appreciate tall, dark and handsome when I see it. If I'm not mistaken, you two shared a moment."

Tansy's cheeks warmed. She hoped she hadn't looked quite as dazzled as she'd felt. "I was trying to mentally place him."

"Don't blame you. Was he on a beach towel in the sand or on a bearskin rug in front of the fire?"

"Rose!" Tansy laughed, bringing an excited bark from Ewok. "I was trying to figure out why he looks so familiar. I swear we've met before."

"Did you tell him so?"

"I did, but apparently we haven't met. He said he would have remembered." Sexual heat curled through her as she thought about the low, intimate way he'd said it.

"Whew!" Rose fanned herself. "A guy who knows how to deliver his lines. And he wasn't wearing a ring. I checked. What's his name?"

"Don't know."

"Why on earth not?"

"Didn't think to ask."

Rose slapped her forehead. "You meet a hero type who rescues precious little Ewok, a man who says he would have remembered if you'd met before, and you neglect to get his name?"

"I'm out of practice with that kind of thing." Though now Tansy wished she had a name to attach to the first man in ages to arouse her dormant libido.

"I know you're out of practice. I've volunteered at the shelter for almost two years, and I don't think you've had so much as a date, let alone a romance. I figured you were either too busy or very picky."

"I'm both."

Rose nodded. "I realize your work brings you joy, and there's nothing wrong with being picky. But FYI, you and that cameraman were giving off sparks." She pulled a phone out of her small messenger bag. "I'm going to call the station and find out his name."

"No!" Then her panic turned to laughter. "Okay, you got me. Very cute, Rose. You don't have the number."

"Yes, I do." She hit a button on her phone. "Yesterday

you asked me to double-check when we were supposed to arrive. The number's still in my phone."

Tansy groaned. She'd forgotten about that. "Rose, hang up. Seriously."

"No worries. I'll just say that The Haven wants to send him a personal note for his part in recapturing Ewok."

"That's a flimsy excuse. Please don't—" But Tansy was wasting her breath. Rose was already talking to someone at KFOR.

"Yes, I mean that quick-thinking cameraman who saved little Ewok after he escaped. We want to send him a note of thanks. Ben Rhodes? Got it."

Nice name, but Tansy couldn't connect it to the dim memory she had of seeing him somewhere before.

Theoretically, Rose should be hanging up now that she'd found out his name, but for some reason she was still talking. "Really? That's too bad." She paused. "Well, if you're considering sending someone out, I can't think of a better choice than Ben Rhodes, if he's available."

Tansy's eyes widened as she glanced over at Rose, eyebrows raised.

Rose pretended not to notice. "Well, good. I hope it works out. I'll check with Tansy. 'Bye."

"You'll check *what* with Tansy? What are you up to, Rose Parker?"

The volunteer's expression was smug as she tucked the phone back into her purse. "You remember those candid photos of the animals you gave them so they'd have something for the promo spots?"

"Yes. I know they aren't great, but it was all I had."

"They didn't pass muster, so they want to send one of their cameramen out to take some better shots."

"And you suggested Ben." She tried to sound disapproving, but that was difficult when she was short of breath and squiggles of excitement were dancing through her system.

"Yes." Rose settled back in her seat with a smile. "He'll be perfect."

CHAPTER TWO

PERFECT. THE WORD CERTAINLY described Ben as Tansy opened the front door of the yellow-and-white Victorian that The Haven used as its administration building. She and Ben had agreed on an early Saturday morning appointment, and she'd turned on the white Christmas lights outlining the house to banish the gloom.

Against the backdrop of those sparkling lights, he looked ruggedly handsome in jeans, boots, a sheepskin jacket and a brown cowboy hat. The scent of the fresh pine wreath hanging on the door came in with him, along with the tang of frost and his minty aftershave.

Tansy greeted him as nonchalantly as she could, considering they were alone for the first time and her heart tap danced with excitement. She'd suggested giving him a tour before The Haven opened for the day, which meant that even Faye, the receptionist, wasn't around.

"Good morning." Tansy extended her hand and Ben pulled off a leather glove to shake it. "Where's your equipment?"

"Left it in the Channel 10 van." His grip was warm and firm, but the brim of his hat cast his face into shadow, making his expression difficult to read. "I wanted to get the lay of the land first."

"Of course. No sense in lugging everything around until you're ready to start." When he let go of her hand, she resisted the impulse to press it against the butterflies circling in her tummy.

Stepping around him, she relocked the door. "I can't tell you how much I appreciate this. I knew my pictures weren't very good. Photography isn't my strong suit."

"Maybe photography isn't, but I can already tell this is." He walked into the reception area. What had once been the house's living room was now divided by a waist-high counter. Two desks and several filing cabinets occupied the larger space behind the counter. In front of it, two sturdy wooden armchairs and a low table created a seating area, and a coat tree stood in the corner.

Ben's gaze lingered on a small artificial tree sitting on the counter. Its only decorations were a strand of multicolored lights and white angel donation cards hanging from the branches. A small sign invited visitors to choose a card and donate the item listed on it.

Unhooking one of the angel-shaped cards, he tucked it in the pocket of his coat. "That angel tree's a good idea. Paul said you've made astounding progress at The Haven since you were hired three years ago."

"He's giving me too much credit. None of this would have been possible without a generous benefactor who donated this land, including both houses, when he died."

"According to Paul, that benefactor was inspired by your enthusiasm for the animals. So you'll have to take some of the credit, Tansy."

Hearing her name spoken in his deep baritone sent a shiver of delight up her spine. "What can I say? I love my work."

"Obviously." He walked over to a bulletin board mounted on the wall to the right of the seating area.

Tilting his hat back with his thumb, he scanned the array of snapshots.

"More bad pictures, I'm afraid," she said.

"Not so bad. The idea of putting up pictures of folks with their newly adopted animals is terrific. You just need a better camera."

"No, I need a better photographer."

Ben scanned the pictures. "Don't sell yourself short. I see potential there." He turned back to her. "So The Haven ended up with these two houses, and you designated the bigger one as your headquarters."

"That's right. It's mainly office space except for a couple of rooms we use as temporary holding areas for incoming animals. There's not much to photograph in here."

"Are you also housing animals in the blue Victorian next door?"

"No, that's where I live, along with whatever animals I'm fostering at the moment. Right now it's Ewok and Wookie."

His eyebrows rose. "No one's taken them?"

"Not yet." She did her best to breathe normally, but her chest was tight with the thrill of seeing him again. "I had hoped their TV appearance would help, and by the way, the camera work on that segment was wonderful. Paul said a good part of it was your doing."

"Animals make great TV."

"Only if the person behind the camera has a feel for them. You do."

He met her gaze. "Thank you. That's nice to hear, but it didn't result in a home for Ewok and Wookie. I'm sorry about that."

She gulped and resisted the urge to fan herself. He was potent. "Many dog lovers prefer a certain size. They want small, big or in between. The big and small combo takes some getting used to. But I'm not splitting them up. Someone will come along." Once again she wondered if maybe Ben would adopt them.

She'd developed a reputation for being able to match animals with their ideal human companions, and her instincts told her Ben would be perfect for those two dogs. He appeared to have the calmness Ewok needed and the athleticism to play with Wookie.

But there was something else, something more subtle that she'd picked up from watching the television clip. He obviously saw the dogs as creatures worthy of notice and respect. Not everyone did, and it was a trait she admired.

She really hoped he'd take Ewok and Wookie, but for some reason he wasn't rising to the bait. Maybe he needed help to figure out that these dogs were meant for him. "Do you have any animals at home?"

"Nope."

She was taken aback by his definitive tone. "Not interested?" Her spirits spiraled downward.

He shook his head.

She waited for an explanation. When none came, her disappointment bloomed out of all proportion to the situation. She wanted to blame Rose, who had woven fantasies all week long about how Ben could be her Prince Charming.

But she was a grown woman of twenty-eight who shouldn't allow anyone to plant ideas in her head. And they'd both been wrong about Ben. He could be the most desirable man in the world, but if he didn't want to share his life with companion animals, he was not the guy for her.

Animals were her life, had been ever since she was

a little girl. Although it might sound corny, she felt that she had a calling to love and protect them. The concept of euthanizing those deemed unadoptable was blasphemy to her, which dictated that she had to work for a no-kill shelter.

Rose's instincts and that wonderful film clip to the contrary, Ben wasn't willing to offer his home to an animal, and he wouldn't reveal why. She couldn't imagine having a close friendship, let alone a romantic relationship, with someone who had that attitude.

She had to write him off as her prince and quit daydreaming. He was here to do a job, and once he had, she'd put him totally out of her mind.

"All the photo ops will be in the buildings out back," she said. "Let me get my coat, and I'll show you the—whoops, hello, Max." She turned to greet the orange tabby that appeared unexpectedly, hopping up from behind the counter. "I'm surprised you made an appearance, kitty-cat."

Max sat on the tan Formica, tail curled around his haunches as he fastened his green-eyed gaze on Ben.

"Max is our office cat," Tansy explained. "Most people think that's funny because office cats are supposed to be friendly and Max certainly isn't. He takes aloofness to a whole new level. If I were to try and pet him now, he'd probably walk away. He's never checked out a visitor, either."

A soft rumble came from Max's chest.

Tansy stared at the cat, who continued to focus on Ben. "Now you're *purring?* What's up with that?" She looked over at Ben. "Max hardly ever purrs."

"Maybe I remind him of somebody he used to know."

"I suppose that's possible. He was a stray, so we don't know his story. Since he's both standoffish and neurotic, it's unlikely he'll be adopted, so we've designated him as our unfriendly office cat."

"What's neurotic about him?"

"When he's stressed, he'll chase his tail and chew on it. Sometimes we have to bandage it and make him wear the cone of shame so he won't chew the bandage." Tansy shook her head and sighed. "But I love him, anyway."

"That's why you're good at your job. You probably have something you love about every dog and cat in the place."

"I do. They're each special in their own way, even curmudgeons like Max." She consulted the clock hanging on the wall. "But enough about that. We'd better get moving if we're going to have any time at all for you to take pictures this morning."

"And I want to make sure I get them before the morning naps start."

"Good thought. Let me get my coat and we'll be off."

So he knows animals tend to grab a midmorning nap. She thought about that as she walked around to her desk and picked up the dark blue parka she'd draped over the back of her chair. He might not want animals in his house, but he was familiar with their habits.

She shoved her arms into the sleeves of her coat and glanced down as she fumbled with the zipper. When she had it engaged, she raised her head, intending to tell Ben to follow her down the back hallway to the rear door.

Her breath caught. He stood at the counter scratching behind Max's ears. Nobody scratched behind Max's ears. He never allowed it.

But the cat was relishing the attention now, and Ben was a natural at giving that attention. Tansy could tell when someone wasn't used to interacting with animals—their movements were hesitant and awkward.

Ben might not have any animals now, but he'd been close to at least one cat in the past, a cat he'd loved. Maybe she shouldn't put much stock in that, but…she did.

Turning away so Ben wouldn't catch her staring, she zipped her parka in one noisy motion. By the time she finished, he'd moved away from the counter and Max, who still seemed mesmerized by the man in the sheep-skin coat and cowboy hat. Now she was really curious about what had happened to Ben that kept him from wanting pets. If she kept her eyes, ears and even her heart open, she might be able to find out.

Taking a deep breath, she met his gaze. "Ready to explore The Haven?"

"Lead the way."

"We'll visit the cats first." She'd thought maybe Ewok and Wookie would touch him the most, but per-haps not. If he could warm up to Max, then he'd be a sucker for the sweethearts he was about to meet.

IN THE GRAY LIGHT OF DAWN, Ben followed Tansy out the back door of the house to the lighted buildings behind it. He hoped she hadn't noticed him petting Max, be-cause she might read too much into it. He should have resisted the impulse.

But Tansy's comment that Max wouldn't let anyone pet him had been a challenge. He'd wanted to test that, especially because Max had looked at him exactly the way his childhood cat, Mickey, used to, with a silent plea for attention.

Mickey had only been able to make that plea with one eye instead of two because he'd lost the right one in a fight. Ben later learned that male cats should be neutered so they wouldn't fight or breed. But as a kid he hadn't known that, and his aunt and uncle certainly wouldn't have wanted the expense of a vet bill.

So he'd allowed Mickey to roam the streets of whatever town they moved to in their vagabond life. Max looked so much like Mickey that if Ben believed in kitty reincarnation, he'd wonder if Mickey had somehow come back in the body of this cat. With his eye repaired.

Didn't really matter if he had, though. Mickey's life had been cut short by a car. He'd been ten—not so bad, actually, for a cat, especially an outdoor one. Ben had heard of indoor cats like Max making it past twenty, or even twenty-five, but that still wasn't long enough to suit Ben. He wasn't into long-lived animals like parrots or tortoises, so he was better off staying out of the game.

Scratching behind Max's ears had felt achingly familiar, though. This gig was already testing his resolve not to form attachments. But petting one orange tabby wasn't the same as forming an attachment, he told himself. It changed nothing.

A light snow the night before had turned to slush, but someone had shoveled the lighted walkway that led from the back of the house to a couple of octagonal buildings. A signpost pointed left to the larger one, christened the Doggie Digs, and to the right for the smaller octagon named the Kitty Condo. Beyond that stood a boxy portable building that must be where the cats from the hoarder were being kept.

The signs designating the cat and dog areas were cute but unnecessary. A chorus of barks from the larger octagon would have clued him in.

"It's feeding time." Tansy paused and glanced toward the Doggie Digs. "One of the high points of their day, obviously."

"I'm partial to a good meal, myself."

She graced him with one of her million-dollar smiles. "Me, too."

And here he was, once again gazing at her expressive face and wishing…what? That he could figure out some stupid reason to spend more time with her? So he could become dependent on that smile for his happiness? No way.

"I should buy you lunch sometime, to thank you for doing this," she said.

"That's a generous offer." Was she asking him out? If she was as interested in him as he was in her, it would be hard to keep her at arm's length. "But I hope you don't think I volunteered my time for this. The station's paying me."

"Well, sure, I thought they probably were, since they insisted on sending someone out to get better shots. But even so, you're giving up your Saturday morning."

"I don't mind." And that was the crux of his dilemma. He'd looked forward to coming out here. Professional pride had something to do with it, because he liked the idea of improving on the photos she'd provided. But he'd also just wanted to see her.

Maybe he'd hoped that she wouldn't be as appealing today as she had been on Monday. Wrong. She fascinated him more than ever. He couldn't figure out how she maintained her bright optimism given the realities of her job. How could she love these animals with all she had when she knew that loving them would also bring pain?

"Sorry." She gave him an apologetic glance. "I'm wasting time gabbing about lunch instead of giving you the tour I promised. Do you have any questions so far?"

He had a million of them, all about her and how she

had come to be the person she was. But that would invite questions about himself, and she would want him to reveal things he'd kept hidden for years. "No questions," he said. Then he decided that sounded abrupt. "I take that back. What about the shape of these buildings? I've never seen an octagon used for an animal shelter before."

She brightened. "Aren't they amazing? We built the Doggie Digs first. We borrowed the octagon concept from a no-kill shelter in Utah called Best Friends Animal Society. I spent a week there and was so inspired. The design allows us to have a central area for organizing food and meds. The pie-shaped enclosures branch out from the center."

Ben nodded. "Looks efficient."

"It is. Once we saw how well it worked, we used the same design, slightly modified, for our Kitty Condo." She walked toward the door leading into the cat building. A sign warned Caution, Loose Cats. She opened it a crack and warm air spilled out. "All clear?"

"All clear," called a female voice from the other side of the door. "I'm cuddling Brutus, and he's the only one out here right now."

Tansy opened the door wider and stepped inside. "Good. I've brought the cameraman from KFOR."

Ben followed her through the door and closed it again. The octagonal room was about the size of an average kitchen and resembled one, too, with its countertops, cabinets, refrigerator, washer and dryer. There was no stove, but he noticed a microwave and a toaster oven. Both the washer and dryer were running.

"Ben Rhodes, meet Cindy Stanton, one of our valuable weekend volunteers. Cindy's a senior in high school, so her weekdays are full, but she comes over every Saturday and Sunday morning to help feed the cats and scoop the litter boxes, even when it's cold and dark outside."

"I want to be here, no matter what the weather is." Cindy, a lanky teenager with a blond ponytail, was wearing a practical outfit of jeans and a long-sleeved rock band T-shirt. She sat on the floor cradling a small black cat with white tuxedo markings. She glanced up at Ben with interest. "Nice to meet you, Mr. Rhodes. Is it okay if I don't move? Brutus finally settled down, and I—"

"Please don't get up." Ben crouched down, reached over and gently stroked a finger down Brutus's soft fur. "He's young."

"He's young and he's a maniac. I'm working to socialize him so he won't bite and scratch people."

Ben looked closer and noticed small red welts on the backs of Cindy's hands. "That's dedication."

"That's love. I adore this little guy. My whole family's allergic except me, or I'd take him home in a second." She grinned. "Actually, I'd take a *bunch* of them home. When I get my own place, I'm so going to have lots of cats, and maybe foster, too."

"I'm going to hold you to that," Tansy said, a smile in her voice.

"No worries. I can hardly wait." She glanced at Ben, who was still stroking the cat. "I'm *so* glad KFOR is helping us with this campaign and that they sent you to take some pictures. Nothing against you, Miss Dexter, but you really need better ones for the promo spots. What they used this week? Kinda lame."

Tansy laughed as if she wasn't the least bit insulted. "I know."

Cindy returned her attention to Ben. "So where's your camera?"

"I left it in the van. I wanted to get my bearings before I started shooting."

She nodded. "Makes sense, but you might as well go back and get it before you head into one of the cat rooms."

"Oh?" Ben continued to run a finger along Brutus's silky fur. He'd forgotten the pleasure of such a simple caress. "Why is that?"

"Have you ever been in a roomful of cats, cats with toys and branches to climb on, not to mention tunnels, and shelves and all that stuff?"

"Can't say that I have." He was intrigued by the concept. "Don't they fight?"

Cindy gave a shrug. "Not so much."

"But they do fight sometimes," Tansy said. "We watch for that and only allow the aggressive ones in for short visits until they settle down."

"Even if they fight a little," Cindy said, "it's still *so* much better than cages."

Ben levered himself to his feet. "Then I'd better go get my camera."

"Good." Cindy seemed pleased with that decision. "If you don't, you're gonna kick yourself, because you'll get in there, and one of the cats, like Moppet or Nifty, will be doing something adorable, because they are *constantly* doing funny stuff, and you'll miss it."

Tansy unzipped her parka as if she meant to stay here while he retrieved his equipment. "I didn't think to ask," she said. "Are you going to take video or stills?"

"Both, but if I get something with the video camera, I'll use a single frame, not a sequence. We're only putting one shot up on the screen at a time."

"Which is why they have to be really *fantastic* shots," Cindy said.

"Yeah, yeah, I get it." Tansy shoved her hands into the pockets of her jacket and smiled at him. "We need someone with a magic touch."

Ben's heart lurched. Unless his instincts were wrong, she was flirting with him. The invitation in her eyes was subtle, but his response wasn't. He wanted to accept the invitation. Good thing Cindy was there, because he had no business accepting anything from Tansy.

But that didn't stop his traitorous mind from imagining what it would be like to step closer and cradle her face in both hands. And then he'd kiss her, very gently, taking it slow at first. After that—

"Ben, do you want me to go with you? I think you can find your way easy enough. There's a sidewalk that leads around the house to the parking lot."

He snapped out of his dangerous daydream. "Not if you have something to do here."

"There's always something to do here. There are path lights, but if you want me to show you I'll be happy to go along."

"I'm sure I can find my way. It's getting lighter every minute. I'll get my equipment and be right back." He slipped out the door, cursing himself for being a fool. Kissing Tansy would be a huge mistake, both personally and professionally.

He was a cameraman on a job, and that did not include getting cozy with the subject. He could get fired for that, and rightly so. But even without considering his job security, he couldn't afford to get carried away.

Kissing her would open him up to God-knows-what. Yes, he was drawn to her and wanted to find out what made her tick. But then she would demand to know what made *him* tick, and he wasn't about to let her or anyone get that close. If she tempted him, he'd just have to get over it.

CHAPTER THREE

"I LIKE BEN. HE'S CUTE." Cindy held Brutus in the crook of her arm as she carefully got to her feet. The little cat worked his way up to nestle against her shoulder but didn't try to squirm away.

"I suppose." Tansy congratulated herself on that neutral response when two minutes ago she'd been on the verge of flinging herself into Ben's arms. Cindy had been an excellent chaperone, for which Tansy was grateful. Mostly.

She took off her parka and hung it on a hook beside the door before walking over to check the towels in the dryer. Ben was not immune to the charms of animals. She'd known that from the way he'd cradled Ewok against his chest on Monday morning, and today he'd voluntarily made overtures to both Max and Brutus. Ben was a real puzzle, one she desperately wanted to solve.

"I think he likes you."

Tansy ducked her head and began pulling towels out of the dryer because she didn't want Cindy to see her blush. "He's just a friendly person doing his job."

"Maybe so, but when he looks at you, there's more than friendship going on. You may have missed it because you haven't been dating recently. I have, and I know that look."

Tansy folded towels as if her life depended on it. "Have you been talking to Rose, by any chance?"

"As a matter of fact, she called me last night."

Tansy stopped folding and turned to stare at the teenager. "About Ben?"

"Yep. We both agree you need a love life, and she wanted me to check this guy out and see what I thought of him. I think he's pretty cool."

Tansy shouldn't be surprised that the two were in cahoots on this. Of all the shelter volunteers, she was closest to Rose and Cindy. "Are you supposed to report back to Rose?"

"Of course. She'd promised that gentleman friend of hers, Mr. Hobson, that she'd help with his Christmas shopping or she would have found an excuse to drop by this morning. She's dying of curiosity."

Tansy picked up the stack of warm towels and hugged them to her chest. "Then tell Rose that we have a potential glitch."

"He's in a relationship?"

"I'm not sure. If he is, that would be a deal killer. I don't poach."

"If he's in a relationship, then he has no business looking at you the way he did. I say he's not. So what's the potential glitch?"

"When he first arrived this morning, he told me point-blank that he's not interested in having animals in his life."

Cindy's mouth dropped open. "Really? After the way he was loving on Brutus?"

"I can't explain that. Or the fact that I caught him scratching Max's head."

"You're making that up. Max never lets us pet him."

"I know, but he hopped up on the counter and started

purring while Ben and I were in the office looking around. That was surprising enough, but then I went to get my coat, and when I turned back, there was Ben, scratching behind Max's ears."

"So why doesn't he want animals? Maybe he lives with somebody who's allergic. Not a girlfriend, but somebody else. I know what *that's* like."

Tansy considered the possibility and rejected it. "He would have said so. I mean, take you, for example. You tell everybody that's why you don't have animals at home."

"Yeah, I do. Wow, it makes no sense."

"It doesn't."

"I'll stick around while he's filming. Maybe I can figure out what his problem is."

"That's an excellent idea." Tansy opened a cupboard above the counter and laid the clean towels inside. "You can supervise while I go back to the office. I need to post an update on our Facebook page and talk to Faye about a few things."

"Wait. I didn't mean for you to leave."

"I know." She grabbed her parka and put it on. "The truth is that I *am* attracted to the guy."

"Aha!"

"But if he's really closed to the idea of having animals around, then it's better if I don't spend too much time with him."

"I guess. If I find out anything, I'll—" She stopped speaking when the door opened a crack, letting in a swirl of cold air.

"All clear?"

Tansy wished hearing his voice didn't make her flush with pleasure. She glanced at Cindy. "Got a tight grip on Brutus?"

"He's secure." She clutched Brutus against her shoulder.

"Come on in, Ben." Tansy's heart thumped as she zipped her jacket. She couldn't remember the last time she'd had such a strong physical reaction to a man. Ben made her feel as if she were Cindy's age again and had developed a major crush on the captain of the football team.

The intensity of her feelings for someone she'd only just met wasn't all that unusual for her. She'd always had good instincts, both for people and animals, and she sensed Ben was a kind person. But there was some issue keeping him from opening his heart. And until she figured out what that was, letting Cindy help with the photography session was the smart thing to do.

Ben came through the door with a digital camera on a strap around his neck and a camcorder in his hand. He looked puzzled when he saw Tansy with her coat on. "Aren't you staying?"

"I have a ton of work to do in the office," she said. "I'm leaving Cindy in charge. You'll be in good hands with her."

"I'm sure I will, but I thought…" His expression went from confusion to resignation. "No worries. I'm sure Cindy can take me over to the dog area when I finish up here."

Tansy nodded. "Absolutely. She's one of our most capable volunteers."

"Do you want to preview what I've done before I go, or should I just head on to the station when I have plenty of shots?" His tone was conversational, as if he didn't care one way or the other.

She didn't believe for a minute that he wanted to leave without showing her the pictures, nor did she want him to. "I'd love to see what you come up with." She might be able to distance herself from the photography session, but she couldn't bear missing the results. He was, after all, filming her babies.

"Okay. I'll drop by the office when I have something to show you." His smile was tinged with sadness, as if he understood perfectly well why she was pulling back. He recognized that they had a sticking point.

Except he knew why and she didn't. "I'll see you later, then." She left, and disappointment sat like a cold lump in her chest.

This was stupid. Why couldn't he just tell her what his problem was? The answer was obvious, though, when she gave herself time to think about it. His uneasiness about having animals around must involve something personal, and he didn't know her well enough to explain. Cindy was good at pulling things out of people, but chances were he wouldn't confide in her, either.

Tansy sighed. If nothing else, she'd get some decent pictures of her furry friends out of the deal. If the station would allow it, she'd like to use some of them on The Haven's Facebook page. Her shots, to use Cindy's term, were lame.

She knew Ben's would be wonderful, and not only because he was a professional. He cared about animals, and that would show in the pictures he took today, as it had in the footage he'd shot on Monday morning.

Her gut feeling about him wasn't wrong. But she didn't have all the facts and might never learn them. Swearing softly under her breath, she walked up the pathway to the administration building.

TWO HOURS LATER, BEN whistled as he walked toward the back door of the yellow-and-white Victorian. He couldn't remember when he'd had so much fun with a camera. With some coaxing from Cindy, the cats had performed like trained acrobats, but he had some sweet and touching shots, too.

Most of the dogs had been hams as well, and he could hardly wait to show Tansy the pictures. Getting good ones had been a breeze, and with the tiniest bit of instruction and a better camera, she would be able to take shots that were just as great. In fact, one of his spare cameras would do if she didn't want to invest money in equipment.

But she might not be willing to have him teach her photography techniques and loan her cameras. Judging from her quick retreat this morning, she'd decided against spending time with a guy who was so obviously wrong for her. Smart move on her part.

He would take his cue from her, show her the pictures and head on out of this place. But the image of those cats frolicking together in an open play area would stay with him for a long time. And the memory of Tansy's bright eyes would stay even longer, though he'd do well to erase it.

As he opened the back door and started down the hallway toward what had been a deserted reception area early this morning, the hum of voices and an occasional dog bark drifted toward him. He walked in on a much different scene than the one he'd left.

On the far side of the counter, two dogs, one a black Lab and the other a cocker spaniel, tugged at their leashes. Because each dog had at least one kid fussing over it, Ben decided these were new adoptions, not animals being surrendered to the shelter.

A plump red-haired woman worked behind the counter, dealing with forms and answering questions. Tansy was helping her, bestowing warm smiles on the adults signing the forms and pulling out their checkbooks. The adults and kids all seemed to know each other, so Ben decided two families had come in together to adopt.

He waded into the confusion, introduced himself and asked if he could film the happy families and their new canine friends. Everyone seemed pleased about the idea, so he got some more footage. Maybe the station could use it and maybe not, but the excitement of the moment was contagious and he thought capturing it might be useful for...something.

Apparently he'd come in on the tail end of the procedure, because within fifteen minutes, the families had driven off with their dogs and the reception area grew quiet again.

Tansy beckoned him over to the counter. "Ben Rhodes, this is Faye Barnard, who presides over the front desk and creates order from chaos."

Ben shook her hand. "I could tell that this was a red-letter day for those two families."

"It was." Faye's cheeks dimpled and her green eyes glowed with satisfaction. "This is what it's all about, settling previously unwanted animals with families who are crazy about them. It's so rewarding."

"And thank you for capturing it," Tansy said. "Do you think KFOR would run something like that?"

"I don't know. I saw an opportunity and grabbed it, but I'm not in charge of what gets shown and what doesn't. I'd love to see that air, though. It would inspire more people to adopt."

"Yes, it would." Tansy's gaze met his, and the question was there, the same question that had always been there. Had it inspired him? Was he ready to take in a homeless dog or cat?

She didn't say that out loud, though, which meant he could pretend he hadn't picked up on her unspoken plea. "Do you have a minute to look at what I have here?"

Tansy glanced at Faye. "Can you handle the phone for a little while?"

"Be happy to."

"Then come on back to my desk, Ben." Tansy motioned him around the end of the counter. "Nobody's scheduled to come in for at least another thirty minutes, but you never know. Anything can happen around here, and usually does."

"I've got it under control," Faye said. "Go preview those pictures. I know you're dying to see them."

"I am."

"I think I got some you'll like." Ben followed Tansy to a desk in the far right-hand corner. Her computer was on and several folders were stacked beside the monitor. A rigid plastic chair sat next to her desk, and he commandeered it, bringing it over so it was close to her chair.

"Was Cindy helpful?" She sat down and swiveled to face him.

"She was great." Setting both the digital camera and the camcorder on the desk, he shrugged out of his coat and hung it on the back of the chair. Then he took off his hat and looked for a place to put it.

"Let me have it," Tansy said." He handed her the hat and she set it down on top of the folders. "I'm glad Cindy was there. She's so good with the animals."

"She is. She played with both the cats and the dogs so I got some terrific action shots." Settling onto the chair, he picked up the digital camera and clicked the preview button so the first one appeared in the small screen. "Can you see that? Here, take the camera and use that button to jump to the next one." He leaned toward her and did his best to concentrate on the images.

But he'd like to see the man who could do that and ignore the flowery scent of her skin and the tickle of her warm breath on his cheek. If he made a half turn, his lips would meet hers. But kissing her at all would be inappropriate, not to mention kissing her in a public office space under the watchful eye of her receptionist.

He reminded himself that he enjoyed his job and would not care to lose it because he'd behaved unprofessionally while on assignment.

She wasn't helping, though, with her little gasps of delight as she scrolled through the pictures. The noises she made sounded way too much like a woman responding to a lover. Knowing how joyfully she embraced life, he imagined she'd be equally joyful when she made love.

"Oh, Ben, these are great!" She clicked to the next frame and sucked in a breath. "Look at those blue eyes. All Siamese are stunning, but Hyacinth has the most amazing eyes."

So do you, Tansy. But he couldn't say that now, and probably not ever.

Eventually she got to the dog section. At one point she actually moaned with happiness. "Wonderful. Just wonderful. You have such a talent."

He'd been told he had talents in other areas, too, but he'd bet money that kind of expertise wasn't Tansy's top priority. Openness would be important to her, and he wasn't a tell-all kind of guy.

So he fought his natural response to being achingly close to her. Anyone would think he hadn't been with a woman in quite a while. And anyone would be right.

Yes, he'd been out of the dating scene for a few

months, but that wasn't the problem. He wasn't some sex-starved adolescent who couldn't go without it. His current need was specifically for Tansy.

He wanted to kiss her until they were both senseless with desire. They had obvious chemistry, so that part of their relationship would go just fine. It was the pillow talk that scared the devil out of him.

As he battled his demons, he was startled by the orange tabby, Max. The cat appeared from nowhere and jumped into his lap. Ben spoke without thinking, giving an automatic response ingrained years ago. "Get down, Mickey." He realized his mistake immediately. "I mean, Max."

Tansy's head whipped around and her eyes grew wide. "He's on your lap."

"So it seems." He started to remove the cat.

"Ben, you don't understand. I've never seen him get onto someone's lap. Could you…could you let him stay there for a little while? I want to encourage that behavior."

"I guess." So instead of lifting the cat down to the floor, he began stroking him. Max purred and kneaded his claws into the denim of Ben's jeans.

"That's amazing. He's acting like a regular cat."

Using both hands, Ben caressed Max in a remembered pattern, beginning at his chin and working his way to the base of his tail. "He probably *was* a regular cat before something happened to make him unfriendly."

"I'm sure you're right." She regarded him silently for a few seconds. "What did you call him when he first jumped up?"

"Oh." He threw the explanation out in an offhanded way. "I used to have a cat who looked a lot like Max.

His name was Mickey. I was concentrating on the pictures and had a memory lapse."

"What happened to Mickey?"

"Got hit by a car. The vet tried to save him, but he was hurt too bad." Twelve years later, and he still hated thinking about that day. So he didn't until forced to, like now.

"I'm sorry."

Fortifying himself against the sympathy he knew he'd find there, he looked into her blue eyes. "It's okay. It was a long time ago, and he was ten. That's not so bad for a cat."

"But not so good for the person who loved him."

"I got over it."

She gazed at him for a moment longer before glancing away. "Yes, I'm sure you did."

She didn't believe him. And that meant more questions would follow. Damn it.

CHAPTER FOUR

TANSY SOMETIMES FORGOT people, but she never forgot an animal, especially when that animal was connected to tragedy. Now she remembered why Ben was familiar. He'd been the sobbing teenager who'd brought his one-eyed orange tabby to the vet's office where she'd volunteered after school.

But she didn't think he'd appreciate knowing that she'd been the sixteen-year-old girl who'd held him while he cried that day, so she kept the information to herself. After she got home, she'd looked for him in her high school yearbook, but he hadn't been there. He'd slipped in and out of her life without a trace.

And now, twelve years later, here he was sitting right next to her. Max continued to attach himself to Ben's lap as if Velcroed to his jeans, while Tansy went back to exclaiming over the still shots. When they finished with those, Ben propped the camcorder on her desk and shared the videos he'd taken.

Although they both behaved as if nothing had changed, everything had changed for Tansy. The pieces of the puzzle that made up an image of Ben Rhodes were coming together. He'd said Mickey died at ten, so he'd likely had the cat since he was a young boy. Judging from the depth of his grief that day, Tansy suspected Mickey had been the only pet and possibly the best friend of a lonely boy.

After Mickey had taken his last breath, Ben had charged out the door, his face contorted with pain. Days later an envelope stuffed with cash had arrived at the vet's office, along with a scrawled note of thanks. The vet had shown both to Tansy, but there was no return address, no phone number, no contact information at all.

With their unconditional love and devotion, it was easy for animals to become a person's lifeline. If Mickey had been that for Ben, she could understand why Ben might have decided that loving an animal made him too vulnerable. She understood, but it made her sad.

She felt especially sad when she looked at Max, who acted as if he'd finally found his soul mate. As he sat contentedly purring on Ben's lap, he wasn't the same cat who refused even the slightest caress from any of the other employees and volunteers. During a break in phone calls at reception, she asked Faye to come over and witness the miracle.

Faye stared at Max in disbelief. "I'll be damned. Ben, you must be a sorcerer. You should see what we go through when we have to bandage his tail and put on his cone."

"I guess there's something familiar about me."

"I don't think he responds to you simply because you're a guy," Faye said. "We've had other men volunteer at the shelter, and Max ignored them the way he ignores us."

"It could be the sound of his voice or the way he smells," Tansy said.

Ben laughed. "Must be the tuna fish oil I rub on after my shower."

"So that's it." Tansy grinned at him, and they were almost back to normal with each other. But she would always look at him differently now that she knew, or thought she knew, why he avoided bonding with animals.

That decision was costing him, too, though she wasn't sure he realized it. The way he interacted with animals revealed how much he hungered for the connection he denied himself out of fear. Yet she had no idea how to fix the situation.

If she asked him to take Max home for the Christmas holidays, he probably would say no. On the other hand, what did she have to lose? She might as well find out exactly how rigid he was on this matter.

The shelter phone line started ringing. "I need to answer that," Faye said. "But don't move. I want a picture of Max sitting on your lap. If I tell the others, they'll think I've been smoking funny cigarettes."

Tansy and Ben finished up the videos before Faye reappeared, brandishing her camera phone. "I'm emailing this to a bunch of people who know how much of a grouch Max is." She aimed the phone at the cat. "They'll accuse me of using Photoshop."

Ben glanced at her. "He's really never been on anybody's lap? That's so hard to believe."

"It's as if he doesn't trust us enough," Tansy said. "We've tried playing with him, giving him treats, catnip, you name it. He tolerates us, but barely."

Faye took another picture with her phone. "Maybe he was just waiting for the right person to show up. None of us were the right person. You are."

"Unfortunately, I'm not—"

"How about just for the Christmas holidays?" Tansy didn't want to give him a chance to finish the sentence that would end all hope. "You heard my pitch at KFOR. There's no expense other than some food and litter, and no obligation. If you could socialize Max, he would be more adoptable. You could help him find a true home."

Ben met her gaze. "I wish I could help you, but I can't."

Anger stirred in her. "You mean you won't."

"All right. I won't." Gripping Max firmly, he pried the cat from his thigh and set him on the floor. When Max crouched as if ready to spring back into his lap, he quickly stood. Max rubbed against the leg of his jeans and continued to purr.

It broke Tansy's heart. She stood and faced him. "Can't you see how much he wants to be with you?"

Ben lowered his voice. "Sorry, Tansy, but I'm not taking Max home with me. I don't want an animal in my house, and besides, I have plans. I'm going skiing with friends over Christmas."

Faye suddenly found chores to handle at her desk.

Taking a deep breath, Tansy curbed her anger. Having an animal did complicate travel plans. No denying it. But animal lovers usually decided the rewards were worth the bother.

Clearly, Ben didn't feel that way, and no good would come of challenging his attitude. He'd spent the morning taking pictures that might help several animals be adopted. Sure, he'd been paid to do it, but he'd thrown himself into the project, and because of his enthusiasm he'd come up with some wonderful shots.

She cleared her throat. "You're right. Sorry. It's never a good idea to coerce a person into taking an animal, even if it's only for a trial period."

"No, it's not."

Doing her best to ignore Max's desperate bid for attention from his idol, Tansy focused on the business at hand. "Your pictures are fabulous. I know the station

owns them, but if they'd be willing to let me use a few
for The Haven's Facebook page, I'd be very grateful."

"I'll check with Paul." Ben put on his sheepskin coat.
"I'm sure you can work something out."

She turned back to her desk and retrieved his hat.
"I'd appreciate it."

He looked at the cat at his feet. "If for some reason
he doesn't want to give you any pictures, I could come
back on my own time and take some for you." He put on
the hat and tugged the brim over his eyes before picking up both cameras.

Although she longed to fling the generous offer in
his face, she couldn't afford to do that. "I'll keep that
in mind. Thank you."

"I'll be in touch." As he walked away, Max trotted
after him.

"Max, no." Tansy followed behind and scooped up
the cat. Max twisted and growled his displeasure. "You
can't go," she murmured into his orange fur. "He doesn't
want you."

And if Ben didn't want Max, then Tansy didn't want
Ben. Simple as that.

BEN KNEW HE'D GONE from hero to jerk in sixty seconds.
But what was he supposed to do? He fumed about it all
the way back to the station and for days afterward. He
kept picturing the flare of anger in Tansy's eyes when
she'd said, *You mean you won't.*

But he hadn't been born yesterday. She was a pro
at this adoption game. She knew as well as he did that
once he allowed Max into his home and into his heart,
the cat would be there for life—Max's life, which would
probably be short. Ben wasn't going through that again.

If Tansy had immunized herself against that pain,

then bully for her. She was definitely in the right line of work. So was he, for that matter. While she was comfortable with the passing of time, he was in the business of freezing it.

The images he captured with his camera stayed that way. The playful cats and the bouncy dogs would be young forever in the pictures he'd created. Maybe he was denying reality, but he didn't care. His decisions worked for him.

He'd be wise to forget Tansy Dexter. She wanted too much of him, and would make him more vulnerable than any animal could.

But she wasn't easy to forget. Besides his own vivid memories, he was assaulted by promo spots for The Haven. Each morning the six o'clock news included a chart showing the number of animals with temporary homes for the holidays and the progress toward reaching the financial goal necessary to build another Kitty Condo.

Both campaigns were going well, which made for a feel-good Christmas atmosphere in the newsroom. Ben was happy for Tansy that the public awareness campaign was working, but he'd be so glad when Christmas was over and he wasn't being constantly reminded of her.

They'd had one email exchange since he'd left the shelter that Saturday morning. On Monday, he'd sent her a file containing the shots Paul had released to her for The Haven's Facebook page and website. She'd responded with her gratitude, copying Paul. But he knew the warmth in the email was for Paul and not for him, though. Although Tansy occupied his thoughts most of the time, Max wasn't far from his mind, either. The cantankerous cat would spend Christmas day alone in that office, no doubt. No one would volunteer to take him home, and he probably wouldn't want to go with them, even if they did.

Max had his preference and it happened to be Ben, or somebody very much like him. His adoration was touching, and Ben had spent more hours than he cared to admit searching through his contacts looking for somebody who might fit a similar profile. He wasn't *that* unique. But he hadn't found a good match.

With all his effort to push Tansy out of his mind, he'd also forgotten the angel card he'd shoved in his coat pocket. On Thursday morning he pulled his gloves out of his pocket and the card he'd plucked from The Haven's tree came out, too, badly crumpled.

Taking the card had been an impulse, but he still wanted to honor it. He wasn't interested in adoption, but there were other ways he could support the animals. After the way they had parted on Saturday, returning with gifts might seem like he was trying to get back on Tansy's good side, but he couldn't help that.

At least Christmas was still a couple of weeks away. He would have hated finding that card during his ski trip. He vaguely remembered what was on the card, but he checked it again to make sure. Yep, a large carpeted cat tree.

He'd seen a couple of them in the rooms of the Kitty Condo. Most of the carpeting had been shredded by busy claws and replaced with remnants, so the cat trees were now a patchwork of colors with a few bald spots. Considering the plans for a second cat building, The Haven clearly needed more of those things.

Mickey had never had one. After the first few times the cat had dug into the furniture, Ben's aunt and uncle had banned him from the house. By the time Ben was old enough to buy Mickey a cat tree for scratching, he preferred the real trees he found as he roamed the neighborhood. It would have been a waste of Ben's hard-earned cash.

But these days he had the money to spend. He could get at least two. He had a truck, so hauling them over wouldn't be a problem.

Seeing Tansy again might be.

And yet he wanted to see her again, fool that he was. He missed her infectious smile and her sunny outlook. He missed *her,* which was not a good sign, but it was the sad truth.

He spent his lunch break dithering over which cat trees to buy and whether he should get more than two.

Finally he settled on just two. Until the new facility was built, The Haven might not have room for more. These two could be used immediately in the existing rooms or in the portable, and after the second Kitty Condo went up, he'd buy more. Or maybe some toys. Or blankets. They seemed to use a lot of those.

Besides missing Tansy, he missed the warm and optimistic atmosphere of The Haven. He kept remembering the way the cats had played their little hearts out as they celebrated the joy of being alive. He wanted another reason to be part of that.

He left the cat trees at the store and arranged to pick them up later. A misty rain had been falling all morning and he didn't want them sitting out in his truck getting soaked while he worked. He'd have to use a tarp when he took them over to the Haven.

He didn't get off until six—was that too late to deliver the trees? He could always wait until Saturday, but he didn't want to. Now that he'd bought them, he was eager to get them over there. And yeah, he was eager to see Tansy, too.

Originally he'd imagined driving up and surprising her with the cat trees. Now he realized that wasn't such a good idea. If he arrived in the middle of a busy time, he'd only add to the confusion. She, or Faye, or someone, needed to know to expect him.

During a five-minute break in filming, he called The Haven, got Faye and told her his mission.

"That's terrific, Ben!" She was gratifyingly excited. "The cats will *love* having those."

"I can get them over there after work, but it'll be around six-thirty."

"We'll be closed up by then. Do you want to wait until Saturday?"

"Not really. I was hoping—"

"Hang on. Let me check with Tansy." Faye put him on hold and he listened to "Jingle Bells" sung by barking dogs and meowing cats. It made him smile.

"Ben?" Tansy's voice wiped the smile right off his face and jacked up his heart rate.

"Hi. I bought these two cat trees, and I—"

"Faye told me, and we really appreciate that."

He wished she'd said *I* instead of *we*. It was a subtle but telling difference.

"Listen," she continued, "I don't blame you for not wanting to interrupt your Saturday again, so let's—"

"It's not that." Great. Now she thought he was worried about cutting into his weekend. "I just figured the sooner the cats have them, the better."

"Well, that's obviously true. They love having new furniture to explore, and we could really use one out in the portable. Anyway, I can take your delivery. That's one of the advantages of living right next door. Give me a call when you're on your way and I'll come meet you. How big are they?"

"About four feet tall and a couple of feet square. I can carry them. Don't worry about getting help to unload the things. If you want, I can even cart them out back."

"Thanks, but that won't be necessary."

Ouch. She *really* didn't like him anymore. He couldn't blame her, but he wanted the other Tansy back, the one with sunshine in her eyes and a smile on her full lips. But to get that, he'd have to do more than buy a couple of cat trees. After she gave him her cell number, they ended the call.

His heart was still beating faster than normal as he put his phone on vibrate and tucked it into his jeans pocket. Even when she was frosty, she still affected him. The strong attraction was damned inconvenient. Why couldn't he feel this way about one of the women going on the ski trip?

But he didn't. His buddy, Justin, had brought him into the group. They were an ever-shifting singles group of six to ten members tied together by their work at the station and a love of outdoor sports. They skied in the winter and enjoyed water sports and hiking in the summer.

One of the women, a good-looking brunette named Janine who worked in the advertising department, had hinted that she'd like to be more than friends with him. Because he valued her friendship, he'd told her gently but firmly that he thought of her as a sister and nothing more. The chemistry wasn't there for him.

Apparently he was like Max. He had his preference, and no one else would do. Tansy was it. Now that he'd experienced the bright sparkle of her personality, other women seemed colorless.

It couldn't develop into anything, of course. But he liked knowing that she existed, that she was here in Tacoma, even if they couldn't be close friends. Thinking of her might be frustrating sometimes, but her very presence in the world gave him joy.

A little after six, he picked up both cat trees from the pet store, wrapped a blue tarp around them and tied it down. The air was wet, misty and cold, but fortunately the hard rain that had fallen during the afternoon had stopped. After climbing back into his truck, he called Tansy.

She picked up immediately. "Hi, Ben. I forgot you were coming."

That was a blow to his ego. "Is it still all right? I already have the cat trees in the back of my truck."

"Sure, it's fine. Come on ahead. I'm in the Doggie Digs mopping, and I need to get that done, so if you wouldn't mind, could you walk down here instead of having me meet you in the office?"

"Mopping? That part of your regular cleanup?"

"Unfortunately not. We have a leak that's only getting worse. One of our volunteers crawled up on the roof late this afternoon and put plastic down, so it's temporarily handled, but there's still a lot of water on the floor."

"Didn't anybody stay to help you mop?"

"They all offered, but it's the Christmas season. Everybody had either parties or relatives visiting or shopping to do, and I sent them home. I can handle it."

"I'll be there as soon as I can."

"Ben, you don't have to help."

"But I will. See you soon." He disconnected and started up the truck. She might not welcome his help, but she was going to get it anyway. He wasn't about to drop off the cat trees and leave when she had a crisis. That wasn't his style.

But helping her tonight wasn't the only issue. Roof leaks were common in a wet climate. If she didn't have insurance to cover repairs…this was not good news for Tansy's already tight budget, not good news at all.

CHAPTER FIVE

TANSY HADN'T EXPECTED to see Ben again, so when he'd called about the cat trees, she'd had to deal with a rush of unwanted excitement. She'd forgotten that he'd taken one of the angel cards when he'd come in that Saturday morning.

She'd wondered if following through on that gesture had simply been an inconvenience for him. Maybe it was, but he'd been generous enough to get two cat trees instead of the single one listed on the angel card. Or had he gotten an extra one to soothe his guilty conscience?

Now, as she mopped up the worst of the puddles, she talked to the four dogs that had temporarily been housed together. The pie-shaped enclosures had side walls about three-and-a-half feet high with chain link above that, so the bigger dogs could put their paws on the top of the wall and look over at their neighbors. Currently all four dogs were watching her mop.

The yellow Lab and Irish setter had always been roommates in this section, but for the moment they shared the space with a husky and a black Lab. The setter, whose name was Bailey, was the only one whining. The rest seemed merely curious about what she was doing. Talking calmed Bailey, but it also helped Tansy sort through her uncomfortable thoughts.

"I screwed up, guys," she said. "If Ben has a guilty conscience, it's my fault."

The yellow Lab named Nugget barked once as if agreeing with her.

"Exactly, Nugget. You never want to bully someone into taking a furry friend home. They could resent being talked into something they weren't ready to do."

The black Lab sneezed.

"Bless you, Charcoal. Anyway, there's no excuse for the way I acted. Maybe Ben has a wonderful way with animals, and maybe I have a little crush on him and wish he'd change his mind about adopting. I'd hoped it would help him deal with the pain in his past. But none of that gives me the right to suggest he has an obligation to take Max home for the holidays."

Squeezing out her mop, she slapped it back down on the floor. "My one little word of *sorry* doesn't cut it. Now that he's on his way here, I'll grab this opportunity to tell him I was out of line. It won't be easy, but I'll make myself do it."

"Anybody home?"

Awareness skittered up her spine at the sound of his voice. The dogs barked in response, so she had to shout. "In here!" Leaning the mop handle against the wall, she walked through the door of the pen into the center section and nearly collided with Ben. She quickly stepped back and staggered.

"Easy." Ben caught her, his gloved hands firm as they gripped her arms.

"Thanks." She gazed into dark eyes that had the power to make her forget her own name. Wow, he was as gorgeous as ever. Same sheepskin coat and brown felt cowboy hat. He rocked that look.

"No problem." He held on to her a little longer than was necessary. Then he let go and moved away. "Got another mop?"

"Ben, you really don't have to help me with the floor. I can take a break from this and open up the Kitty Condo so we can put the cat trees in there and you can be on your way."

He went very still. "Do you want me to be on my way?"

No. "I hate to hold you up. I'm sure you have things you'd rather do than help me mop the floor."

He tipped back his hat and regarded her steadily. "Actually, I don't. But last time we talked, you were upset with me. Maybe you'd prefer that I drop off my donations and leave."

"No, I would not prefer that." She took a deep breath. Now or never. "I had no right to be upset with you. And I had no right to put pressure on you to take Max for the holidays. I violated my own rule by doing that, and I hope you'll forgive me. It was inexcusable."

His expression relaxed. "Not inexcusable," he said. "You adore these animals. You love Max and want the best for him. You saw a chance for him to bond with someone, and you wanted to encourage it."

"Loading you up with guilt in the process."

"No, I don't feel guilty, Tansy. I'm only sorry that I'm not the ideal match you and Max think I am."

"Me, too." She wondered if he realized that statement could apply to her as well as Max. Probably not. He didn't know Rose had once had high hopes for a romance between them.

"Friends?"

She nodded. "Friends."

"And friends don't let friends mop alone." He shoved his gloves in the pocket of his coat before unbuttoning it. "Where can I put my coat?"

"I'll take it." She smiled as a weight lifted off her

heart. She'd apologized and he'd been more than gracious. Maybe they could be friends, after all. "You can have my mop and I'll get another one from the storeroom." She took his coat, which was still warm. To her credit, she didn't hug it close, but she did take some guilty enjoyment in appreciating the snug fit of the long-sleeved T-shirt he had on underneath.

"Might as well give you my hat, too." He took it off and handed it to her.

"Be right back." She hurried into the octagonal space that mirrored the one in the Kitty Condo, except this one was bigger and had one whole wall devoted to leashes. Two raised dog beds plus food and water dishes sat in a corner, waiting until the mopping was finished to be put back in their rightful places.

Tansy hung Ben's coat and hat on a hook next to where she'd left her own parka. Before she walked away, she held the soft sheepskin to her nose and inhaled. Ahhh.

Visually he was a beautiful man, but she'd always been sensitive to scent. A man could look like a Greek god, but if he didn't appeal to her nose, she wasn't attracted to him. Ben passed the scent test with Max, apparently, but he passed it with her, too.

Grabbing another mop from the storeroom, she headed back into the flooded area. Moments later they were working side by side as they attacked the remaining puddles.

He mopped with long, sure strokes. "When did you find the leak?"

"This morning when we opened up." She resisted the urge to watch him instead of working. Concentrating on the floor was a challenge when the alternative was ogling the shift of his muscles as he wielded the mop. "When Rose reported it, we didn't think it was too bad, but in the afternoon, when it rained harder, the leak got worse." She glanced up at the stained ceiling. "The plastic seems to be holding the water at bay for now, but I've asked a roofer to come out tomorrow and give us an estimate."

"Insurance?"

"We have it, but last year I raised the deductible to lower our monthly bill and help keep us in the black. Obviously that was a mistake."

"Do you have enough to pay the deductible?"

She sighed. "No, we don't. And I can't dip into the money earmarked for the second Kitty Condo. We've almost hit our goal, which the station will announce very soon, and donors will expect to see the building go up."

"And I guess you can't suddenly announce another fund-raiser for the roof."

"It's Christmas, and people have already been more than generous. I can't go back to them again so soon. This is just a bit of bad luck. I'll figure something out."

She just had no idea what that could be. What if she couldn't find the money? What if the shelter went bankrupt, the animals became homeless…and it was all her fault?

"I'm sure you will. I just wish I could help."

She couldn't ask for what she really needed—to be held. In her fantasy, he'd put down the mop, wrap her in his strong arms and cradle her against his chest while he smoothed her hair and told her everything would be all right.

"You did help," she said. "You took some great pictures that are making our Facebook page and website shine. I've had so many compliments on those photos, Ben. Contributions through Facebook and the site for the Kitty Condo are definitely ahead of where they were before I added your pictures."

"Good."

From the other side of the wall, Bailey whined and shoved his nose against the mesh.

"Almost done, Bailey."

"Yeah," Ben said. "I think we've got it handled. If you'll take the mops, I'll empty the bucket."

"Thanks. We'll need to move those beds and their food and water dishes back in here before we transfer the dogs."

"No problem." He sounded cheerful, as if he might even be having a good time.

They were finally able to return Bailey and Nugget to their rightful spot, and Ben was a hands-on helper, petting all the dogs and talking to them as if they were his buddies. The husky, Yukon, seemed especially taken with Ben, but all of them responded with wagging tails and doggie smiles.

The longer Tansy observed Ben's behavior at the shelter, the more she became convinced that all Ben needed was a chance to hang around animals for a while and get past his fear of becoming attached. He might be a lot tougher about such things than he gave himself credit for.

Ben was in an excellent mood as they put on their coats and headed into the misty night air. "Here's my thought," he said. "I'll unload the first cat tree while you open up the Kitty Condo. Once we've got them in place, I'll take you to dinner."

"All of that sounds good except the last part."

He paused on the sidewalk and stared at her. "You're refusing my dinner invitation? I thought we'd signed a peace treaty."

"We have, but I don't think it's fair for the guy who brought over two cat trees and helped me mop the floor to also buy me dinner. I have some homemade veggie soup and a loaf of homemade bread at my house. Why don't you come over?"

He hesitated for a fraction of a second. Then he smiled. "Sounds perfect."

She caught her breath. She'd been doing fine, keeping her balance and congratulating herself on how well this friendship thing was working, until he smiled. Just like that, she became a molten mass of hormones. And she'd just invited him to share an intimate dinner in the privacy of her home. What had she been thinking?

BEN HADN'T EXPECTED his dinner invitation to become something even cozier than a shared table at a restaurant. He'd taken a chance offering that, but she'd had a tough day and it had seemed like the right gesture. A friendly thing to do.

Sharing a meal in her house was riskier, and for a brief moment, fear of that type of intimacy had made him hesitate. Then he'd decided it wasn't a romantic gesture on her part. She wasn't a temporary fling kind of woman, and she'd definitely avoid getting involved with a guy who'd declared he wouldn't be adopting any animals.

They were friends, nothing more. He kept that firmly in mind as she exclaimed over the beauty of the cat trees he'd bought. Her appreciation felt great after all the time he'd spent agonizing over which to buy. She continued to rave about them as he carried each one into its designated space.

Anyone listening to her would have thought he'd brought her diamonds. Though he couldn't imagine her getting this excited about mere jewelry. In fact, she'd probably hock it and put the money toward something for the animals.

When the second cat tree was settled in the portable building, they stood together and watched the cats adapt to their new climbing and scratching structure. Even though the cats had been through tough times, they were recovering their natural instinct to have fun. A few held back, but within minutes the carpet-covered towers were play central.

Ben laughed as a black cat chased a tabby in, out and around the tower. Then they reversed roles and the tabby became the aggressor until a calico joined in, making a three-way game of it.

"Wish I'd brought my camera."

"I think that all the time, but even when I do remember to bring my camera, the results aren't as good as yours." Tansy stood beside him, her expression animated, her eyes bright with pleasure. She'd left her parka on, but it was unzipped.

He was resigned to having her as a friend and nothing more, so he shouldn't notice how her red turtleneck sweater hugged her breasts. But he did. He shouldn't have watched her during the mopping session, either, but he had. The fit of her jeans had affected the fit of his.

He wasn't sure how he'd deal with his response to her when they were tucked inside her little blue Victorian house. He'd have to leave early if he found himself wanting to act on his feelings.

For now, though, he chose to make conversation and pretend that he could ignore the urge to kiss her.

"I really can teach you how to take good pictures," he said. "It's not that tricky."

She glanced over at him. "I'm not sure I believe you. Some people are talented in one thing and some in another. I have an affinity for animals. You're a genius with a camera."

"Thanks for boosting my ego, but I'm no genius, Tansy. It's a skill like any other. It can be learned."

"I'm sure it can, but those who are gifted will always do a better job than those who aren't. I know my limits." She paused, her gaze tentative, her body language hesitant. "Maybe you would…no, that's asking too much." She looked away.

"You can't leave me dangling like that. Tell me what you started to say."

"Okay, but it's fine if you say no. We'll still be friends."

"Tansy."

"Would you consider volunteering to be our official photographer?"

His pulse leaped. Volunteering to take pictures for the shelter would mean he'd see her on a regular basis. His heart wanted to, but his brain said it was a bad idea. "It's a thought."

"Never mind. It would be an imposition. I'd offer to pay you, but as you know, money's in short supply."

"I didn't say I *wouldn't* do it."

"But you didn't jump at the idea, either. I'm sure it's a lot to ask."

It was, but not for the reason she thought. He was already becoming too attached to the shelter and to her. And that led only to pain. Yet refusing to help because he was conflicted about their relationship seemed petty, especially when he was fascinated by the kaleidoscope of cats arranging and rearranging themselves.

He'd had fun capturing the changing expressions

on the faces of the dogs. But his photographer's soul belonged to the cats. They were art in motion, a feline version of Cirque du Soleil. They begged to be photographed, and good pictures would go far to getting them new homes. Fortunately, it wouldn't take any emotional involvement on his part. He was a professional; he knew how to keep his distance from his subjects.

He took a deep breath. "I'd be honored to be your official photographer."

She turned to him, her eyes shining. "Oh, Ben, that's so awesome. The cat trees are wonderful, and I would never want to discourage you from donating such things, but you have a skill that no one on our staff has. Eventually the pictures on the website and on Facebook will be dated as the animals are adopted. We need to give the newcomers their fifteen seconds of fame."

"I'll take care of that. But I'm still buying more cat trees when the new Kitty Condo goes up. These things are amazing."

"And I'll happily accept them. Oh, look! Casper's stalking the others. Too cute."

He'd noticed that she called each cat by name, and she'd done that with the dogs, too. "You have so many animals at The Haven. How do you remember who's who?"

"That's part of my talent, just like knowing how to frame a shot is part of yours."

He nodded. "Point taken." He continued to stand there, and the urge to cup the back of her head and taste her mouth became stronger. They needed to move on. "Anything else we should do?"

"Oh!" She turned to him. "I'm so sorry. I could stand here for hours watching the cats play, but you must be starving."

"Hey, I understand. When I'm shooting something that fascinates me, a bomb could go off and I wouldn't notice." He'd had that reaction the morning of her TV appearance, but he decided not to mention it. He didn't want to upset the delicate balance they'd achieved.

"Nevertheless, I promised to feed you, and it's past time to honor that promise. Let's go."

He wasn't about to argue with her. He'd eaten a quick lunch on the fly because he'd been buying cat trees, and food sounded great right now. Maybe a filling meal would curb his appetite for other things, things he shouldn't be hungry for.

CHAPTER SIX

EVERY CHRISTMAS SEASON, Tansy anticipated that special moment when she felt the spirit of the holidays for the first time. As she and Ben walked through the parking lot toward the flagstone path connecting the administration building to her house, their breath fogged the air. They talked about the resilience of the cats who'd been taken from the hoarding situation, and the great photo ops that would be possible with so many fascinating subjects.

Fat snowflakes drifted down, sparkling in the white lights outlining the yellow Victorian and settling like bits of lace on Ben's hat and coat. Tansy glanced over at her house, where she'd strung tiny multicolored LEDs along her porch railing and placed a small decorated tree on each side of her front door.

Both houses looked festive and ready to celebrate. The crisp scent of damp evergreens hung in the air. As a delicate snowflake landed on her cheek like a kiss, a rush of joy told her that once again, Christmas had arrived in her heart.

"It feels like Christmas," she said.

Ben laughed. "Is that all it takes? A couple of cat trees?"

"No, I wasn't thinking of the donation you made, which is wonderful. It's the combination of the snow, and the Christmas lights...." *And you walking beside me*. But she wasn't about to say that, so she improvised. "And how generous everyone has been to The Haven. All of a sudden the Christmas spirit hit me like an incoming snowball."

"That's great." His tone was wistful. "I envy you."

She wasn't sure how to respond to that. "Hey, it's only the middle of December. You have lots of time to get in the mood."

"Not everybody gets in the mood, you know."

She hesitated. "You don't?"

"No."

"Not ever?"

"Can't say that I have."

She thought she should drop the subject because it seemed to be a touchy one, so she remained silent.

"The thing is…"

"Mmm?" She didn't even want to use an actual word to prompt him, for fear he'd clam up completely. She sensed that whatever he'd started to say wasn't something he mentioned to many people. Maybe not to anyone.

He sighed. "Never mind."

He'd retreated. His behavior reminded her of animals who'd come from bad situations and were afraid to trust. She let the silence stretch between them and figured that was the end of his willingness to share something personal. Then, to her amazement, he spoke again.

"I think you have to have a store of good Christmas memories to draw on from when you're young." He cleared his throat. "That's how I think you get the Christmas spirit, tapping into that."

Her heart ached for him, but she kept her voice light. "I've never looked at it that way, but that could be true." What had his childhood been like, that he had no happy memories of Christmas? More than anyone she knew, this man needed the unconditional love of an animal... or a person.

She led the way up her porch steps and reached for the front door latch.

"You don't lock it?"

"I don't bother if I'm right next door and I have an alarm like Ewok and an enforcer like Wookie in residence. Besides, I'm sure even burglars know that anyone running an animal shelter is probably broke. Don't expect cut crystal wineglasses and fine china at my house. My family and friends know to give me stuff for the shelter or a donation to whatever fund-raiser we have going."

Ben smiled. "I can hear your fan club coming."

She could, too. Ewok's toenails scrabbled on the hardwood floor as he raced toward the door. Wookie was coming, too, but he signaled his happiness with a noise in his throat that was somewhere between a moan and a whine. She opened the door. "Honeys! I'm home!"

Ewok danced with joy and she gathered him up in her arms, but she managed to reach out a hand and stroke Wookie's head at the same time. "Good to see you, guys. And look who I brought with me, Ewok. Your friend from the TV station. Doggies, meet Ben Rhodes, top-notch photographer. Come on, Ben. We need to let them out in the yard for a bit, and then we'll get started on dinner." She set Ewok back on his feet.

The dogs knew the routine, so she followed them through her living room with its secondhand furniture and the small dining room with more of the same. Then she turned left into the kitchen. The door at the end of it opened onto a porch and a fenced yard. Both dogs stood waiting impatiently in front of the door.

"Cozy place," Ben said as he followed her.

"I actually love it. The house belongs to the founda-tion that runs The Haven and can't ever be *mine,* ex-actly, but it's mine for as long as I do a good job."

"Then it should be yours for a very long time."

"Not if we go broke with the roofing repairs." Tansy opened the back door. "Okay, guys, out you go!" Ewok shot out first, and then Wookie padded through the doorway and took the porch steps in one bound. She stepped out on the porch and glanced over her shoulder at Ben. "I usually stand out here until they're ready to come in, but you don't have to."

"Sure I do." He joined her on the porch and closed the door behind him. "I'm not going to cower in the warm house while you're out here in the cold. In fact, if you want to go in and start heating up that soup, I'll supervise the operation here."

She gazed over at him. "You really are famished, aren't you?"

"Yes."

Something in the way he said it made her heart beat faster. But he was probably talking about food. It was late, well past most people's dinner hour. "Okay, if you're willing to watch them, I'll go turn on the stove."

"Excellent."

Ducking inside, she took off her coat and hung it on a peg by the back door. Then she pulled the soup pot out of the refrigerator and set it on a burner. Soon the aroma of carrots, onions, diced tomatoes and potatoes filled the kitchen.

She buttered several slices of her favorite cheddar cheese yeast bread, wrapped them in foil and popped them in the oven. The meal wasn't fancy, but adding a bottle of wine would make it a little more gourmet. She wondered if he liked wine, and whether he preferred red or white.

Opening the back door, she stuck her head out to ask him and discovered he was no longer on the porch. The sound of his laughter filled the air, mingled with happy dog barks. When she walked out onto the porch, the glow from the porch light revealed a scene that made her heart squeeze.

Ben, who professed not to want animals in his life, was romping with her dogs. Snow fell around them as all three leaped and ran through the cold night air.

As if sensing her presence, Ben skidded to a stop and glanced in her direction. "They were really amped up and I figured they'd give us some peace if I played with them a bit. Was that okay?"

"Of course it's okay!" She smiled. "But dinner's ready."

"We're a mess."

"Don't worry about it. I'll get some old towels. Be right back." Still smiling, she went inside to put on her coat and grab the towels.

No matter what Ben might say, his actions proved to her that he would be a happier man if he allowed animals into his life. But she wouldn't try and convince him anymore. She'd let Ewok and Wookie do it for her.

AFTER HELPING TANSY with doggie cleanup, Ben gestured toward the wood in a metal rack on the back porch. "Do you use your fireplace?"

"I sure do."

"Mind if I build us a fire and we eat dinner in front of it?"

"Sounds great to me."

He left his wet boots on a mat in the kitchen. Then

he busied himself with logs, kindling and newspaper. Having something to do kept him from thinking about the bonehead comments he'd made about his lack of happy Christmas memories. He had no idea why he'd felt the need to reveal something so personal. Luckily she hadn't pressed for details, but he'd have to watch himself from here on out.

The fireplace was great, and made him wonder why he'd never had one in any of the places he'd rented over the years. He'd seen them as an amenity for a vacation cabin or a ski lodge, not a home. He needed to remedy that.

While he tended the fire, she set up their dinner arrangement. Soon the fire was crackling nicely and they were sitting on the floor in front of it, bowls of steaming soup and warm bread laid out on her coffee table. She'd fed Ewok and Wookie when they'd come back inside, and they were now both zonked out, Wookie next to Ben and Ewok next to Tansy.

Ben sat beside Tansy with a few inches between them. He'd left that space on purpose. This was a dinner shared by friends, not lovers.

The energy in the room might go a notch past friendship on the relationship meter, but that only served to sharpen his enjoyment of the food and the cozy setting. He couldn't remember ever being happier. "This is great." He sipped his red wine and took a bite of the fragrant bread. "Thank you."

Pausing with her spoon in midair, she gazed at him with softness in her blue eyes. "Got to treat my volunteers right."

He wasn't sure if he was the reason for that look in her eyes, but he liked thinking he made her happy, even if it was a friendly kind of happy. "I'm glad I played with the dogs, it seemed to be good for them."

"It was, and I'm thrilled they got the exercise. They'll sleep well tonight."

"Good." He took a mouthful of soup and realized exactly how hungry he was. He finished off more than half of what was in his bowl before he spoke again. "Does it ever get to be too much, living right where you work?"

"Never. This is my dream. I've wanted to help animals ever since I was a kid."

"Brothers or sisters?"

"No, although my parents had planned to have more than one kid. It took them forever to have me. They were both in their forties. So they filled the house with dogs and cats, instead. Having a lot of animals around seemed normal to me." She chuckled. "My folks still have quite a menagerie."

"Here in Tacoma?"

"No, they got tired of the winters and moved to Arizona. They'd love it if I'd move down there, too, but I've found my bliss with this foundation. I'm not going anywhere."

He was glad to hear it. As much as he worried about his intense emotional reaction to Tansy, he didn't want her to leave town. "I'm pretty settled here, too," he said.

"It has lots of good points."

"Yep." Tacoma had always felt like home to him, maybe because it was the last place he'd lived with Mickey. So, once he was on his own, he'd moved back here. His aunt and uncle had continued to roam, and last year they'd headed to Mexico in an RV. He'd had no word since then, but they'd never been big on keeping in touch.

"It's great, what you're doing with The Haven," he said. "But don't you ever get discouraged?"

She turned her head to look at him. "You mean because I can't save them all?"

"Something like that, yeah."

"The fact is, I can't save them all, but if I let myself dwell on the negative side of the ledger, I'm wasting valuable energy. Instead I think about all the ones I have saved."

"The glass-half-full theory."

"That's me."

Indeed. He looked into those luminous eyes and finally began to understand how strong she was and how perfectly suited to the work she'd chosen. "That's inspiring."

"Thanks, but *I'm* inspired by what *you* do, which seems a lot more complicated to me."

"It's not. I keep saying you could learn it." He tried to keep from staring at her mouth, but it was so tempting. And so very close.

"I could learn the basics, but your talent can't be taught. You work instinctively to capture the essence of your subjects. I can tell you operate by instinct—so do I with the animals."

"I'm not always successful."

She laughed. "Who is?"

"I know, but I get impatient." He'd made a copy of the footage he'd taken of her at the station. He wasn't satisfied with it. "Like with you, for example."

"Me?"

"The camera work I did when you came to KFOR was okay, but you're so much more…filled with light than what I managed to record. I need another chance."

Her breath hitched and her eyes grew dreamy. "Filled with light?"

"Mmm." He realized that he'd moved close enough that their shoulders touched. He risked a lot being this near to her and saying these things, but he couldn't seem to help it. "You give off this subtle glow. I didn't capture that in the footage I took."

"That's very flattering." She spoke in hushed tones as she drifted toward him, closing the gap. "But I don't think I glow."

"Yes, you do. You're glowing now."

"I am?"

"Yes." He breathed her in. "Here." He touched his lips to her cheekbone. "And here." He pressed his mouth against the space between her brows. "And here." He feathered a kiss along her jawline.

He would have missed her soft gasp if he hadn't been so close. But he didn't miss it. "Tansy, if I don't kiss you right now, I'm going to explode."

Her lashes fluttered down, concealing those incredible eyes. "Ben, if you don't kiss me right now, I'll explode, too."

"Can't have people exploding, can we?" He cupped her cheek, his fingers sliding over the silky temptation of her skin. His heart threatened to pound right out of his chest as he hovered nearer. At last, when his breath mingled with hers, he closed his eyes and sought the velvet softness of her lips.

And when he settled his mouth over hers, his sense of homecoming nearly overwhelmed him. Risky or not, he needed to be with this woman, to absorb her warmth and bask in the light that surrounded her.

Then she moaned softly, and the surge of desire that roared through him left him trembling with the effort to keep his pressure light, his touch gentle. But he managed it. She'd yielded this much to him, but if she sensed that his control could snap any second, he might lose her trust.

With great effort, he lifted his head and gazed down at her. Her eyes opened slowly. He waited, breath held, for what they would reveal.

At last, with a quivering sigh, she let him see what he'd dreamed of, but never dared hope for. Passion blazed there…for him.

"I shouldn't want you," she murmured.

His voice was husky with need. "No, you shouldn't."

"But I do."

He closed his eyes and took a long, shaky breath. He would do the noble thing. "I'll go."

"Don't you dare."

His eyes snapped open. "What?"

"Don't you dare kiss me like that and walk out my door, Ben Rhodes."

"But you said you shouldn't want—"

"Some things defy logic." Her hand cupped the back of his head, drawing him down. "And this is one of them."

CHAPTER SEVEN

To Tansy, the positive view was always better. Maybe she was rationalizing asking him to stay—and the hotter Ben's kisses became, the more that was likely—but she had to believe that Ben cherished animals the way she did and was capable of loving pets and people.

So when they stood and carefully navigated around the sleeping dogs on their way to her bedroom, she told herself that she didn't have to worry. She wasn't giving her heart and her body to the wrong man. Ben was moving closer to an epiphany every day.

She wanted him so desperately that when he mentioned that he wasn't prepared, she pushed past her embarrassment and admitted she had condoms in her bedside table drawer. Fortunately he didn't question their presence in her bedroom. Neither did she take the time to explain that Rose and Cindy had conspired to put them there, just in case.

After they turned on the bedside lamps and closed the bedroom door, he began to undress her with murmured words of praise and more kisses from his talented lips. Only a few minutes of that and she abandoned all debate. Something basic in him awakened something basic in her and she couldn't fight it anymore.

Maybe they would forge a bond strong enough to withstand any challenge, and maybe they wouldn't.

When he stripped off his clothes and urged her back onto the cool sheets, she no longer cared to worry about it.

For now, there was only Ben, loving her with a tenderness that brought tears to her eyes. He was a man who knew the meaning of the word *cherish*. He didn't rush.

She was the one who begged him to hurry. She'd imagined making love to him ever since they'd met, and she'd despaired of it ever happening. Now that it was about to, she couldn't wait.

Covering her with his warm, muscled body, he rested his weight on his elbows and gazed into her eyes. "I don't want to hurry," he murmured. "I want to savor you, Tansy."

"You could savor me later. During round two." Now that he was in her bed, she wasn't in any hurry to kick him out.

His beautiful mouth tilted in a smile. "I could, but we'll only have a first time once." He leaned down and feathered a kiss over her lips. "I want to make it memorable."

She groaned and ran her hands up his sculpted back. "We have all night."

"Do we?" He nuzzled her throat. "Are you inviting me to stay?"

"Yes." She arched upward as he kissed his way to the swell of her breast. "Please stay. Please…" Her request became a whimper as he found her nipple and drew it into his mouth.

Stay. The word vibrated through her as he continued his unhurried exploration. Her heart beat a wild rhythm punctuated with that single word. *Stay…*

He seemed to know exactly how to touch her, where to touch her. Her skin flushed in response and moisture sluiced downward. She shifted restlessly as he dipped his tongue into her navel.

He held her hips still and shifted his weight until he lay between her quivering thighs. And then…sensation rocketed through her as his mouth made contact. His intimate kiss was bold, thorough, devastating.

Gasping, she surrendered to the assault. He brought her quickly to the brink, and when she tightened, ready for that exquisite release…he eased back.

"Ben."

"Take your time." His warm breath caressed her damp skin. "Pace yourself."

"But I want—"

"Don't run to meet it. Let it roll toward you." He used his tongue to tease her.

"It's a tsunami."

"Not yet. It will be." He settled his mouth over her and coaxed her to the edge…and paused. Again.

"You're torturing me." She moaned and tried to wriggle out of his grip.

He held her fast. "I want you to remember this, Tansy. Every second."

"I *will*." She was on fire, burning with frustration. "But please…"

"Yes. Now." The fierce pressure of his lips and tongue catapulted her into a whirlpool of pleasure more intense than she'd ever known. She lost all control as her climax rocketed through her with a force that left her dazed and breathless in the aftermath.

Sinking back onto the damp sheets, she flung her arms out and closed her eyes. Rainbows danced behind her eyelids, and a slow, lazy smile touched her lips. *Oh, yeah.*

"You look happy." He slid up beside her and stroked wet tendrils of hair away from her temples.

"Ecstatic."

"That's what I was going for."

She kept her eyes closed, still enjoying those rainbows. "What…about you?" Vaguely she realized he must be in a world of hurt right now.

"You, um, mentioned condoms?"

"Left-hand bedside table drawer." She was amazed she remembered considering that she had a minimal number of brain cells operating.

The mattress undulated as he turned over, opened the drawer and found the box. Cardboard snapped and foil crinkled.

Her dazed mind began to recover, allowing her to imagine him tearing open a condom package and rolling the latex over his rock-hard penis. He'd kept her so busy with her own orgasm that she hadn't been able to fully appreciate the special equipment he brought to the party. She was appreciating it now, however.

Moments ago she'd been sated, sure that another climax was impossible after the way he'd pleasured her. Maybe not. As he flattened a palm on either side of her shoulders, his expression focused and his eyes hot, her body clenched and moistened, wanting more, wanting him.

But on her terms. She placed a hand on his chest. He had a terrific chest—firm, warm and lightly sprinkled with dark hair. "Wait."

He paused, his gaze locked with hers, a question lurking in the dark depths of his eyes.

"Lie down. I want to be on top."

He hesitated a moment more. "All right." His voice

was gruff with the effort to control himself. But he stretched out on his back.

Scrambling up, she surveyed him from head to toe. He was magnificent, a virile male with strong calves, muscled thighs and impressive family jewels paired with a proud erection. She ached to have him deep inside her, but if he could insist on giving a memorable experience, so could she.

"Will I do?"

Heart pounding, she gauged his taut expression and judged that he was near the breaking point. "You'll do very nicely." She closed her fingers around the rigid evidence of his arousal.

His chest heaved. "Is this payback?"

"Maybe." Caressing him lightly, she straddled his thighs.

He groaned and squeezed his eyes shut. "I'm really close."

"Pace yourself." She stopped touching him and eased onto his thighs.

He gave a choked laugh. "So my words come back to haunt me."

"I want this to be memorable."

Opening his eyes, he allowed her to see the fire blazing there. "It already is."

Her breath caught. She'd never been with a man who brought such emotion to the act of making love. This man who'd seemed so reluctant to share, to trust, had opened himself completely here in the privacy of her bedroom. She'd meant to tease him some more, but suddenly that seemed like a waste of time, just to prove a point.

"Come to me, Tansy. Please."

Holding his gaze, she rose over him. He bracketed

her hips with his strong hands and guided her to that ultimate connection. As she eased down, her blood pounding through her veins, the heat in his eyes intensified.

His jaw clenched. "So good."

"Yes." Her breathless answer seemed inadequate. Her body hummed with joy at having him deep inside her. All her instincts about him were right. They were perfect together.

Bracing her hands on his powerful shoulders, she began to move.

He sucked in a breath and his grip tightened. "Even better."

"Uh-huh." She loved watching his eyes darken as she initiated a slow rhythm. He matched her movements, thrusting upward as she bore down. She reveled in the intense pleasure of that steady friction.

The room filled with their ragged breathing and the provocative sound of love being well and truly made. She pushed him to go faster, bringing a groan from deep in his chest and a flash of fire in his eyes.

"Tansy."

She heard the desperation in his voice, knew he was losing control. But so was she. She gulped for air. "Let go, Ben."

"But…I want…"

"I'm there…I'm…" She erupted, and her cry of release blended with his as they tumbled into the abyss together. With a soft moan, she sank down against his damp chest. Nestling there, she listened to the rapid beat of his heart.

He wrapped her in his arms and rested his cheek against her hair. "You're perfect," he murmured.

"No, *we're* perfect."

He hugged her close. "Mmm."

It wasn't quite a murmur of agreement, but it wasn't exactly a denial, either. She smiled. He might think they were too different, but she knew those differences were evaporating like rain puddles on a sunny day. Eventually he'd figure that out, too. She could wait.

As she lay there pondering the wonder of their lovemaking, she gradually became aware of scratching at the bedroom door.

"Ewok?" Ben's voice was lazy with satisfaction.

"Yes. Ordinarily they spend the night in here with me." She decided to leave it at that and see how he reacted.

"In the bed?"

She detected no disapproval in the question, only curiosity. "Not Wookie. He's way too big. His dog bed's over in the corner. But I admit I've let Ewok get up here with me."

"Hmm." He stroked her hair, his breathing steady.

The scratching stopped. "See? He gave up. They're fine out in the living room for tonight."

"If you say so."

"I do."

He sighed with obvious contentment. "I hate to ask you to move, but it has to happen sooner or later. It's a drawback of the system."

"I know. I'll let you up. Bathroom's through that door on the right." Easing away from him, she rolled sideways so he could get out of bed and deal with the condom. Without his warmth, she shivered and pulled up the covers. In the frenzy of their lovemaking, they'd kicked them to the bottom of the bed.

Closing her eyes, she listened to the creak of her house's old floorboards as he walked into the bathroom.

She was glad he liked this house. She might be getting way ahead of herself to imagine him living here, but she didn't think so. It was only a matter of time.

The floorboards creaked again, and she expected him to climb back into bed with her. Instead she heard the unmistakable sound of her bedroom doorknob turning.

She sat up and blinked.

A gloriously naked Ben opened her bedroom door and called to the dogs.

"Ben, are you sure you want to do that? I warn you, Ewok will—" Before she could finish the sentence, Ewok tore through the open door and scrambled up beside her, tail wagging, button eyes bright with happiness.

Wookie ambled through the door, gave a low, guttural sound of pleasure and went straight to his bed in the corner.

Ben left the door open and turned back to her. He glanced with amusement at Ewok, who had taken his usual position on top of the covers, but smack in the middle of the bed.

"I warned you," Tansy said. "I've indulged him, and when he's in here, this is where he sleeps."

"Then he should get to sleep there." Ben walked back to the bed and climbed in on the other side of Ewok. "It's his house, after all."

"For now it is, but I'm only fostering."

Ben propped his head on his hand and studied her. "No, you're not."

"What do you mean? Of course I am. That's why I brought them to KFOR, in hopes someone would decide to take them."

He smiled. "Someone has. You."

"No, not me. I have to keep my house open so I can take in those who need extra care and attention for a little while. These two were traumatized by being left, even more so than most dogs are, so I brought them over here."

"I understand the concept, but you sure love having these two around. You would be sad to see them go."

"Of course I would, but…" Ewok watched her with bright eyes full of devotion. She looked over at Wookie, sprawled contentedly on the giant bed she'd bought him. "I would," she said softly. Her throat was tight.

"I know they'd be sad to leave you."

Thinking of that, she blew out a breath to release some tension. "I took this job right after I'd lost a dog and a cat, a few months apart, to old age. Right away I was tempted to adopt at least one of the animals, but then I thought that was silly. I was surrounded by furry friends all day. Keeping my house available for special cases seemed reasonable."

"I'll bet by now you have plenty of backup for those special cases."

"I do." She grinned sheepishly. "I could have found Ewok and Wookie a foster home. And to be honest, they might have adapted to the Doggie Digs just fine. Instead I kept them here."

"Where fewer visitors actually meet them."

With a groan she flopped back on the bed. "At least I took them on TV!"

"Yes, and that was brilliant showmanship on your part, but you were secretly worried somebody would adopt them after that, weren't you?"

Turning her head, she met his knowing gaze. "I've never admitted that, either to myself or someone else.

But yeah, I was dreading that phone call and relieved when it didn't come. How did you figure all this out?"

"Observation. It's what I do for a living, after all. I get behind a camera and watch what happens in front of it."

"So you do." She reached a hand across the bed. "You're awfully far away."

He laced his fingers through hers. "Call me old-fashioned, but I don't think I could get too friendly with you while there's a dog in the bed."

"And I wouldn't let you, either, which is why I was so surprised when you let them in."

"I'm the one intruding on their territory. Didn't seem fair to keep them outside."

She wondered if he realized the depth of his empathy for other creatures. "Yes, but now that we have a chaperone, we can't do anything fun."

"We can lie here and talk. That's fun."

She smiled because he was absolutely right. She loved the cozy intimacy they'd established. "Any special thing you want to talk about?"

"As a matter of fact, there is." He gave her fingers a squeeze. "As your official volunteer photographer, I have an idea for a fund-raiser to fix your roof."

Her eyes widened. "Is that so? What, pray tell?"

"I'll make a holiday DVD featuring the animals at The Haven. You can sell it at the front desk, but you can also sell it online. It would be good for next Christmas, too."

"Ben, that's a great plan! So you'd make it right away, while we're decorated for the holidays?"

"That was my thought. This weekend, in fact, if you're willing."

"More than willing. I love the idea." Her mind raced

through the possibilities. "Besides what we've already done, we can do a few extra things, like put bows on some of the dogs' collars, the way I did for Ewok and Wookie."

"Or you could get one of those plastic mistletoe balls and hang it from a string for the cats to play with."

"Or buy various sizes of Santa hats and see if we can get any of the dogs and cats to wear them long enough for a picture."

He laughed. "I can imagine a cute video of a million attempts to put a cat in a hat."

"Me, too! Oh, Ben, this will be awesome." She leaned over, brought their joined hands to her mouth and carefully kissed each of his fingers. "Thank you for being so creative."

"You inspire me."

She glanced down at Ewok, who was fast asleep. Then she lifted her gaze to Ben's. "I'm having a moment of inspiration, myself. Think we can sneak out of here without waking the dogs?"

His dark eyes glittered with interest. "Possibly. What did you have in mind?"

"Oh, building up the fire and spreading a blanket in front of it. Would you go for that?"

"In a heartbeat. Lead the way."

Her body began to tingle in anticipation as she eased out of bed and crept toward the door. This was quickly becoming the most amazing night of her life.

CHAPTER EIGHT

BEN HAD ALWAYS THOUGHT Tansy was a beautiful woman, but as she lay on a soft blanket with firelight gilding her body, she was breathtaking. When he finished rolling on the condom, she lifted her arms and parted her thighs in a seductive invitation that sent lust slamming into him like a body blow. He fought to keep from grabbing her and burying himself in her wet heat without foreplay or finesse.

Moving over her, he gazed into blue eyes sparkling with firelight. "That was incredibly sexy, what you did just now. You almost made me forget myself."

She ran her palms over his chest, stoking the fire. "How do you mean?"

"I wanted to ravish you."

Her full lips parted and her breath quickened. "I like the sound of that." Sliding her hands lower, she began to fondle him in ways that made his eyes roll back in his head. "I think I'd enjoy being ravished by you."

"Do you? Keep that up and it's liable to happen."

She moistened her lips with her tongue as she continued to use her hands in ways guaranteed to drive him around the bend. "Ravish me, Ben."

"I will." Sitting back on his heels, he captured her hands, circling her wrists with his fingers. Then he drew them over her head and leaned down, his mouth barely touching hers. "You drive me crazy."

Her breath was warm and sweet. "Maybe I want to."

"Prepare to take the consequences." Adjusting his position, he probed gently, but once he found what he wanted, he thrust home with enough force to lift her from the blanket. It felt so good he nearly came. But he controlled the urge, because he wanted this to last.

She gasped and shivered against him.

"Too much?" He nipped at her lower lip.

"Nooooo."

"Then wrap your legs around my waist. I want more of you, Tansy Dexter."

When she did, he pushed forward, going even deeper. Her muscles clenched around him, telling him she was already close. Drawing back, he began to pound into her, making her breasts shake with every stroke. Within seconds she climaxed, arching against him with a keening cry, but he kept going.

Her eyes grew wild and she began to pant. He shifted his angle. Ah, there. Another trembling response. He bore down, driving into her with relentless purpose, and she came again, thrashing her head from side to side and dragging in air.

Gradually he eased up on the pace until finally he slid into her drenched channel almost lazily, as if he had hours to do this. He didn't. His control was slipping fast, but he wasn't ready to surrender just yet.

As he pumped, he settled his mouth over hers and kissed her slowly, deeply and thoroughly. Then he lifted his head just a fraction. "Once more," he murmured.

Her reply was breathless. "I can't."

"Yes, you can." He kept moving, making steady contact right where it counted, rubbing that precious little spot at the entrance to paradise. "I know you can."

She moaned softly and raised her hips, meeting him halfway.

"There, see?" He brushed his lips over hers. "You want to."

"Yes… Oh, Ben…it's so…good."

When he felt her spasm, he let his control slide away. Once again he drove into her, and her orgasm triggered his. Gasping, he shoved deep one last time as waves of pleasure rolled over him, incomparable pleasure.

As the first rush of feeling passed, he had to face the enormity of it. He'd never made love like this. He'd never felt so open, so completely connected. Tansy had learned how to cope with devastating loss and grief. Maybe if he was with her he could learn how to cope with it, too.

The idea scared him spitless.

LATER, THEY PULLED A second blanket over themselves and cuddled next to a fire that had burned down to a bed of glowing coals.

Tansy nestled her cheek against his chest. "I loved being ravished."

"Good." He chuckled and caressed her shoulder. "I'll have to do it again sometime."

"All I need is a few minutes' notice, and I'll make myself available."

"You'd better not say things like that. I'm liable to become a pest."

"That sounds lovely." She relaxed against his comfortingly solid body.

"Yeah, it does. I'm thinking I'll cancel that ski vacation."

"Mmm, I'd like that. I'd like that a lot. My folks are staying in Arizona for the holidays, so having you in town would be excellent." The thought flooded her with happiness. "You might even consider taking Max, after all."

He stopped stroking her shoulder. "What?"

Uh-oh. He wasn't ready to hear a suggestion like that. She'd been feeling so mellow that the comment had slipped out. " It's just that your ski trip was an issue and now it's not. No pressure—"

"Oh, I think there's pressure, Tansy." His voice had lost some of its warmth. "You're determined for me to adopt that cat, aren't you?" He sat up.

So did she. She scooted around so she was facing him. "Not determined. Never that. But tonight I watched you with the dogs who'd been flooded out, then the cats with their new playground, and Ewok and Wookie here in my house. You have an affinity for these animals, Ben."

"I never said I didn't like them. That doesn't mean I'm ready to take on their care and feeding."

"That's not what's got you spooked." She'd started this discussion, and she had to finish it. Despite evidence that attachments could enhance his life, he continued to avoid the risk of loss.

He frowned. "I'm not spooked, either. I just don't want to rush into—"

"I was there when you brought Mickey in."

He jerked as if she'd reached out and slapped him. "What do you mean?"

"I doubt you remember because you were so torn up, but when you carried him into the vet's office after he was hit by that car, I held you while you cried."

A look of panic was replaced by cool reserve. "So what?"

"So what?" She wanted to shake him, but she kept

her hands to herself. "Losing him was horrible for you! I know that because I was there. You hinted that you didn't have a wonderful childhood, and I'm guessing Mickey was the one bright spot for you."

His expression closed down. "I didn't have a wonderful childhood, but it wasn't as bad as some. My mother wasn't interested in me, so she left me with her sister and brother-in-law. At least I was raised by relatives instead of shoved into foster care."

Her chest grew heavy with dread. This was not going well. "Was Mickey your only pet?"

"Yes. My first and last. We moved around a lot, and he was the one constant, the only one I could rely on to always be there. And then he wasn't."

"Ben, you were only a kid. Of course it hit you hard. We're all more emotional at that age. But if you'd give Max a chance, I think the two of you would—"

"I can't believe this."

"Believe what? That I can see your love of animals shining in your eyes? That I know the joy that can bring? Yes, we usually outlive the animals we love, at least until we're seniors ourselves. But you can handle that, Ben. I know you can. And the rewards are huge!"

"You're trying to rescue *me,* aren't you? First I let down my guard to a pet, then to people?"

She stared at him. Her blood felt like snowmelt running through her veins. "Maybe I am trying to rescue you. Maybe I hate to see what you're missing and hope you'll change your mind."

He met her gaze for several endless seconds. "Right." He stood and headed for the bedroom. Once he opened the door, both dogs came out, Ewok in the lead. He closed the door after him.

Wrapping a blanket around herself, she gathered

Ewok into her lap. Wookie flopped down in front of her and rested his head on her knee. "Oh, guys." She rubbed Wookie's large head with one hand and scratched behind Ewok's ears with the other as she blinked back tears. "This isn't going to be good."

Sure enough, it wasn't. Not long afterward, Ben came out, fully dressed. "I've been kidding myself, Tansy. I thought you cared about me. I didn't realize I was a project."

"A project? No, you're not! I just figured that—"

"A little TLC and a revelation about my tortured past, and I'd be all fixed up, right? I'm not one of your rescue animals, Tansy!"

Oh, God. She had screwed this up. "I never thought you were. I shouldn't have mentioned taking Max."

"No, I'm glad you did. I'm glad you finally told me the dark secret about that day in the vet's office." His expression remained closed. "Now I understand why you took pity on me and invited me here."

Tears choked her, making her words come out as a croak. "That's not why."

"Sorry, but I don't believe you." He glanced around. "Where the hell is my coat?"

"In the kitchen." Misery tightened her chest. She had pushed him and ruined everything. Nothing she said now would convince him that she hadn't plotted to *fix* him. And maybe he wasn't completely wrong about that, which made her even more miserable.

"Thanks." He went in, flicked on a light, then turned it off again as he came back out wearing his coat and hat. "Look, I keep my promises. I'll still be your official photographer, and I'll create the holiday DVD we talked about. I'll do it Saturday, if that's all right."

She swallowed. "Fine. I'd love to let you out of that

agreement because I'm sure it doesn't hold the same appeal, but I need both those things desperately, so I accept your generosity."

He stood there a moment longer. "I'd appreciate it if you'd tell me one thing, since you were there that day. And then I don't want to talk about it ever again."

"Okay."

"What happened to him? I mean, after..."

"I talked the vet into letting me take him and bury him with my family's pets in our backyard. Unfortunately, that house doesn't belong to my folks anymore, so you can't visit—"

"No, no. I wouldn't want to do that. But I wasn't thinking at the time, and when I finally realized that I hadn't taken care of everything, I worried that maybe he'd ended up in a landfill or something. Thank you for making sure that didn't happen."

"It wouldn't have happened. Dr. Horton was a wonderful vet. Still is. He donates a few hours to The Haven every month."

Ben nodded. "Good. That's great." He backed toward the door. "I need to go. Have to be at work early."

"I understand." Sadly, she did understand. She'd taken the possibility of something wonderful and crushed it by pushing her own agenda. "Goodbye, Ben."

"See you Saturday. I'll come early, if that's okay."

She swallowed the sob that threatened to escape. "Sure. Early's fine."

He looked at her once more before heading for the door. The lock clicked as he closed it behind him.

Ewok whined, and she glanced down. Her vision was blurred by tears, but she could see that she was holding him way too tight. Hysterical laughter bubbled up. "Me and Lisa the anchorwoman, huh, Ewok. Thank you for not peeing on me."

Ewok licked her hand as if to say that she was forgiven. Then Wookie let out a huge doggie sigh.

"One good thing came out of Ben Rhodes spending time here tonight," Tansy said. "He made me realize that I don't want either of you going anywhere. Tomorrow I'm taking both of you off the adoption list."

But there was more than one good thing that had come out of the evening she'd spent with Ben. They'd shared laughter, sex and a connection that she'd thought might last. Instead it had been over mere hours after it had begun, and it was her fault. She wasn't dealing with that very well, either.

Ewok put his paws on her chest and began licking the tears from her face.

"Thanks, sweetie." She cuddled the dog close, but not too close. She didn't want to get peed on. "Looks like it's going to be the three of us for Christmas, after all."

BETWEEN THE TIME BEN left Tansy late Thursday night and the time he parked in The Haven's lot Saturday morning, he went through hell. And it was a hell of his own making. He'd known, *known* not to get involved with her. But he had ignored his own warnings and made love to her. Twice.

Even worse, making love to Tansy had given him the best memories of his life. What had he been thinking? Apparently he hadn't been thinking at all. He'd been so besotted with her that he hadn't seen the trap closing around him.

Oh, she hadn't deliberately set it. At least he hoped not. The condoms had been damned convenient, but there could be an explanation for the unopened box in her bedside table drawer. The decision to have sex had been spontaneous. He'd bet money on that.

He'd been the one who'd mentioned giving up his ski trip so he could spend time with her, which had opened up a can of worms he should have anticipated. He shouldn't have said anything about staying home, but once again, he'd let his libido run the show.

He wondered how different everything would have been if she'd told him a week ago that she'd been there when Mickey died. But he could see why she hadn't said anything. Not blurting it out in the office had been the sensitive way to handle the situation. He should have known she would push the adoption. She thought his decision to avoid bonding with animals was a mistake, a symptom of his deeper pain. She wanted to rescue him from that mistake, heal him—for his own good, of course. That really stuck in his craw. He didn't need rescuing, by her or anyone.

Now if he could only forget the intense joy he'd felt when he was with her, he could move on.

In the past couple of days, though, he'd had zero success with that, and if he continued on as the shelter's official photographer, he might never get over her.

So once he'd completed this DVD, he'd scout around for someone else to take the assignment. Surely someone in Tacoma had camera skills and was itching to donate those skills to helping homeless animals.

Bolstered by that plan, he took a deep breath, grabbed his backpack full of camera equipment and climbed out of his truck. A couple of cars were in the lot, and lights were on inside the yellow Victorian. Fresh snow had fallen during the night, but the steps were already fairly tracked up.

He was surprised that people had been coming and

going from the shelter so early. Last Saturday at this time, Tansy had been alone in the office and only two volunteers had been working, one for the cats and one for the dogs, but when he walked in the door he noticed Faye behind the counter.

She glanced up. "There you are. Tansy's not here."

"Oh." Disappointment sliced through him. He was angry with Tansy, but he was still desperate to see her again. She'd probably made herself scarce on purpose. After all, she didn't have to be here to help. He could handle it alone.

"She asked me to come in early this morning and help you set up." Faye gestured to a couple of canvas shopping bags sitting on her desk. "She bought some props for you to use, if you want them."

He nodded, but the more he thought about Tansy's being AWOL, the more irritated he became. Coming here hadn't been easy for him, but he had because he'd made a promise. They'd brainstormed the project together, and even though they both might feel a little awkward, they should work on this DVD together. Besides, he wanted to see her, needed to see her. Fool that he was.

Faye took her coat from the back of her chair and put it on before picking up the bags. "Where do you want to start, cats or dogs?"

"Cats. Just out of curiosity, where is Tansy this morning?"

Faye paused to gaze at him. "It's Max."

"What about Max?"

She regarded him with caution, as if debating what to say. "He has an abscess at the base of his tail where he bit himself. We didn't notice it right away, and now…

well, I'm afraid it's an emergency situation. Tansy rushed him to the vet."

A band of fear closed around his chest. "But he'll be okay, right?"

"I don't know. The abscess is poisoning his system, and they'll have to do surgery. It depends how that all goes. Anyway, ready to start shooting?"

"No. I'm going to have to come back later." He pictured Tansy alone at the vet's office with a cat she loved, one who might not make it. He knew what that was like. "Where's the vet's office?"

"It's Dr. Horton. He's on—"

"I know where his office is." He'd avoided driving past it whenever possible. He wasn't looking forward to walking into it now. But he couldn't let Tansy sit there alone and worried. He wanted to be there for her, no matter what.

CHAPTER NINE

ALTHOUGH TANSY WOULD have preferred to be right there while Dr. Horton and his assistant operated on Max, they didn't really need her. After helping out in the office when she was a teenager, she'd decided against going to veterinarian school, so she didn't have the training to be of any real help. All she could do was sit in the waiting area and worry.

When the outer door opened and Ben walked in, she thought she was hallucinating. Tossing her magazine aside, she stood. "What are you doing here?"

He crossed to her, taking off his hat as he walked. He stopped in front of her, his dark gaze troubled. "I... Oh, hell, come here, Tansy." He pulled her into his arms.

She went willingly, wrapping her arms around him. He tucked her head against the wooly softness of his sheepskin collar. "I'm so sorry about Max."

She'd held it together until then, but in the comfort of his arms, she let the tears fall. "That ornery cat had better not die on me," she said in a choked voice. "Especially when he did it to himself!"

"He's not going to die." Ben laid his cheek against her hair and rubbed her back. "You said yourself Dr. Horton's the best. He'll fix Max right up."

"I blame myself." She sniffed. "I should have noticed he was getting sick, but he's never perky, even under the best of circumstances. Silly old cat."

"Tansy, nobody deserves the blame less than you. You've given Max a place to stay and a job to do."

She gave a watery laugh. "Yeah. His job is to ignore everybody who comes into the office, and he does it brilliantly."

"He's an original. A conversation piece."

"Guess so." She took a shaky breath and sniffed again. "Thank you for coming."

"I had to." He kissed the top of her head. "I couldn't let you be here alone."

Leaning back, she looked into his eyes. "Kind of ironic, isn't it? Twelve years later, here we are in Dr. Horton's office, but our situations are reversed."

"Life's crazy that way." He brushed a tear from her cheek with his thumb. "But this time, the cat's gonna make it."

She knew he had no inside information, but she needed someone to tell her it was going to be okay. Ben looked so sure that Max would live, she chose to believe he would be right.

"Tansy?" Dr. Horton walked out into the waiting area. Tall and thin, he was a little grayer, a little balder, but his blue eyes were still kind behind his wire-rimmed glasses.

She let go of Ben. Steeling herself for whatever was coming, she turned to face the vet.

"I think he'll be fine," Dr. Horton said.

Relief made her sag. "Thank God."

Ben put his hand on her shoulder and gave it a squeeze.

"You'll have to watch him and make sure the antibiotics are doing their job," the vet said. "And of course he has to wear the cone. He won't be very happy for a couple of weeks, I'm afraid."

Tansy smiled. "So he'll be a little grumpier than usual. I'm used to that. Max is not what you'd call a cheerful cat." Although he had been, briefly, when he'd settled himself on Ben's lap. She turned back to Ben. "Dr. Horton, this is Ben Rhodes from K.FOR. He's offered to make a holiday DVD to sell as a shelter fundraiser."

"Excellent." The vet beamed. "Glad to see Tansy has another supporter."

Ben stepped toward him and held out his hand. "I'd like to add a personal and long-overdue thank you. When I was seventeen, I brought my one-eyed cat in."

Tansy glanced at Ben in surprise. She wouldn't have expected him to mention that.

"Oh?" Dr. Horton studied Ben as he shook his hand. "You do look familiar. What was the situation with your cat?"

"Accident with a car. He didn't make it, but I appreciate all you did trying to save him. I left rather… quickly after he died."

The vet looked over at Tansy, then back at Ben. "Were you the one who sent an envelope full of cash with no note?"

"Yeah. I hope it was enough. I should have stopped by long before this to find out."

"It was more than enough. I wanted to return the extra money, but we didn't know how to get in touch with you. I think Tansy tried to find you in her high school yearbook."

"I enrolled midyear and we left for Spokane before the semester ended. I wasn't in the yearbook."

Tansy remembered he'd said he'd moved around a lot. A hard way to live for a child. Now was not the time to ask him about his past, though.

"Well." Dr. Horton glanced at Tansy. "Mystery solved at last. And now you two have become friends, I see."

Tansy nodded. "We have." She hadn't thought they would be after Thursday night, but Ben had come to support her through Max's surgery. He must care about her, after all.

The vet turned to Ben. "Come to think of it, wasn't that cat of yours an orange tabby like Max? I could be wrong, but some cases stick in your mind."

"He looked a lot like Max, except for having both eyes," Ben said. "Oh, and my cat was still a tom. I'm going to bet Max is not."

Dr. Horton laughed. "That's a given with any of The Haven's animals. And if I know Tansy, she's already talked you into taking at least one home with you, if not more."

Tansy sucked in a breath.

"She's tried." Ben glanced at her. "It's not for me."

The vet looked startled. "Allergic?"

"No, I just…don't care to do that."

The uncomfortable silence that followed was interrupted as Dr. Horton's assistant, Nancy, a middle-age woman with dark hair, came out with Max's carrier. "He's pretty woozy," she said. "I doubt he'll put up a fuss on the way home."

Tansy was glad for the change of topic. "That'll be a relief. He yowled all the way here." She started to take the carrier, but Ben reached for it.

She let him do the honors, but his gallantry didn't fool her into thinking he'd forgiven her for what he considered a serious case of meddling in his life. Maybe she'd mishandled the situation, but if he was using her bungled attempt to help as an excuse to cling to his isolated lifestyle, then he wasn't the man she'd thought he was.

She had an account with Dr. Horton, so she didn't have to mess with paying for Max's surgery. After thanking him and Nancy for pulling Max from the brink, she walked out with Ben. A light rain had begun to fall, and she put up the hood on her parka. Then she quickly unlocked the shelter's van and opened the passenger door so Ben could set the carrier on the seat.

"Want me to belt him in?"

"Please."

He reached for the seat belt, wrapped it around the carrier and snapped it into place. "That should hold him." He turned to her. "I didn't do any shooting, so I'll head back over and get started. I might have to finish up on Sunday, if that's okay."

"Fine. Just let me know when you're coming and I'll be over there to let you in. Thanks for everything." She started around to the driver's side.

"Wait." He caught her arm.

"What?" She turned back to him.

"I'm sorry for being so harsh on Thursday night. I know you're only trying to help."

"Thanks for that." She waited, hoping against hope that he'd say he was rethinking his position.

"It's just that whenever I consider taking in an animal, I don't like the odds."

"Odds?" She stared at him as the rain pelted down. "When you're talking about love, you don't play the odds."

"You make it sound so easy, but it's not."

"I didn't say it was." Anxiety over Max had sapped her patience, and as she stood there gazing at this stubborn, wounded man, she lost it. "You know what, Ben

Rhodes? You're a damned coward. You don't have the guts to face the possibility of pain. I'll see you back at the shelter." She marched around the front of the van, wrenched open the door and climbed in.

As she backed out of her parking spot, Ben continued to stand where she'd left him. Rain fell in silvery drops all around him, but he stayed motionless, as if he were a granite statue.

Unless he changed his approach to life, and that didn't seem likely, he might as well be stone. Then nothing could touch him, which seemed to be what he wanted.

BEN WASN'T SURE HOW long he remained standing in the parking lot, but eventually the amount of water cascading from the brim of his hat made him realize he needed to move. He got into his truck but didn't start the engine. He wasn't sure where he wanted to go. He'd promised to create a DVD for Tansy, but he wasn't in the mood to be creative right now.

Pulling out his phone, he texted her that he would be back early the next morning and would work all day. Maybe by the next morning he'd have recovered from being called a coward.

He'd been accused of many things in his life, but never that. He liked to think he was as brave as the next man. One summer while out waterskiing with his buddies from KFOR, he'd rescued a kid who was drowning. No one else in his group had leaped into the water to grab the kid, but he had.

Then there was the time he'd come upon a burning wreck on the freeway. He'd pulled the passenger out because the driver had been too hysterical to do it. In both cases he'd acted without hesitation. So how could he be a coward?

He refused to accept that label. Instead he drove home and called Justin, his friend from the station. They played racquetball until they were exhausted, and then went for beer and pizza.

After his second beer, Ben turned to Justin. "Would you say I'm a coward?"

Justin stared at him in confusion. "Why are you asking me such a dumb question?"

"I want your opinion, bro. We've worked together for three years, and we've gone on all those adventure travel trips. In that time, did you at any time think I was a coward?"

"Hell, no, dude! You were the one who had the balls to tell Lisa her skirt was too tight when she walked on the set a couple of weeks ago. She could have got you fired for that. Coward? I don't think so!"

"Thank you." Ben lifted his beer bottle in Justin's direction. "Thank you very much."

The next morning, fortified by Justin's evaluation, Ben arrived at The Haven in the gray light of dawn. Tansy was polite, but reserved.

"How's Max doing?" Ben really did want to know. He'd thought about the cranky cat quite a bit since yesterday.

"He's fine."

"Is he here?" Ben looked around the deserted office.

"Oh, no. I took him over to my place so I can monitor his progress."

"How do Ewok and Wookie like that?"

She folded her arms and glared at him. "None of your business."

"I see." His jaw tightened. The party was over. "I'd like to start with the cats."

"I'll take you out there." She put on her parka and picked up the two canvas bags full of Christmas props. They walked in silence to the door of the Kitty Condo. Opening the door, Tansy called out to Cindy, who confirmed that she was ready for Ben to start.

Tansy glanced at him. "Are you going to need my help?"

"No." Two could play this game. "I'll handle it."

"Then I'll leave you to your work." Handing him the bags, she turned and walked back down the lighted path.

Ben told himself that her attitude was for the best. She expected things of him that he wasn't willing to give, so reverting to a business relationship would help them both get through the making of the DVD. After that, he would find another photographer to help her.

LEAVING BEN TO PHOTOGRAPH the animals without her was sheer torture, but necessary. Tansy needed to put some distance between her and the sexy man in the sheepskin coat. Despite her rant about his cowardly nature, she still hoped he'd somehow become the man she knew he could be.

When he'd walked through the door in the cold of dawn, she'd longed to throw herself into his arms and share his heat. He might be a coward, but boy, was he a hot one. She hadn't been able to forget the glory of their lovemaking.

But she had to be strong. She was firm in her beliefs, and this wasn't a time to compromise. Animals were her life, and hooking up with someone with Ben's attitude would only lead to heartbreak. If he made her feel like a goddess whenever he touched her…well, that was lovely, but not enough. But, ah, how she missed him.

At noon, Cindy walked in the back door and Tansy peppered her with questions about the shoot.

"It's going great." Cindy took the elastic from her hair and redid her ponytail. "It's as if he thinks like a cat, if you know what I mean. He's there one second before they do something, so he captures the moment."

Tansy felt a rush of pride, even though she'd told herself that she only cared about the value of his skill. "Good. Then this DVD will be special. Lots of people take videos of animals, but we want to stand out from the pack."

"He showed me some of what he had, and it's amazing. I'm telling all my friends to get this DVD."

"Seriously?" Tansy had trouble imagining teenagers who were into zombies and aliens wanting to see a cute video of cats.

"Oh, yeah. There's this one part where Atlas was poised to jump and Ben got underneath him. Atlas looks like Supercat flying to the rescue. It's awesome. So funny!"

"Great. That's really great." Tansy's heart ached for what might have been. She could have been there watching Ben as he captured Supercat with his deft use of his camcorder. She could have rejoiced with him and shared the experience.

But she knew he was a fraud. He worked magic with his camera but his heart wasn't in it. Ben Rhodes kept his heart locked away, protected from all harm.

"I have to go," Cindy said. "I've left him in Shelby Conrad's capable hands at the Doggie Digs. I'm sure he'll get some terrific stuff over there, too. But between you and me, I think he's a cat person."

"Maybe so." Tansy didn't consider him either a dog or a cat person. He wouldn't commit to caring for either species, so he didn't get the designation. But she wouldn't say that to Cindy, who was smitten by the talented Ben Rhodes.

He'd better not let on to Shelby Conrad that he wasn't planning to adopt an animal. That woman was devoted to her rescue work, although Shelby seemed to need the animals as much as they needed her. With no kids and a husband who'd been deployed to a combat zone, Shelby had thrown herself into volunteering and fostering. Tansy was extremely grateful for her help.

Cindy headed for the door, but turned before she reached it. "Too bad it didn't work out for you and Ben."

Tansy wasn't sure how to respond to that statement, so she said nothing.

"I mean, he's great, and you're great, so I still think you'd make a good couple."

"Cindy, he absolutely refuses to allow animals into his life. Do you see me with someone like that?"

Cindy hesitated. "I don't think he's clear on what he wants."

"I agree." Tansy wanted to scream or pound on something. A teenager had more insight into the problem than the man himself. "But until he is, we're at an impasse."

"I've seen him with those cats." Cindy fiddled with her ponytail. "All I'm saying is, don't give up on him yet."

"I'll see how it goes." But Tansy had already gone a few rounds with Ben, and her heart was bruised. She didn't hold out much hope that their story would have a fairy-tale ending.

CHAPTER TEN

BEN DIDN'T STOP BY THE office when he was finished at
the end of the day. He'd been frosted by Tansy's icy
attitude that morning, and he saw no reason to subject himself to it again. After packing up and thanking
Shelby for her help, he walked to the parking lot and
got into his truck.

No lights shone from the windows of the yellow Victorian, but even from here he could see the cheerful
strand of LEDs strung along Tansy's porch rail. He
caught the scent of a wood fire. She was tucked into
her little house with Ewok, Wookie and Max. He wondered if she still had soup and homemade bread left.

Okay, this was truly pathetic. He was sitting in his
truck and fantasizing about what was happening in Tansy's house. What was wrong with him? Turning the key,
he started the engine and pulled out of the lot.

He had a long night of editing ahead of him if he
planned to have something to show Tansy during his
lunch break tomorrow. That was his goal, to get this
damned thing done and end the torture of constant contact with her.

By eleven that night, he was bleary-eyed from editing, but he couldn't ignore the truth anymore. Tansy
had nailed it. He was a coward. The proof was in every
frame of every video.

All day he'd been dealing with abandoned animals.

If they hadn't been abandoned, they wouldn't be at The Haven. Once upon a time they'd been living in a cozy setup that they'd expected would go on forever, and then, boom! They became excess baggage, ending up homeless and unwanted.

And yet, despite that, these creatures had not given up hope that life could be good again. He was humbled by the sheer volume of optimism on the videos he'd shot. These animals had more courage than he did.

Today he'd dealt with cats who'd been left by the side of the road. Yet they'd come over and rubbed against his leg, wanting to be stroked. He'd met dogs who'd been jettisoned because their family was moving and didn't want the inconvenience of taking them along. Those same dogs still wagged their tails and affectionately shoved their noses into his hand.

Maybe their previous situation hadn't worked out, but they had great expectations for the next one. Sure, a few of the animals moped in a corner, but Cindy and Shelby had told him how diligently Tansy worked with the depressed ones to bring them out of their shells.

She'd tried to do the same with him, and he'd rejected her attempts. He'd retreated, like the coward that she'd so rightly labeled him. But if these dogs and cats who had been rejected could bounce back, what was wrong with him?

He worked on the DVD all night, and then he had to go to work. Surviving on caffeine and sugar, he made it through the six o'clock morning news. Then he told Paul he had a personal issue and needed the rest of the day off.

At first he thought Paul wouldn't let him go, so he played his ace. "It's a project for The Haven," he said. "Yesterday I shot footage for a holiday fund-raising

DVD, and Tansy needs to approve it so I can get it into production and up for sale."

Paul's expression mellowed, but he remained skeptical. "That will take all day?"

"I'm afraid so." Ben kept his expression neutral. "There's a lot of detail to be covered." Was there ever. And he had no idea if he'd succeed, but he had to try.

"Okay," Paul said at last. "Why do I feel like Ebenezer Scrooge granting Bob Cratchit a holiday?"

Ben shrugged. "It's Christmas. We're surrounded by those traditional stories." But in truth Ben was Scrooge, and instead of being instructed by the ghosts of Christmas past, present and future, he'd been taught to cherish life by a host of furry friends.

"Guess so. Take off, then. And say hello to Tansy for me."

"Will do."

With the video on the seat next to him, Ben drove to the pet store and loaded up. He needed cat litter, a litter box, a pet carrier, a cozy bed, a cat tree and some toys. He went somewhat overboard on the toys. He took the clerk's advice on what food to buy. If Tansy had a different favorite, he could always switch it out.

By the time he arrived at The Haven, it was nearly noon. He hoped to God she hadn't left for an appointment, or worse yet, caught the flu. She had to be there. She simply had to.

He walked into the office with the DVD rough cut in his hand and sighed in relief. Tansy and Faye were each at their desks working. Tansy looked up first, and he told himself it was because they had a connection and she sensed his presence.

But her expression was guarded. "You must have the DVD ready to preview."

"I do."

She took a deep breath. "Come on back and let's see what you have." She acted as if it would be a chore that she had to get through.

He chose not to be offended. She had every reason to give him a hard time. Rounding the counter, he proceeded back to her desk, commandeered the same chair he'd used the last time, and sat down. "Here you go." He handed her the DVD in its hard plastic case.

"Did it take you long?" She popped it out of the case and inserted it in her disc drive.

"All night."

She glanced over at him with grudging respect. "You must be tired."

"Some." He unbuttoned his coat and took off his hat, propping it on his knee. "But it was worth one sleepless night, all things considered."

She waited while the video loaded, and he sat quietly, enjoying being close to her, being able to breathe in her special scent and admire the curve of her throat and the pink tinge of her cheek. Her lashes fluttered, as if she sensed his gaze on her.

The video began. It was a love letter, and he hoped she'd see that. She did seem entranced—her lips were parted and her breath was shallow as she studied the images. He was proud of what he'd done, and judging from her rapt attention, he'd captured the concepts of optimism, hope and joy.

The whole thing took more than thirty minutes, which gave him plenty of time to bask in her glow and realize that any man who was privileged to be with her should thank his lucky stars every day. If she gave him a chance, he'd do exactly that.

When the video ended, she turned to him, eyes shining. "Incredible. I love it."

"And I love you." He hadn't meant to bust out with it, but the words came without him realizing they would.

She gasped and her eyes widened.

"Didn't mean to say that quite yet," he murmured. "But it's true, Tansy. I'm in love with you."

Her bright eyes grew even brighter and a pink flush spread over her cheeks. She swallowed and cast a quick glance at Faye.

Ben noticed the receptionist was paying considerable attention to her computer screen, but chances were she was listening to every word. He didn't care. He wanted to tell the whole world.

"I realize you don't love me," he said. "Because who would love a coward? But I'm working on that, and maybe in time you'll come to love me back."

She cleared her throat. "I've tried really hard not to love you," she said in a low voice. "I haven't been particularly successful."

"Really?" His heart thumped crazily in his chest.

She nodded. "You're all wrong for me, and yet I—"

"Not all wrong." He reached for her hand and held it between both of his. "But I did have to evolve quite a bit to meet your standards. I want to adopt Max."

Her eyebrows lifted. "You do? Are you sure?"

"As sure as I am that I love you, and that's pretty damned sure. I've bought all the stuff I need for him and it's out in my truck. You might not want me to take him yet, but I wanted to be ready in case I could. You can come and look in my truck if you want, make sure I've got everything."

"I don't have to." Her eyes sparkled with that sunshine he loved so much. "I only have to look at you. There's something different about you today."

"I am different, and it's because of you. You and the animals. Your bravery and theirs put me to shame, and I'm determined to change my attitude."

"My sweet Ben." She cupped his face with her free hand.

He smiled. "That sounds promising."

Faye pushed back her chair with a loud, scraping noise. "Okay, you two." She stood and faced them. Although her voice was stern, her expression was not. Then she started to laugh. "I'm thrilled for you both, but I think you might want to take this party over to Tansy's house before you embarrass us all."

Tansy's rosy glow deepened as she looked at Faye. "I doubt Ben has that kind of time." She gently extracted her hand from his. "He probably has to get back to the station."

"Actually I took the day off."

Her gaze swung back to his. "You did?"

"I wasn't sure how long it would take to get Max settled in, assuming you'd let me have him today."

Faye nodded. "Could take a long time, considering how cranky Max is right now. I warn you, he's not in a good mood."

"That's okay," Ben said. "I am."

Tansy glanced at Faye. "I hate to leave you alone to handle everything."

"Hey, consider it my Christmas present. Take Ben down to greet his cat and then you can…discuss the adoption procedures."

"All right." Tansy pushed back her chair, and when she stood, so did Ben. "You've never adopted an animal before, so we'll need to go over everything carefully."

"Very carefully." Ben took her coat from the back of her chair and helped her into it. Then he smiled at Faye. "Thanks."

"No problem. I always thought you'd come around. You're not the hardest case we've ever come across. I can think of one who's a lot worse." She winked at Tansy.

Tansy laughed. "Me, too."

"Oh?" He glanced from Faye to Tansy. "Who's that?"

The two women spoke together "Max!"

THAT EVENING, TANSY cuddled on the sofa with Ben as a fire crackled in the fireplace and the Christmas lights glowed from the tree in the corner. Tansy's head was tucked against Ben's shoulder, but she made sure not to crowd Max, who was firmly ensconced, cone and all, on Ben's lap. Ewok had curled against Tansy's other side, and Wookie was stretched out by their feet.

Fortunately Max had been asleep when she and Ben had first arrived, which gave them plenty of time to make long, sweet love to each other. But after Max woke up and discovered that his soul mate had reappeared, he'd been unwilling to let Ben out of his sight.

Ben laid his cheek against Tansy's hair. "Do you think he'll expect to be attached to me like this 24/7?"

"He probably won't be as needy once he knows you'll come back."

"Good, because although I like having him on my lap, I have…other things I want to do that require Max to be somewhere else." He tightened his arm around her.

Desire stirred. "Me, too. Fortunately, adult cats sleep eighteen hours a day."

"That's good news, too."

"He'll probably sleep most of the day while you're at work. He should be fine alone in your apartment."

Ben sighed. "Speaking of that, I suppose I should think about packing him up and driving home."

She'd been thinking about that all afternoon and evening. Their love was very new, but it didn't feel that way. Sitting here with him, her world made sense at last.

She took a deep breath. "If you're not ready for this, just say so, but I was wondering if you—"

"Yes."

"Yes?" She lifted her head to look into his eyes. "You don't know what I was going to say."

His gaze was warm. "I'd say yes to anything you asked me right now, but I'm hoping…I'm hoping you're asking me to move in."

Her heart beat faster as she realized her dreams really were about to come true. "I am asking you to move in."

"Thank God. Because I was sitting here trying to figure out how this was going to work. I want to be with you, and you need to be here with Ewok and Wookie, and I should be home with Max. I could trundle him over here every night in his carrier, but that didn't sound like a very—"

"He would hate that."

"Yeah." He smiled. "And we sure don't want to cause Max any stress."

"We sure don't." She returned his smile.

"I'd do anything for that cat." He lowered his head, and his breath was warm against her mouth. "After all, he led me to you."

"He definitely deserves special treatment."

"So do you, Tansy. And I'm just the guy to give it to you."

"I believe you are." As she surrendered to his kiss, joy spilled over her in a glittering cascade. She had it all—her precious animals and the man who would love them, and her, with all his heart. At last she'd found her forever home…with Ben.

* * * * *

To Daisy and her forever family.

I'm honored to have been a part
of your journey to find each other.

HOME FOR CHRISTMAS

USA TODAY Bestselling Author
Catherine Mann

CHAPTER ONE

Shelby Dawson-Conrad waited inside an airplane hangar to welcome home her husband, as she'd done for at least half a dozen military deployments. Their two dogs sat beside her, wearing matching Christmas collars with bells.

The band, the families and banners were the same year after year, their anticipation echoing up to the steel beam rafters. This chaotic lifestyle had become the norm for her.

But one thing was glaringly different. She was wearing underwear.

Usually before she welcomed her husband home, she shimmied out of her panties in the car and stuffed them in her purse. Today, her underwear was so totally in place she might as well have put on a chastity belt.

She and Alex had been married for nearly eight years. They'd loved each other for most of that time. Until things started to fall apart. Four months ago, just before he'd left for another deployment, they'd contacted lawyers about a divorce.

So welcome-back sex was definitely out of the question.

Still, honor dictated she greet Alex returning from his deployment. Even if the marriage was all but over, she refused to be like her mother who'd left her husband to return home from war unwelcomed. Shelby would not be that callous. She had worked hard to be the perfect wife, to be the antithesis of her own mom.

And yet it still hadn't been enough.

The band transitioned from "The Star Spangled Banner" to "I'll Be Home for Christmas." She arched up onto her toes to stare over the press of other families gathered in the heated hangar at McChord Air Force Base. A toddler girl twirled in a candy-cane-striped dress, with elfin snow boots on her feet and a "Welcome Home, Daddy" poster in her hand. A little boy in a Santa hat leaned against one of Shelby's dogs, burying his chubby fingers in Samson's fur.

Her heart squeezed tight. She and Alex had dreamed of starting a family…but it had never happened, despite countless and costly fertility treatments.

The holidays would be awkward with the looming divorce and no children to focus on, but Shelby had a plan to ease that unbearable tension. She'd volunteered to use her holiday break from teaching to drive three shelter dogs from The Haven to each of their adoptive families around Washington State. If Alex came with her, they could use the time to talk through their unresolved issues on neutral ground and end their marriage on a positive note. Getting Alex to discuss their problems was like pulling teeth, but she figured if she had him alone in a moving car, it would be a helluva lot tougher for him to bail on the conversation.

Hopefully he would sign on for her idea, rather than insist on spending Christmas in the home they'd bought with such hope when they'd moved to Tacoma, Washington.

Finally, Shelby saw him. Her husband.

Alex loped through the open hangar door toward her, his flight suit rippling with each confident step.

The frenzy of reunions melted away as her eyes locked on him, drawn by an attraction that refused to fade no matter how bad things got between them. His flight bag dangled from his hand, his helmet was under his arm. Sweat from wearing his helmet plastered his blond hair to his head. He could have been the quarterback for a pro football team striding, victorious, across the field. A five o'clock shadow bristled his jaw, giving his poster-boy-handsome face a rough-around-the-edges air that only deepened his appeal.

Without question, the chemistry between them when they'd met at nineteen years old had been combustible. But along with his hot body and seductive hands, she'd fallen for his dry wit and determination. He excelled at his job as an in-flight mechanic on C-17s. And he was in demand—the massive cargo plane was part of most military operations around the world, transporting troops and equipment.

His calling was to serve his country, something he'd made clear to her from the start. She couldn't even claim ignorance of the sacrifices that being a military wife demanded. Her father had flown the same aircraft and Shelby had grown up in the military lifestyle. She'd lived through her mother's inability to cope with the stress, her parents' divorce and her mom's abandonment of both her daughters as well as her husband.

Yet in spite of Shelby's best intentions, she'd failed just like her mother. The weight of that shook her to her core.

Her fists tightened around the leashes hooked to her German shepherd and springer spaniel, Samson and Delilah. The dogs had both been adopted from a shelter, both were their children.

Alex stopped in front of her, the scent of musk and

hydraulic oil clinging to his unzipped parka. He didn't reach out and neither did she. Awkwardness hovered between them. Nothing new. Samson and Delilah, on the other hand, moved in sync, tugging and whining to get closer in a display of undiluted joy so dear her throat clogged with emotion.

Dropping his bags, Alex sank to one knee and wrapped an arm around each dog's neck. The bells on their collars jingled in time with their yipped greetings.

"Hey, there, buddies," he said, his drawl drifting over her senses like a pure shot of Southern Comfort. "Missed you both every day."

She watched without speaking, letting the tears flow because hey, no one would judge her for it. Everyone would attribute her tears to homecoming joy rather than a breaking heart.

"Yeah, I know," he said soothingly as the dogs put their paws on his shoulders, barking their heads off, but he didn't so much as wince. He just took the leashes from her hands and continued to talk to Samson and Delilah. "Thanks for getting baths, you two. We'll have fun messing you up again later when we play in the snow."

He continued his calm monologue until Samson and Delilah settled down, each dog plastered against one of his legs. Now there was nothing left but for the two of them to speak. To pretend. Tougher than ever to do with all the couples around them embracing with happiness and a promise of passion.

Alex rose, standing eye to eye with her, then taller. She toyed nervously with the feather in her hair. His indigo blue eyes held a flash of guardedness, a hint of anger—and unmistakable desire. She couldn't stop the answering reaction inside her, accompanied by a ridiculous sense of relief that she'd changed out of the jeans she'd been wearing when she'd washed the dogs. She'd put on a green cashmere dress and knee-high leather boots.

All in the name of pride.

A wasted emotion most of the time, yet right now it was the only thing keeping her spine upright as the silence stretched. She had to do *something* to ease the uncomfortable distance between them. Her mind full of all their past passionate reunions, she leaned in to rest her cheek to his, using the excuse of the dogs between them to keep from moving any closer.

"Welcome home," she whispered, her skin sealed to his by the dampness of her tears.

He thumbed dry her other cheek with the barest hint of a stroke, so brief and yet utterly stirring. "I didn't expect you to be here waiting."

"Of course I'm here." She angled away, scrubbing her face with the back of her wrist, the cashmere sleeve tickling her senses, still on fire from his touch.

She had to ask him about the dog transport, to ask whether he would spend several days in a car with her, talking, but nerves pranced in her stomach. She'd given up trying to repair their marriage. Still, she hoped they could talk through things for…what? If not friendship, at least they could ease the rawness of emotions between them, ease the pain.

"Right, you are always the perfect wife—and I mean that." His face tugged with a self-deprecating smile. "I'm the one who screwed things up between us."

"We both made mistakes." Too true. She crossed her arms, hugging hard against the regret swelling in her chest. Last December, she'd lost her temper with him because they were spending yet another holiday apart.

She still cringed over her loss of control, when she'd always prided herself on being *the* supportive military wife, unlike her mom. "I'm hoping we can put that aside for now and just get through the holiday."

"Just call me Scrooge." He passed her the leashes as he scooped up his bags and helmet again.

"I guess I've called you worse." Much worse. Her temper and her mouth betrayed her too often, racing ahead of her brain.

A dry laugh rasped from him. "Why do you have to be so funny and hot?"

Before she could pick her jaw up off the floor, he nodded toward the door. "Let's find your coat and get the hell out of here. All the merriment in this place is Grinching me out."

Tech Sergeant Alex Conrad shouldered through the mass of his brothers and sisters in arms reuniting with their families and friends. As they walked, his wife kept up a steady stream of conversation to fill the awkwardness. He had no family other than Shelby, and soon, he wouldn't have her at all.

He loved her. He just couldn't fail her any longer. So he was going to grit through one last holiday together, buttoning his mouth and emotions up tight, and then set her free.

"Alex, you must be starved. Steaks are marinating in the fridge and I made your favorite turtle brownies with extra pecans."

"Sounds great. Thanks." God, he hated small talk. Although it beat the hell out of arguing with Shelby.

"How was the flight?"

"Smooth. Long. Glad to be home."

"Of course." Her dry tone hinted at the subject of their last—and worst—argument.

The trouble in their marriage had started after their fourth infertility treatment failed. They were out of hope and out of money for more expensive procedures the doctors didn't think would work anyway. Even with his paycheck and her job teaching biology at a private school, it wasn't enough to cover the treatments. He'd told himself he needed to sign up for extra deployments to bolster their bank account. But when Shelby had found out he was volunteering to go overseas, she'd seen right through him. She'd known he was using it as an excuse to escape the tension between them.

By the time he'd returned from the last tour she'd deflated. Given up on him. Given up on them. They'd barely even spoken when he'd been back in the summer, and he'd been relieved to deploy again. Their marriage had fallen apart and a baby wasn't going to hold them together. With tears of pain and anger streaking down her face, Shelby had demanded a divorce. He'd given her the only thing he could.

His consent.

They'd started proceedings just before the last deployment—a non-volunteer one. The minute she'd heard he was flying out for four months, she'd shifted back into perfect wife mode to prove to the world she wasn't like her mom. The world might be convinced, but he'd known Shelby was only going through the motions, then—and now.

She snagged her dressy black coat off the edge of the bleachers, still peppering him with benign questions. "What do you think of Samson's fur? I'm trying a new all-natural shampoo for him."

"Nice. Soft." It stabbed him clean through that things

were so awkward he couldn't even hold her coat while she slid her arms inside.

"The conditioner's really helping with his dry skin."

She flicked her auburn hair free of the collar, a tan feather peeking free as she smoothed down the static. She had a natural beauty, a confidence and strength that shone a helluva lot brighter than any makeup. God, he loved seeing her face beside his on the pillow when he woke up in the morning… There just weren't words for how much he loved her.

And she was mouthwateringly hot in that soft sweater dress, the Christmas-green color turning her eyes a deeper shade of emerald. Just one look at her legs in those knee-high boots…damn. She slayed him.

Before he did something dumbass like sweep her up for a kiss, he shifted his attention to their dogs while she buttoned up and adjusted the reindeer pin on her lapel.

When he and Shelby were newly married, they'd wanted to add a pet to their family, so they'd headed to the animal shelter. Unable to decide between a neglected German shepherd mutt with matted fur and a springer spaniel with a broken leg, they'd come home with both.

He'd grown up with cats—lots of them. He'd never had a dog before, but Shelby had never lived without one. In fact, even though she'd started college with the idea of becoming a military doctor, she'd quickly changed her goal to becoming a civilian veterinarian…a dream she'd abandoned shortly after recuperating from her second miscarriage. Rather than pile on the debt of attending veterinary school, she'd become a high school teacher to help pay for the fertility treatments she would need to get pregnant again.

Zipping up his parka along with too many memories, he ushered Shelby out into the parking lot full of ice and snow flurries, continuing to shoot clipped answers as needed. The sun was dropping fast and so was the temperature, holiday lights on lampposts reflecting off the snow.

She led him to their Ford Explorer, parked three rows in, his boots crunching each step of the way. Their dogs kept pace alongside in their snow booties…so damn cute and Shelby-like. Regrets piled on him faster than a snowplow slapped sludge onto the sidewalk.

He just wanted this day to end so he could hole up alone.

"We're away from the rest of the crew, so let's cut the small talk. You can drop me at the BEQ." The Bachelor Enlisted Quarters. "There's no need to put on an act anymore."

She pivoted to face him in front of their SUV, her jaw jutting. "Are you kidding me? We should be able to live in the same house for a few more days without being acrimonious."

"But it would just be pretending. I'll be moving into my own apartment on January first. That's our reality. Can't we at least be honest with each other?"

"Honestly? It's almost Christmas. I am *not* dropping you off anywhere." She tossed him the car keys.

Sighing, he snagged the keys in midair and unlocked the back of the Explorer. He waved the dogs inside. He hefted his bags in after them and sealed the vehicle shut. "Because that wouldn't be right, and you always do what's right."

"And nitpicking at me like that makes me want to drop you off in a snowy ditch." She slid into the passenger seat.

He stopped by her side of the vehicle. Holding on to her door, he leaned in, their faces so close he could feel the cloudy puffs of her breaths. God, he wanted to kiss her one last time.

"Damn, Shelby, there you go with your spunky hotness factor again."

She exhaled a long breath, the puff of air stroking over him like a phantom brush of her lips. His whole body went rigid in reaction. Her pupils widened in response. He knew her body so well, he could envision the flush spreading over her lightly freckled chest when he touched her. He wanted his wife.

"Alex," she warned, yanking her seat belt on. "I said we should stay together for Christmas. That didn't include sex under the tree." The way they'd celebrated most holidays in the past.

"What did you have in mind? Hot cocoa by the fire like some Norman Rockwell painting?"

His Christmases growing up had been about as far from Norman Rockwell as a kid could get. No wonder he'd failed at making a family with Shelby. He didn't have a clue how to put a real one together. He'd grown up with a chronically depressed mother and an absentee dad who paid the bills as long as he didn't have to darken their gloomy doorstep too often.

Shelby's cheerful optimism had been intoxicating after his somber childhood. But then she'd started pushing for soul-searching, marathon conversations about everything wrong with their marriage. God help him, he just couldn't go down that dark path again.

"Alex, my family has invited us up to their house for Christmas and New Year's."

"Great." He would rather eat nails.

He closed her door and rounded the front of the vehicle where she'd attached a perfectly aligned wreath to the grill.

He hoped like hell she wasn't serious about going to her parents' in upstate Washington. Her dad had built the house after retiring from the air force.

Alex slid behind the steering wheel, reined in his frustration and cranked up the heater.

Shelby held her hands in front of the vents. "About hanging out with my family…"

"It's generous of them to offer, but it'll be awkward as hell and you know it."

Her dad—a full colonel, now retired—had made no secret of his disapproval of them marrying before Shelby had finished college. Then when she hadn't gone on to become a veterinarian, her dad's silent disapproval had felt all the heavier.

She shifted in her seat, the leather of her killer boots squeaking against the leather upholstery. "It would be even more awkward sitting in our quiet, barren house eating turkey while we pretend we aren't weeks away from signing our names to the bottom of a divorce decree."

He flipped on the windshield wipers to slap away the snow that had accumulated as they'd sat in the parking lot. "So which is it? Pretending everything's okay at our house or at theirs? Your choice, Shelby."

She chewed her lip—her first sign of nerves since he'd stepped into the hangar. "Actually, I have a different idea for how we can spend the Christmas holiday." Pausing, she angled closer and gripped his arm. "An idea that will be a great distraction from the tension in our relationship."

Her grip seared clean through his jacket, branding his arm with her touch, firing through him. There was only one way he could think of to distract himself from all their problems and it involved getting her in bed as soon as possible.

Please, Lord, let her be thinking the same thing because the prospect of never making love to Shelby again was killing him. "What kind of idea?"

Her smile went wobbly, hesitant even, but her green eyes were bright with hope. "Wanna take three homeless shelter dogs on a road trip?"

CHAPTER TWO

SHELBY SCRUNCHED HER toes inside her boots, nerves trotting in her stomach as she waited for Alex's reaction to her blurted suggestion.

The heater blasted from the floorboards, their SUV engine idling in the parking lot. She hadn't realized until now how much this trip meant to her, to have something positive happen in their marriage even as it ended. Not that saving these three dogs would erase months of arguments. The ones that had started when she'd learned it wasn't just duty calling him away, he was *volunteering* for extra assignments and deployments. He'd said it was to bring in more hazardous-duty pay, but he hadn't denied it when she asked if he was merely using the travel to avoid facing their troubles.

Over time, anger had shifted to pain, then numbness. But she wasn't letting him avoid her any longer. She refused to let their marriage end with so much unsettled. They could and would finish on a strong note, damn it.

Words tumbled from her mouth in her rush to persuade him. "You know I've been volunteering more and more at our local animal rescue when I'm not teaching. The shelter director—Tansy Dexter—has had an especially challenging month. We've had to take in sixty cats seized from a hoarder, which means we needed a temporary facility to house them until they're healthy and socialized enough to mingle with the others in the Kitty Condos. We also had a leaky roof in the Doggy Digs—"

"What does all that have to do with a road trip and three dogs?" He draped his wrist over the steering wheel in a manner that was too casual.

She could read him well. He was ramped up and tense.

So was she. "Because at the shelter—"

"The Haven."

"Right." She paused, surprised. "Wow, you remember the name?"

"In spite of what you may believe, I do listen to you."

Ouch. "I never said you didn't listen."

"Do you want to stick with that statement?" He smiled, *really* smiled for the first time since he'd returned.

His deep blue eyes sparkled with dry humor, reminding her of when they'd met. She'd seen him at a picnic by the lake when she'd been home from college for the summer. He'd looked across the rows of tables directly at her, and without missing a beat, he'd simply walked away from the people he'd been talking to. With bold, determined strides, he'd approached her as if nothing and nobody else mattered.

Then he'd smiled and she'd forgotten to breathe. He'd knelt to pet her dog—a senior golden retriever. Her gaze had been drawn to the rest of him. A hot, muscled body, heart-stopping eyes and he loved dogs, too. She'd melted right then and there.

Warmth curled in her stomach now as well, and it had nothing to do with the heater. She forced her mind back to their conversation and how touched she was that he'd taken note of her volunteer work at the shelter. "Okay, sometimes—lots of times—I don't feel heard, maybe because *you* refuse to talk. Apparently, though, you are listening to some of what I say, even when you're staring at a book."

"Thanks. I think." He put the SUV in Reverse and eased out of the space before pulling forward, tires crunching on ice.

"Hey, about my road trip," Shelby said, needing to return to level ground, away from emotion-laden memories. "The Haven has a program right now where we're trying to find foster homes for all the animals over the holidays so none of the fur babies have to spend Christmas in a shelter. We've lucked into lots of coverage from KFOR TV."

"How's it working?"

"It's been crazy lining up enough families, checking them out, making sure everyone understands the special needs of some of the animals." Her mind swirled with the details as fast as the snowflakes spiraled in front of the headlights. "Such as the calico kitty, Katie, who has diabetes, and the mama rottweiler who has puppies—"

"We're not road tripping with those puppies, are we?" He raised an eyebrow.

"No. Three other *dogs*." Did that mean he was already on board? He hadn't said so, but the implication was there. Her heart raced faster. "As for the reason for the road trip, these three dogs already have families who want to do more than just foster them for Christmas, they want to adopt them. But the families don't live in the area."

"The shelter expects you to give up Christmas to deliver these dogs? That seems unreasonable."

"Nobody asked," she rushed to reassure him. "This was my idea. I offered to foster the dogs until after the holidays, then drive them to their new homes. But the more I considered it, the more I liked the idea of a road trip to deliver them before Christmas. The families were thrilled when I floated the possibility, though I told them I'd have to confirm later. If we pick up the dogs at The Haven tomorrow, we'll have them all delivered before Christmas Day. So if you're on board…?"

"And if I'm not?"

Her skin prickled with an icy chill. Was he really asking her to choose? Or pushing her away completely? She was all the more determined to push for a real and open conversation with him. "Do you want to spend Christmas in our house alone? Or at my family's house pretending for days and days?" She swallowed hard. "Or I could go by myself, if you would prefer. I would rather do that than just sit around and hurt the way I'm hurting today."

His head snapped back, then his hand lifted, reaching for her. "Shelby—"

If he touched her, she would melt right into his arms just as she always did. "Alex, no. Please don't. Haven't we wounded each other enough already?"

Beyond their rocky Christmas last year, she had many more regrets. Such as the times she'd been so baby obsessed that she'd barely said hello to him before she'd rushed him into the bedroom. Not that he'd ever complained. But she'd realized in her heart she'd shortchanged them both by focusing so completely on a baby that wasn't meant to be.

A tic tugged at the corner of one of his eyes, but he put his hand back on the steering wheel, accelerating as the light turned green. "You're the one who insisted I not spend the holiday alone in the BEQ. So, now I'm saying I won't let you spend Christmas alone, either."

Her heart squeezed tight with a hope she should have

been long past feeling and a long way from wanting. But damn it, his words touched her all the same. "I am going on this trip, and I'm hoping you'll come with me."

"Okay then. That's where I'll be. With you."

Her heart sped and she eased away from the door, her arms aching to just hold him and say to hell with pride and worrying about being hurt again. She swallowed down the lump in her throat and started to lay her heart out there as he wove through holiday shopper traffic.

"Shelby, I'm glad you're being reasonable about this. It's not safe for you to be driving on icy roads, not to mention delivering three dogs to total strangers."

Icy roads.

Meeting strangers.

He was simply protecting her the way he would anyone else. Nothing personal. No lingering romantic feelings.

The warmth inside her faded. "The Haven takes the safety of the animals very seriously. The adoptive families have to submit extensive applications. These abandoned and abused creatures have been through enough without submitting them to another bad situation."

Shaking his head, he drove through rush-hour traffic, the holiday lights blinking in shop windows. "I don't care how good someone seems on paper or how many neighbors have vouched for them—"

"Reputable vet references as well—"

"Fine. Vets, too. But…" He changed lanes, passing a sedan with a fir tree strapped to the roof. "Do you honestly imagine I'll ever stop worrying about you?"

Damn it, why was he twisting her inside out saying things like that? Why hadn't he cared this much all those weeks she'd been alone and he'd chosen deployments over being with her? "If you care so much, why did you agree to a divorce in the first place?"

"Are you saying you've changed your mind?"

"Don't toy with me this way, Alex, it's not fair." She refused to let him break her heart again. She'd cried herself dehydrated over this man more times than she could count. She'd vowed the tears would stop, and yet today still more had trickled down her face. "I mean it. No games. We need open, honest communication."

"I thought you said you wanted me to go along on the road trip. So why are you arguing with me now?"

"Because that's what we do, Alex. We argue. And you're right, I *do* want you to come with me," she said, digging into the conversation, grabbing hold of the opportunity to talk to him openly. "I would feel guilty if I left you alone on Christmas, so you're doing me a big fat favor by coming along on this trip where we can be marginally less miserable than if we sit in the house. Last Christmas was particularly tough, and I'm sorry for how I unloaded on you over the phone, making it even tougher. Long-distance arguments are the worst. But we can do this. Sure, it's not a traditional holiday, but by saving these three lives, we'll be making a beautiful memory for our last Christmas together."

He didn't bail out the window when she'd blurted out that little bit, and that gave her hope for this trip.

"Carting dogs around the country for Christmas, that's definitely a break from traditional." He half grinned again, easing some of the tension in the air.

"Not around the country." She shot right back, letting herself smile, even if there was a touch of irony to it. "Just around the state, and then a quick stop by my parents' at the end."

His face went guarded in a flash. "A quick stop?

Don't you think that'll be awkward with your folks, no matter how short the visit? I could catch a plane once you get there and cut out on that part."

"We won't be there long. Just on Christmas Day, rather than for a whole week as they originally suggested. A day shouldn't be that difficult to get through. And, uh, I haven't told them about our breakup yet." She knew she would have to explain to them about the divorce eventually. She'd just expected to have more time.

"What?" He glanced over quickly before looking back to the busy road. "When *did* you plan on telling them about the divorce?"

"Once it's final." Was she hoping for a last-minute reconciliation in spite of everything she said? That their conversations might lead to finally resolving their differences?

"Won't they be upset you didn't say anything before?"

Like he was the king of openness? "*My* family. *My* problem. All I'm asking is that you leave the timing to me."

"Fair enough." He nodded tightly. "What about our dogs? Five dogs in one car is a lot."

"The Bennetts have offered to watch them. Samson and Delilah play with their dogs and children at the dog park, so it'll be familiar and fun for the dogs."

"The Bennetts." Alex's face shut down even more. Yet another sticky subject between them.

Lieutenant Colonel Tanner Bennett was Alex's squadron commander and an old family friend of her father's. Kathleen Bennett was also a lieutenant colonel—and a flight surgeon. No matter how often Shelby told Alex she was proud of him, that it didn't matter to her whether he was an officer or enlisted, apparently it mattered to him.

But he didn't argue. He just drove on in silence down the darkening street toward their three-bedroom house. Samson and Delilah rested their noses on the backs of the seats, eyes going from Alex to Shelby.

His hand went up to rub each dog along the neck as he drove. He had so much love to give, yet he'd shut himself off more and more from her as the years passed, the conversations shorter and shorter, those smiles fewer and fewer until she didn't know how to reach him anymore.

She looked away sharply, preferring to gaze out the window rather than at her husband pouring affection on their dogs. That hint of emotion in him tore at her. Her panties might be well in place.

But her emotions were far from safe tonight.

GOD, IT WAS GOING TO be a long night.

Alex wrapped a towel around his waist after his shower and tucked it securely at his hip. Scooping his flight suit off the floor, he pulled the patches off, stacking them to the side. He tossed his sweaty uniform into the laundry.

In years past, Shelby would have been in the shower with him. They would have celebrated his homecoming against the tile wall and then again in bed. Sex had always been the one arena where they communicated exceedingly well.

But when the sweat cooled on their skin, reality set in. He couldn't ignore their problems, her anger over his deployments, his fear that he wasn't good enough for her. She'd accused him of dodging conflict by disappearing. And he had, to a degree.

But in spite of what she said, they had needed the extra money. The fertility treatments had put them thousands of dollars in debt, and when the treatments hadn't worked, he figured if he couldn't give her a baby, he could give her other things—the house, maybe even vet school. She was an awesome high school teacher, but he knew that wasn't her dream. She'd given up a lot to allow him to follow his dream. To an extent, she'd even given up her family, since things remained strained between him and her father.

Now all he could give her was a divorce.

By habit, he wiped the bathroom mirror clear of steam the way Shelby preferred. He stopped as he heard the phone ring. The chimes ended and the muffled sound of Shelby's voice filtered through the door. When she didn't shout for him, he finished cleaning up the bathroom. The call only served as a reminder that she'd built a life of her own here, and he wasn't part of it.

What would her life be like after the divorce? He didn't have a clue. And although he wanted her to be happy, the idea of her with someone else sent his blood pressure spiking.

He scrubbed a hand over his freshly shaved jaw and padded out of the guest bathroom, all too aware that he'd been relegated to the guest *bed*room, as well. Soon, he wouldn't even be welcome there. He wouldn't have any right to be inside their three-bedroom ranch-style house.

Would she remember how they'd enjoyed painting the walls together? Something he'd lost sight of when it had come to decorating—he'd become increasingly frustrated as she'd dragged him to yard sales and thrift stores to create a Pottery Barn–look he couldn't afford to give her.

Maybe if they'd been able to afford for her to go to veterinary school…

And there his brain went again, churning over might-have-beens when he should be focused on the present. On getting through Christmas.

In spite of Shelby's road trip plans, the house was decorated with colored lights outside and a tree inside. The fireplace was decked out with garlands and a crèche. He thought of how he'd grouched about all the gear they'd hauled out each Christmas in the past, even though he knew how important it was to her.

But each red bow, every gumdrop on a gingerbread house, reminded him of when he'd decorated alone as a kid, his dad hiding at work and his mom too depressed to leave her room, preferring her cats to people.

After a couple of years, Shelby had quit asking him to help and now he felt guilty as hell envisioning *her* decorating alone.

A gust of wind rippled down the hall a second before he heard the back door close. Shelby's voice echoed softly as she talked to their dogs.

"Hold still just a second so I can dry you off. Good boy. Good girl."

Her nonsensical cooing continued and he found himself leaning against the wall to listen to her. While her voice filled his ears, he took in the scattered framed photos of them—their wedding by the water in Charleston, South Carolina, mountain climbing with their dogs on vacation, military reunion photos. A lot of "welcome home" pictures.

"Alex?"

Her husky voice pulled his eyes from the pictures to her.

Damn. Just damn.

She stole the air from the hall simply by standing there. Her wet auburn hair trailed over her shoulders, and she wore a terry cloth robe.

Except she never wore robes.

So she'd obviously put it on as a barrier against his gaze, while he wore only a towel. She swallowed hard and pinched her collar closed.

Memories tormented him of her grinning as she'd tugged him into Victoria's Secret one day to help her choose lingerie, then to help choose a new scent for her body spray and lotion and wash.

He could smell it now, and he swallowed hard.

"Shelby, even if you layered a sweater on top of that robe, I would still remember what you look like wearing nothing at all. My only question would be, is your belly button ring a diamond or a sapphire?"

Her eyes flickered over his chest like the edges of a flame. "Sex was never a problem for us."

"You've got that right." And in a few more seconds that would be all too apparent.

"But it was just a Band-Aid that held our relationship together for too long." She folded her arms over her chest. "We should both just turn in."

Drawn by the memory of that day in the store, as she'd closed her eyes and inhaled the different body wash scents, he walked quietly toward her. "I guess that means a holiday quickie is out of the question."

"Afraid so." Sighing, she cupped his cheek. "You still have the power to break my heart again if I let you. I can't let you."

Damn it. Life was supposed to have gotten better since they'd made the decision to move on. Right now, he didn't want to move on with jack. He wanted to live in the moment, making love to his wife.

He slid a hand around her waist, palming her spine. The scent of her body wash—raspberry, he could still envision the bottle they'd chosen together—teased and tempted his nose. His body went hard in reaction, and he accepted it had nothing to do with his abstinence for the past four months and everything to do with his wife standing less than an inch away. Each breath she took grew heavier until her breasts brushed his chest.

A kittenish moan rolled up her throat. He recognized the sound well and couldn't resist. He angled his head and she tipped her face up, just enough that their mouths met in a familiar fit that he'd never expected to experience again. Then he wasn't thinking at all, just feeling. The give of Shelby's breasts against him. The glide of her soft hands along his shoulders. The sweet sweep of her tongue along his.

Fire surged through him, pulsing, demanding that he say to hell with walking away. This was his wife, his woman, and he wanted her in his arms and in his bed.

His towel slid down and off. Her hands tapered down until she gripped his ass, urging him closer in unmistakable encouragement. Passion stoked higher, hotter, and then his feet were moving, hers, too, as they stumbled toward their bedroom. He hadn't expected they would end up here, but he wasn't arguing with the direction.

Then her mouth eased from his as she angled backward toward their sleigh bed, and he damn near shouted ooh-rah until he realized…

Samson had tripped Shelby, pushing between the two of them. Delilah sailed past, landing in the middle of the thick comforter. Shelby squealed, sagging onto the mattress beside the dogs. Already, he could see doubts filling her eyes as she pulled her robe closed.

Biting off a curse, Alex yanked open a drawer to get a pair of sweat pants. "I should apologize."

"You have nothing to be sorry for. It's every bit as much my fault." She pushed back her tangled damp hair. Delilah pressed to her side while Samson curled up beside the bed.

He looked around the room—their room. Suitcases and two empty boxes were stacked beside her reading chair, reminders of how he would be clearing out after New Year's. That day would come soon enough. For now, he had a mission. Make this last Christmas together as peaceful and non-confrontational as possible.

He scratched his shoulder. "After I finished showering, I heard the phone ring. Was that your folks?"

She sat upright, her eyes going wide. "I almost forgot. It was Tansy from the shelter. She was calling to let me know that she'd finalized the details with the adoptive families, but there's been a slight change in plans. Good news, actually."

"No dog transport?" Which meant what? Pretending in front of her parents for a week?

Hell.

"Oh, the dog transport is still on. But Tansy has an in with the station now because of her friendship with cameraman Ben Rhodes—well, they're *more* than friends, really, but that's beside the point." She waved a nervous hand. "Ben was able to convince the station manager to send a freelance cameraman along with us on our road trip. He'll be shooting footage for a special on the shelter, something to keep interest up after Christmas. They're really stoked about the angle—us spending our Christmas together, driving the dogs."

Her words sunk in, deep and heavy, settling in his gut like stale fruitcake. "So let me get this straight. We were making this road trip so we didn't have to pretend here at home or in front of your family. And now you're saying we have to pretend for the whole damn world?"

Wincing, she shrugged. "Merry Christmas?"

CHAPTER THREE

CHRISTMAS LIGHTS OUTLINED the yellow-and-white Victorian house The Haven used as its administration building. The twinkling brightness reached through the late afternoon haze. Shelby slid from the front seat of the SUV, slamming the door behind her. The crisp air carried the scent of fir trees and the symphony of barking dogs.

She searched for the comfort she usually found here. But her mind was still a jumble over the shocker that a reporter would be going with them. It would be good for the shelter, but it complicated her plans for this trip. Her jaw clenched in frustration. Another person would make it all the tougher to talk to Alex.

But she wasn't giving up.

With determined steps around a small snow drift, she charged toward the shelter door. When she wasn't teaching biology at a local private school, she spent almost all of her free time volunteering here or with fosters at home. She understood she was lucky to have a job in her field, utilizing her college major. She reminded herself of that every morning as she dressed for work, but she still found herself living for the hours she spent here. The part of her that had once yearned to be a veterinarian still ached inside her.

Would she stay in the area after her divorce? She wasn't sure, and right now, she couldn't bring herself to plan beyond Christmas and making one last positive memory with her husband.

But after their impulsive kiss in the hall last night, she wasn't confident she could keep her panties in place around Alex. Maybe it was a good thing that the freelance cameraman would be coming along after all.

Picking her way along the shoveled and salted walk, she was ever aware of Alex's quiet presence behind her. Only the steady sound of his footsteps assured her he was following. Neither of them had spoken much since she'd dropped the bombshell about their extra passenger. They'd gone to their separate, cold and lonely beds for the night, where she'd tossed and turned until nearly sunrise, then ended up sleeping late.

In the morning, she'd found a note on the counter that he'd taken their dogs out for a run, but he would be back in time to pick up the transport dogs. She'd almost laughed at the predictability of his avoidance.

The front door of the shelter opened, sending a fresh pine wreath swaying. A man held the door open for his wife and daughter. The teenager cradled a fluffy bichon puppy against her chest.

Inside the shelter, the warmth wrapped around her like the feel of Alex's leather jacket on a late-night beach walk. She glanced over her shoulder. Her eyes collided with his.

She swallowed hard and pushed words free. "This shouldn't take long."

"I've got nowhere else to be for the next two weeks."

"We'll be done long before that." The double meaning hitched her breath.

But how could she build a marriage with a man who refused to meet her halfway in their life together? How could she build a marriage with a man who seemed to have forgotten all the dreams they once shared? A man who took every opportunity to cut and run, literally and emotionally?

She shifted her attention back to the present as they walked deeper into the reception area. What had once been the house's living room was now divided by a waist-high counter. Two desks and several filing cabinets filled the larger space behind the counter. She waited with Alex on the other side. Sturdy wooden armchairs and a low table in the seating area were packed with people filling out paperwork. An overburdened coat tree stood in the corner.

Shelby waved at the bubbly receptionist who was popping candy cane bark into her mouth, one broken piece at a time.

"Hello, Faye, we're here to pick up the three transport dogs."

"Tansy already went with Cindy to get our lucky trio." Standing, Faye pushed aside the display with info about a local TV fund-raiser and extended her hand. "And this must be your husband. Hello, Sergeant Conrad."

"Alex," he said simply, shaking her hand.

"Alex, then. Glad to finally meet you. We've had a running bet around here as to whether or not you were a ghost."

At least he didn't wince. "Nice to meet you, as well."

Faye paged Tansy then lifted the gift box of peppermint chocolate candy from beside a small artificial tree sitting on the counter, an angel tree with ornaments listing donation needs. "Some peppermint bark? Dogs bark, get it? Woof woof."

"Thanks." Shelby popped a piece into her mouth since it seemed rude not to.

Faye filled the awkward silence. "Sorry for the wait. Things have been especially hectic around here since we picked up all those cats from the hoarding situation—"

Her ramble was cut short as Tansy Dexter walked briskly inside with two dogs on a leash, a teenage volunteer behind her carrying the third. Always approachable, Tansy wore jeans, gym shoes and a blue sweatshirt with a shelter logo on the front. She had curly black hair and an ever-ready smile. Shelby envied the ease with which Tansy approached life, the joy and calm that radiated from her to the animals she rescued.

Tansy held out the leashes. "Shelby, Alex, I can't thank you both enough for this. Meet your charges. This is Trooper. We're pretty sure he's a beagle/basset mix, around two years old. Animal control picked him up wandering without a collar or microchip. He's such a sweetie they called us with a hefty plea to take him in."

She passed over the leash and Shelby dropped to her knees. The hound dog bayed once then swiped a doggie kiss on her cheek before she could blink. "What a loveable guy. I've been hearing good things about you, buddy."

Tansy continued, gesturing to the teenager behind her. "This is Cindy. She's helping out on her Christmas break since we're a bit overwhelmed getting all the animals settled into foster homes for the holidays. She has Prince."

The teenager in a long-sleeved concert tee carried a Pekingese. "Prince is eight years old." She rested her cheek against his fur, her blond ponytail swishing forward. "His owner had to go into a nursing home and no one else in the family would take him."

With a final quick kiss on top of Prince's head, Cindy passed him over to Alex, who seemed totally underprepared for the fur ball thrust into his arms. Before Shelby could offer to hold Prince, Tansy passed her the other leash of a black Lab puppy.

"And this is Daisy." Tansy's brow furrowed, her eyes sad. "Daisy was brought in with her mother and the rest of her litter when she was only two days old. Daisy was the last of her litter, adopted at twelve weeks old, but her family returned her when she was five months. They said they didn't have time for her. She really misses the family that gave up on her, and she hasn't warmed up to anyone since. She's been here almost four months this go-round."

Shelby passed the beagle's leash to Alex and focused her attention on the Lab puppy. Daisy was more interested in exploring under Faye's desk than coming out for a belly rub. "We'll work on winning her over."

"You'll do great—as always. You've got the Dr. Doolittle touch," Tansy said. "It'll translate well for us in the TV feature. Oh, which reminds me. The freelance camera guy, Gene Watts, will meet you at your house at eight tomorrow morning."

Alex checked the office clock mounted on the wall and extended his hand for the other leash. "Shel, take the Peke and I'll load up the bigger two while you finish with the paperwork."

They swapped dogs, hands brushing, awareness snapping even through the gloves they still wore. She pulled away quickly, tucking Prince to her chest. Her eyes followed Alex as he nodded a quick farewell to Faye and Tansy before slipping out the door. And she couldn't help thinking that he really was like a ghost, briefly drifting in and out of her life.

Tansy pulled three manila envelopes from under Faye's box of peppermint bark. "These are the adoption papers and vet records for each dog. You know the drill. And thank you again, hon."

"I wish I could do more." She tucked the papers to her chest, holding them so tightly her parka crackled and Prince squirmed. "I'll email you the details and post photos on Facebook from the road."

"That would be super. Seeing the happily ever after helps us get through those heartbreak days." Tansy grabbed a jacket from the behind the counter and followed Shelby out the door. "Are you okay, hon? Really?"

"Of course." She paused in front of the building. "It's the Christmas season."

"But you'll be spending it on the road when your husband just got home, and now Ben wants to send the cameraman with you, too."

Shelby glanced over at her husband. He sat just inside the back of their Explorer with Trooper and Daisy. Guilt swamped her again at stealing his Christmas, but she had to believe this was their best chance at real closure. "You know things have been awkward between Alex and me. This trip is a blessing. Even the cameraman will be a welcome buffer, like the dogs."

"Still, you two deserve to relax and celebrate his homecoming as well as the holidays." She pushed her moppish curls from her face as the wind tore at them.

"We all do, but believe me, I'll be celebrating when I have these three sweet dogs settled with their forever families."

Prince snorted in agreement, his big tongue sweeping over his smooshed face.

"You deserve that happiness, too."

"I'm happy." *Liar.*

Tansy fished a dog biscuit from her jeans pocket and passed it to Prince. "Shelby, you know one of the

things I like most about you? You're an open book—
but that also makes it impossible for you to hide when
you're fibbing."

A car door slammed, pulling their attention to the
parking lot again. A man hurried toward the Victorian
building and Tansy straightened. "Gotta get back to
work. That's the guy who agreed to foster the St. Bernard mix puppy."

"Good luck." Shelby adjusted Prince in her arms
and picked her way across the parking lot toward the
Explorer.

Toward Alex.

A wave of nostalgia swept over her as she remembered the day they'd adopted Samson and Delilah seven
and a half years ago. If Alex was a ghost today, he was
the Ghost of Christmas Past, tempting her all over again
by reminding her of how good they'd had it. It would
be a long night in their house since their cameraman
chaperone wasn't coming until the morning. Shelby
hoped he came early.

ALEX PARKED HIMSELF in front of the computer in his
home office, mapping out the route for their drive
around Washington State. As long as the weather cooperated, they would be finished with their deliveries and the cameraman could fly home to Tacoma by
Christmas Eve. Then he and Shelby would arrive at her
family's house later that day, suffer through Christmas
Day then hit the road to come home.

Just as Shelby had predicted, Samson and Delilah
were fine with staying with the Bennetts. Apparently
the dogs knew the family there better than they knew
him, these days.

Now it was just him and Shelby in the house. Alone.

He thought about his marriage and he didn't have a clue what he could have done differently. There must be a missing cog in him that made him unable to put a family together. He'd tried, checking in on her during the fertility treatments, comforting her when they'd failed, although he'd never found the right thing to say and somehow always brought her to tears…which inevitably sent his mind racing back to the days when his mother had locked herself in her room, depressed and crying.

Rather than risk hurting Shelby again, he'd panicked and signed on for another deployment. At least then he could offer her space and more money. As things worsened between them, yeah, he'd hit the road for himself, too, for the escape as much as the paycheck, just as she'd accused him of doing. Emotional confrontations weren't his gig.

But he was good at his job, damn good, and now it was all he had left. A sound from the door drew his attention. Shelby padded into the room, her fuzzy socks silent against the carpet. She carried a tray with sandwiches and steaming soup. Trooper and Prince trailed her. Daisy was probably still hiding out, being antisocial.

Alex took the tray from her and set it on the ottoman in front of the futon. "Thanks. You didn't have to go to the trouble, though."

"It's just potato chowder." She stuffed her hands into her jeans pockets. "I needed to use up the milk before we leave."

He nodded to the pair of dogs on her heels. "Those two have been shadowing you since we left The Haven."

"They've been through a lot of change." She sat on the futon and patted the space beside her for both dogs to jump up. "Some separation anxiety isn't unusual."

"And Daisy? Where's she?"

"Totally uninterested in having anything to do with me or the other dogs. She loped around the backyard on her own until she wore herself out." Shelby tucked the Pekingese in her lap while scratching the beagle/basset's floppy ears. "Now she's sleeping under the coffee table with your gym shoes."

"My Nikes?"

"Just joking. Sorta. You only lost a shoelace before I rescued your shoes." She pointed to the computer. "What are you doing?"

"Mapping the route so we have a backup if bad weather puts the GPS on the fritz." He held up a folder of maps and contingency plans in case of closed roads.

"You sound like my dad. Always with plan A, B and C."

"No need to go for the jugular." He scratched his neck.

She toyed with the feather in her hair, studying him through narrowed eyes. "It was a compliment. I wish you and my dad had taken the time to get to know each other."

Frustration and even some anger nipped inside him as she pointed out another way he'd let her down. No matter how hard he worked, no matter what he did, he would never measure up to her father, the great Zach Dawson. But arguing with her wasn't going to change a thing.

"Thanks for the soup." He spun the office chair to his computer again, hoping she would take the hint.

Her heavy sigh only gave him a moment's warning before she walked past him to lean against his desk. She folded her arms over her chest and stared him down.

He couldn't stop his gaze from settling on her

breasts, plumped above her arms. He would give his right nut to be able to peel that white cable sweater over her head and kiss every inch of her.

A year and a half ago, that would have distracted her from her anger. Tonight? He knew better.

"Shel? Problem?"

"Damn straight there's a problem. It's going to be a long, awkward, miserable drive if you keep ignoring me. Can't we at least have a civil conversation with each other?"

Her green eyes sparked with a heat he was tempted to flame. Eight years together had taught him a thing or two about her. If he rose to the bait they would follow a familiar pattern. They would argue. Or she would argue, and he would shut down. She would get so frustrated tears would shine in her eyes, all but bringing him to his knees because he'd hurt her again. He would haul her close.

Clothes would fall…

Blood pumped through him, leaving him impossibly hard.

Her eyes fell to his lap and widened. "Oh, uh…"

"Right, we can keep talking. But I want you to be clear that in every second of that very polite exchange, my brain will be filled with how much I'm aching to take you. On the desk. Now."

She rubbed her palms along her jeans legs. "You're doing it again, Alex, shutting down any chance of a real conversation. That's not fair to me."

A distant corner of his brain had held out a hope she would say something like, *sure, sex on the desk is a super idea.*

No such luck.

Silently, he pivoted away from her and resumed typing on the keyboard, double-checking for rest stops on their trip. Willing away his body's reaction to her and his own disappointment over how he'd obviously screwed up again.

She gave another heavy sigh and shoved away from the desk. "Fine then. Be that way. I have some last-minute Christmas gifts to wrap."

She raced out of the room a second before it hit him. He hadn't bought her a present yet. He'd been clueless on what to get an almost ex wife. He'd been planning to figure it out in the days before Christmas, but now they would be on the road, together. Just not how he wanted them to be together.

His office chair creaked long and slow as he eased back, screen saver bouncing a photo of Samson and Delilah dressed as Mr. and Mrs. Santa Claus. What the hell was it about Shelby Dawson-Conrad that still rocked the ground under his feet like he was nineteen again?

CHAPTER FOUR

EACH BRISK BREATH OF morning air iced her lungs as Shelby picked her way along the slick walkway, adjusting her hold on the sacks of Christmas gifts. Prince, Trooper and Daisy raced around the yard, burning energy they'd stored up in the shelter kennel runs. She stared through the light swirl of snowflakes to her husband securing the luggage carrier on top of the Explorer.

There was no room in the car—the SUV would be full enough with Shelby, Alex, three dogs and a cameraman, plus the winter survival gear, an ice chest of food and thermoses of coffee and cocoa. Trooper and Daisy would ride in the cargo area of the SUV with a fence barrier between them and the seats. Prince would ride up front with her and Alex. She ticked through her mental list and couldn't think of anything else to do or bring.

She'd had a restless night, and now exhaustion tugged at her, the cold air only increasing her urge to hibernate with hot cocoa in front of the fire. With her husband. All she'd been able to think about last night— all she could think about *now*—was how much she'd hoped he would talk to her over dinner. They would share the meal and…what? Find answers?

At least come to some sort of truce so that she could do what she really wanted to do: make love with Alex on his desk. Or the office chair. The floor, the futon.

Her body clearly hadn't fallen in line with her brain in accepting that her relationship with Alex was over.

But he hadn't wanted to talk. He'd shut down, like always, and she was beginning to lose hope that a conversation could make this any less painful.

This morning her eyes were drawn to him as they always were. His parka hit the waistband of his jeans, leaving her with too perfect a view of his narrow hips, his perfect butt. Her gaze traveled to his broad shoulders and she ached to walk up behind him and rest her cheek on his shoulder, pretend they were a happy couple getting ready for a holiday trip. The neighborhood hummed with so much normalcy she wanted to shout in frustration at how out of control her life had become.

She actually envied her neighbor clearing the dusting of snow from his driveway with a snow blower, and the harried mom across the street taking trash out in her slippers and a long overcoat.

The decision to divorce had seemed so clear-cut when she'd learned he was voluntarily putting himself in harm's way. Being a military spouse was difficult enough, but the fact that he'd deliberately added to that stress had been the last straw for her. How could he be that desperate to avoid true emotional intimacy with her? How could he have disregarded her worry, how deeply it tore at her? She feared each knock on the door could be an official notification of his death.

Alex turned to take the sacks from his wife. "Good God, what's in here?"

"Stuff for my family and things for you. It would look strange to my family if we didn't give each other anything." She glanced down at their gloved hands, both holding the handles to the bags without touching. "I, uh, wrapped up a couple of presents for you to give to me."

"What makes you think I didn't take care of that myself?"

She looked up quickly, guilt tweaking, along with a whisper of something that felt too much like hope. "I'm sorry. I didn't mean to insult you."

"Forget about it. You're right. I haven't shopped yet." He took the bags and pivoted away to stow them in the car-top carrier. "You didn't say anything wrong."

But she obviously had. She searched for the right words so she wouldn't derail her chance to talk things out with him later, so she didn't wreck any chance at a peaceful journey before it even began—

A Yukon hybrid veered off the road and into her driveway.

Shelby stepped aside quickly, almost slipping on the ice. "That must be the camera guy."

The driver's-side door opened and the driver slid out in a smooth blur of dark jeans and black wool duster. In his late thirties probably, the man had dark hair pulled into a ponytail. From the backseat, he hefted out a massive camera bag and duffel.

"Morning, folks," he called over his shoulder with a flat Midwestern accent. "I'm Gene Watts, your freelance cameraman for the KFOR piece."

Her husband stepped forward. "Alex Conrad and my wife, Shelby—"

The reporter continued without pausing, "I would shake your hands but mine are full, and honest to Pete, I'm not a chatty guy. I consider myself an artist with my camera. So while my lens and I become one, you just go about your life as if I'm not here."

Shelby laughed in a cold puff. "Okay, Mr. Watts. Thank you. And while you're sitting in the back becoming one with your camera, if you get hungry or thirsty, help yourself to something from inside the cooler."

Alex reached for Gene's duffel. "I'll stow that on top. We're a little short on space until we start delivering our three wise men."

"Wise men?" Gene looked up from inspecting the contents of the cooler.

"Three dogs. Three wise men. Speaking of which, time to load up Melchior, Caspar and Balthazar."

She smiled, realizing she'd lost sight of how witty her husband could be. She missed the laughter from the early days of their marriage when they'd both been lighter hearted, less jaded. Sure that they would have the white-picket-fence future with two kids who would play with their pair of dogs.

But that dream had died along with the laughter Alex hadn't cared enough about their marriage to really work at saving it, to talk to her, to explain why he'd taken all those extra deployments, let alone to promise her he wouldn't do it again. He'd let her go with both hands, not even bothering to make a last-ditch effort.

Seeing the family with Trooper would no doubt be a great big dose of Ghost of Christmas Present. But she would just have to deal with it. She'd settle for delivering dogs to other families, giving them the future she'd once planned for herself and her husband.

ICY ROADS, HOLIDAY TRAFFIC and three dogs on board made for slow going, adding extra hours to their drive to Spokane. Alex flexed his hands as he released the steering wheel, then threw the SUV into Park outside the upscale pet supply store. They'd designated the shop as a neutral place for Trooper to check out his new family and for Shelby to go over the paperwork.

Ever aware of the cameraman, Alex stayed silent. He couldn't help but notice Shelby's practiced smile over the past several hours, her deliberately breezy voice and how she did her best to position the dogs in front of the lens whenever possible. Her years teaching high school biology had given her confidence with public speaking. He regretted costing Shelby her dream to be a vet, but he admired her success in the classroom.

She pulled out Trooper's leash. "I'm going to take him for a quick walk before I go in to meet the family. Would you mind exercising the other two dogs? As you can see, there are plenty of folks around. We plan our meet and greets carefully for everyone's safety."

This time she smiled for him and the camera.

Alex had to admit, they'd taken care of the security angles by meeting in a well-populated, public place. "Sure." He reached for the leashes. "I'll hook up Prince and Daisy for a bathroom break in the bushes."

Outside, the air was freeze-your-ass-off cold. Not that the weather stopped the shoppers streaming in and out of the row of stores as Christmas carols were piped through the outdoor plaza's sound system—currently "Greensleeves" was seguing into "We Three Kings."

Some folks trailing into the pet store brought their canine pals along, as well. Shelby attached Trooper's leash before starting toward the front door. Gene walked backward ahead of her, documenting.

Alex didn't have to be a media professional to see she would look amazing on camera with her vibrant auburn hair and natural beauty. Images of her had filled his dreams last night, leading him to reach for her—only to find her side of the bed cool and empty.

He hung back with the other two pooches and a handful of plastic waste bags. From the painted stencils on the plate-glass windows, it appeared the doggie boutique sported all-natural foods and earth-friendly gear. Through the glass he could see it was a large store with concrete floors and areas sectioned off for the pets to socialize, even an agility course. The place was a sanctuary for indoor play in the winter.

And there was Shelby.

God, everything always came around to Shelby for him.

She spoke with a woman in an apron who directed her over to the play area. After he tossed the waste bags into a trash can, he rushed through the door, drawn to her even more than the warmth of the place. The bells chimed as he walked inside with Prince and Daisy.

Still, he held back and scanned the room, his eyes landing on a family of five. The dad held a collar and leash with no dog at the end. Alex's hand tightened on the leashes, bringing Daisy and Prince in closer. God, he envied that father with the kids tugging at his hands, even jumping on his feet.

The dad's voice carried over the buzz of other shoppers. "You must be Shelby Conrad. We're the Richardson family. We're here for Trooper."

The mom knelt beside the dog, stroking his head. "Our beagle passed away three months ago. I'd had her since I was a teenager. It's difficult, we still miss her. But the children begged…"

"I understand completely." Shelby tucked the envelope of papers under her arms. "Please, take as long as you need meeting with him. We want the match to be right for everyone. We'll walk the other dogs while you and your husband talk."

Shelby eased away until she stood beside Alex near the door, bringing with her the scent of raspberries. She eased Prince's leash from him. "Sorry about the delay on the road today."

"You can't control the weather. Stopping for the dogs slowed us down, too." He nodded toward the family and Trooper. The three kids were taking turns feeding him treats, hugging his neck, squealing over slobbery dog kisses. "Watching them go nuts over him makes the drive worthwhile."

"Tansy said their application and phone interview were really great. Today's meet just confirms it. Gene's going to get some heart-tugging footage from this adoption."

Her eyes glittered with a happy/sad mix that stabbed him clean through. This cheerful family image is what he'd wanted to give her on so many Christmasses. Now the chance was gone.

She cleared her throat and blinked fast. "Tomorrow there will be less pressure. The Swensons worked an extra day into their road trip, just in case we ran behind. We're meeting them at the RV park where they're staying."

"No schedule to follow. What a concept."

She looked up sharply. "Is that a dig at me now that we're off camera?"

He raised his hands. "Honest to God, I was talking about myself. Work."

She deflated. "Sorry to be defensive." She pulled two dog biscuits from a free sample bin. "One good thing about the bad weather, the longer our trip takes, the less time we have to pretend in front of my family." She offered a treat to Prince, who sat on command. Daisy ambled away, not interested, tugging on the leash.

Alex pulled in the slack and guided the black Lab

puppy toward the door. "Luckily Gene seems more interested in filming the dogs than us."

"Maybe we should skip going to my family's house altogether. Just go home and hang out…talk."

Talk?

She zipped her parka up again, the cinched-in waist drawing his eyes to her curves then down to her long legs. What he wouldn't give to tug those fuzzy-topped boots off her, then peel her jeans down while he kissed his way up.

If he was alone with her, talking would be the last thing on his mind. Bad idea.

"You want to visit your family. We're going."

"I don't want to go if you'll be miserable."

This holiday was going to suck no matter what they did, or where they went. He'd already accepted that, and he was doing his best to salvage something for her. He understood this dog transport was important to Shelby; that made it important to him.

His wife really did have a knack with animals, and while he'd known she was spending much of her free time volunteering at The Haven, he was only beginning to realize what a large part of her life this had become.

And as for going to her family's house…that was important to Shelby, too. He could put up with Zach Dawson one last time. He owed her that—and a helluva lot more.

The door opened again, the sound of a Salvation Army bell growing louder and faster before the door closed.

"We'll stick to our travel plan. Mailing all those gifts will cost a fortune. We're committed." He nodded toward the family with Trooper. "And it appears they're committed, as well. Go enjoy your success."

"Don't you want to meet them?"

And face more reminders of the family he'd never managed to give Shelby? No thanks. "I'll just hang here with Prince and the pain-in-the-butt puppy."

She rolled her eyes. "Shh! Daisy might hear you. Poor girl's already sad enough."

Shelby pulled out the papers and met with the mom and dad at the counter while the kids made a Hallmark moment with Trooper, sliding a red holiday bow around his collar. After the last of the adoption papers had been signed, the mom hugged Shelby hard, tears in her eyes. "Thank you. We love him already. You really went above and beyond for my family." Pulling away, she swiped her fingers under each eye then reached into her purse. She pulled out an envelope. "Here's a donation to the shelter. It's not much, but—"

Shelby closed her hands over the young mother's. "This is wonderful. The Haven will put it to good use. I promise."

The youngest of the children raced by in a blur of purple snowsuit and wrapped her arms around Shelby's legs. "Thank you for my dog, lady."

"Merry Christmas, sweetie."

To Alex, the whole exchange was a never-ending punch in the gut. He kept imagining how things might have been if they'd spent time together this way in the past, while they'd still had a connection. While they could have shared the happiness and Christmas cheer they were spreading.

He cupped Shelby's shoulder. "We should get checked in to our motel."

She glanced back at him, her hair gliding along his hand like silken fire. "I just have to thank the owner of the store and I'll be right with you."

Crouching, Gene trained his camera on the family hustling out the door. Looking up at Alex, he said, "Gotta wonder what kind of hotel or motel lets you bring a couple of dogs."

"You would be surprised." He and Shelby had brought their dogs down the California coast one summer and they'd found plenty of mom-and-pop inns that were happy to host them *and* their dogs, even a couple of major hotel chains had, as well. What the hell had happened to the guy he'd been back when he and Shelby had taken that trip? He'd sure screwed up since then. "The kicker will be wearing the dogs out after they've been cooped up all day in the car."

"Lucky for me that I'm the cameraman, then. I'm locking myself in my warm room with carryout and a remote control."

Alex pushed open the shop door. Time was, he would have welcomed the space to get his thoughts together. Level his head. Do anything to avoid more controversy.

But right now, he could only think how the time left with his wife was ticking away, and he wanted to spend every last second with Shelby.

Plus two dogs.

CHAPTER FIVE

KILLING TIME UNTIL ALEX returned with their carryout supper, Shelby squeezed a squeaky toy shaped like a snowman at the Lab. "Daisy? Come on, girl, you can even destroy the toy. Just come play with me."

Prince leaped off the bed and snagged Frosty from her hand then raced in crazy circles with the squeaking toy. That crazy energy sure denied the dog's senior status. Daisy harrumphed, chewing her rawhide bone in the corner. She'd shown more excitement and personality trying to tug Alex around the store. Shelby stroked the black Lab's sleek coat, hoping Daisy would warm up to her. She just couldn't figure this pup out, and that worried her. Would another family give up on Daisy, just as the first young couple that had adopted her?

She inched closer to Daisy, continuing to pet her without pushing her to play. And she couldn't deny that stroking the dog soothed her own nerves, reminding her how much comfort her childhood golden retriever, Aggie, had given her.

Aggie had soaked up a lot of tears in her fur over the years—when Shelby's mom had left, when she'd broken up with her high school boyfriend, when she'd realized moving into the dorm at college meant saying goodbye to her dog.

Once she'd married Alex, she'd tried to talk her father into letting her take Aggie, but her dad had said it wouldn't be fair to her younger sister and stepbrother. Her sister would have understood...but Patrick? He was a sweet kid, but change was especially tough for him as a special-needs child. So she'd left her childhood pet with her dad. Aggie had passed away three years ago and Shelby missed her still.

The door to the hotel room opened and Alex backed inside, carrying a sack and sodas from a local Mexican food chain. Her favorite.

Cold air blasted in until he forced the door closed again.

"Thanks for braving the elements."

"We all gotta eat." He set the bag and drinks by the television, filling the room with the clean scent of snow and his broad shoulders.

"I'm sure you would prefer home cooking after on during mess hall food for the past four months." Guilt gnawed at her harder than Daisy on her chewy.

"Don't worry about me." He started pulling wrapped food from the bag.

Could she just shut down those concerns with the signing of the divorce papers? Or would she spend every Christmas wondering if he'd put up a tree or if he'd retreated even further from any kind of traditional celebration? Who would try to make him smile when he came home from work with the weight of the world on his shoulders? And most gut wrenching of all, she would be giving up her rights to hear if anything happened to him in the line of duty...

Maybe if they resolved some things, she'd be able to find closure. "Thank you again for driving with me. Seeing the Richardsons so happy with Trooper today and knowing I played a small part of that is the best Christmas gift I could get."

Watching the family together hadn't sent her into the old spiral of emptiness she'd sometimes felt about her infertility. Losing Alex had given her a different perspective, made her reevaluate her insistence they weren't a real family unless they had a child together. It took losing everything to make her appreciate what she'd had.

He tossed a tortilla chip to each dog. "It's clear we both want to go out on a good note."

She'd thought the same thing from the start, but hearing him say it out loud…the finality of it hurt.

Her chest tightened, feeling frighteningly like an impending panic attack. Not that she'd ever had one before. Damn it, she wouldn't freak out now. She stroked Daisy faster and faster.

"Shelby?"

She didn't realize she'd closed her eyes. She opened them and found Alex kneeling beside her, burrito and soda in hand. Her panic eased with each deep inhale of his crisp scent.

"Oh, uh, thanks."

He didn't let go of the food. "You can relax. I'm not going to hit on you again. I'm going to eat my supper and find something to watch on TV. Okay?"

She didn't trust herself to speak so she just nodded, fearing he might hear in her voice how much she wanted to be with him right now. How much she needed to get everything out into the open. "Uh-huh."

"I'll take the bed by the door. It's a guy thing, being closest to a possible intruder." He held up his hand. "I bet Prince could take down anyone stupid enough to risk frostbite creeping around out there. But humor me."

He angled closer, offering the burrito. She took the food from him and yet he leaned nearer still…reaching under Daisy's belly for the remote control just peeking out. Standing, he strode away, leaving her with a big fat steak burrito and even bigger regrets.

Not to mention a very clear *back off* message. He was not going to talk tonight. And for once, she chickened out, too, unsure if she could face the fallout if hashing things out didn't end peacefully after all.

THE WEATHER WASN'T ANY kinder to him today than yesterday. It made for slow moving traffic along the interstate, the Christmas lights on distant houses occasionally piercing through the haze, haze and more haze. But, by God, he would make it to the damn RV park before sunset. They would deliver Prince late this afternoon and Daisy first thing in the morning Christmas Eve. The cameraman would fly out and they would drive on to her family's house. Then it would be done. Finished. Thank God.

Because the charade was taking a toll on them both. He was pretty sure Shelby hadn't slept any more than he had last night, the tossing and turning a constant reminder of all he couldn't have as he listened to each shift of her beautiful body against the sheets. Now, Shelby was so exhausted she'd opted to sleep in the back, sending Gene to ride up front.

Alex scowled, his own exhaustion stripping him of the social skills for small talk.

"What, dude?" Gene peeked around the camera, the red record light blinking.

"I'm creeped out by that lens jammed in my face all the damn time," he hissed through gritted teeth. "Isn't there a law against distracting the driver?"

Gene just pushed some buttons without lowering the load from his shoulder.

Sighing, Alex put a hand in front of the lens. "Come on, dude, shut it down, okay? The dogs and Shelby are all out for the count."

"Sure, no problem." Gene set the video camera in his lap. "Mind if I change the radio to a music channel?"

"I'd rather hear the weather."

"Sounds wise." As they passed a minivan, Gene waved at a kid pressing his nose and mouth against the window, steam spreading.

Alex shot a glance at Gene, suddenly wondering… the station had thrown a lot of money behind a small new spot. Was there some other angle going on here? "Have you filmed the shelter for the station before?"

"I'm a freelancer," Gene reminded him, reaching for a bag of trail mix on the dash. "This whole promo gig is Ben Rhodes's baby."

"Ben Rhodes? I seem to recall my wife mentioning him." Alex frowned, not at all happy with the path his brain was taking.

"Rhodes is the head cameraman at KFOR—and he's dating the shelter's director." Gene scooped a handful of trail mix. "Every guy is not after your wife, dude. I mean, she's hot and all, but she's totally gone on you."

Alex grunted.

Gene hmmed, chewing. "Want to talk about what's got you strung so tight?"

"Not really. Roads suck, I should pay attention to my driving. And we might wake up Shelby."

"Your tight-lipped attitutde makes you a tough guy to interview. But hey, I can take a hint, I'll leave you alone." Gene hefted up the video camera again, shifting to angle the view toward the back.

"Damn it, could you quit videotaping my wife?"

"But that's why I'm here. To capture this journey on

film, help with positive promo for the shelter, increase donations and get more animals adopted."

"She's *napping*." He was the one who would watch her as she slept—not some other guy. "Filming her now doesn't help the dogs, and it's an invasion of her privacy."

Gene rested the camera on his lap. "Now you're jealous of me?"

"Do I have reason to be?"

"Are you blind? I already told you, she's clearly crazy about you."

Then why did she ask for a divorce? Alex gripped the steering wheel tighter to keep from shouting it out loud.

"You've got nothing to worry about." Gene shook his head sympathetically. "Even if she hit on me—which she has not—I bat for the other team, if you catch my drift."

Alex scrubbed a hand over his head then grabbed the wheel again. "I just made an ass of myself. I'm sorry."

"Your words. Not mine."

It was perfectly clear Shelby wasn't seeing anyone else, and he'd never once had cause to wonder in the past. But now that they were splitting, she had every right to move on with her life.

His nights of watching Shelby sleep were coming to an end. And he had no one to blame but himself.

SHELBY SCRUBBED THE SLEEP from her eyes and realized the vehicle had stopped. Had she been out that long? All the restless nights must have caught up with her.

She worked the crick from her neck and peeked through the wire divider at Prince and Daisy in the back. "Alex?"

He stretched his arms overhead. "The GPS says this is the place."

About a zillion RVs filled the park even with the frigid temperatures. Gene leaned forward to pull something out of his camera bag.

She fished her phone from her pocket. "I'll text the Swensons that we're here. Would you mind walking Daisy and Prince?"

Mere seconds after she'd hit Send, her phone vibrated with the Swensons' return message telling her to meet them at the clubhouse. She looked out the window at Alex steering the dogs into the trees with such patience in his big burly body. The sense that someone was watching her brought her eyes up. Gene had the camera trained on her face. Keeping up the happy act was starting to really wear on her nerves.

Forcing a smile, she pointed to the window. "The pooches are over there."

"It's cold outside," Gene answered without moving from the front seat.

"That's why you get paid the big bucks. I'm just a volunteer."

Chuckling, he relented and stepped out. She grabbed her jacket from where she'd wadded it up to use as a pillow. She shook the wrinkles from her parka and slid her arms inside.

She opened the door, bracing for the cold. "Alex," she called. "The Swensons are going to meet us in the clubhouse."

On cue, an older couple came out from behind a tricked-out RV decorated with stickers from around the country. Christmas icicle lights dangled across the front windshield. Three small dogs on leashes trotted closer to Shelby, all wearing matching plaid sweaters. Gene went into silent cameraman mode, videotaping…Daisy?

Playing in the snow with a couple of kids?

Grumpy Daisy, who would refuse a squeaky toy soaked in beef broth, was downright prancing around two elementary-aged kids waddling in thick snowsuits. Alex stood to the side, holding the leash, keeping a watchful eye on the playful pup.

A lightbulb went off in Shelby's mind. Daisy loved kids, not adults. She felt dizzy with relief. If her hunch was correct, the Lab puppy would be fine in the morning when she met her new family, since they had two little girls.

But as much as she hated to miss out on watching Daisy shine, it was time to secure Prince's future. Shelby started toward the couple near the clubhouse.

Alex scooped up Daisy and came to stand alongside Shelby at the steps. "The Swensons seem eager to meet Prince."

"I feel guilty making Daisy come inside." But it really was bitterly cold, and she didn't want to risk the Labrador puppy getting sick, especially not when she was so close to her happily ever after.

"Daisy will have kids of her own tomorrow. Kids for keeps. Let's focus on getting this little man settled." Alex held up the leash, the thin silver-studded handle looking tiny and incongruous in his large, callused grip.

Prince approached the nearest pooch—a poodle— warily.

Mrs. Swenson was short, currently sporting fuzzy earmuffs and matching snow boots. She extended her hand. "I'm Louise and—" she paused, gesturing to the wiry man towering beside her "—this is my husband, Skip."

He nodded silently.

Louise patted his arm. "He doesn't talk much. Never has. But I chatter enough for both of us."

Shelby extended her hand. "It's a pleasure to meet you both. I'm Shelby, this is my husband, Alex, and that's Gene, he's filming an animal adoption special for our local TV station. I assume that's okay with you?"

"Of course. Anything to help get more poochies adopted." Louise reached out to the Pekingese, offering her glove for him to sniff before she picked him up. "And this must be Prince."

The Pekingese snuggled into her arms. What a perfect suck-up move. Good boy.

Starting up the stairs into the log cabin clubhouse, Louise crooned to Prince, "Once we get inside, we'll introduce you to the rest of our pack."

Skip followed with their festive pups—a Chihuahua, a Cairn terrier and a poodle. Gene was all over, filming the little guys in their plaid Christmas sweaters and booties.

Louise glowed for the camera. "I sewed one for Prince, too."

Inside, the clubhouse sprawled out to a wide-open space with two long tables by a kitchenette on one side and leather sofas around a stone fireplace on the other. A massive Christmas tree filled one corner. A sound system piped in "Jingle Bells" while a fire crackled in the hearth. A half dozen other campers were scattered in the room, curious about the camera but keeping to themselves.

Louise set Prince down near the Chihuahua...

The Pekingese growled low and long. The pooch was all but claiming Louise as his now. The Chi-Chi growled right back.

Crap.

Alex shot a panicked look her way.

Louise waved a hand. "Don't you worry about a little grousing. We'll just take our time here, no rushing the first meet. You two have a cup of cocoa over there and watch while we work this out."

Nerves pattered in her stomach as she followed Alex to the corner kitchenette, Daisy trailing. She'd been so worried about making this trip perfect with Alex, even fretting about Daisy, but she hadn't considered that cute little Prince's adoption might fall through. What if the rest of the trip was a failure?

Alex passed her a cup of cocoa while Daisy crawled under the table to eat a broken sugar cookie on the floor. "Hot chocolate with extra marshmallows."

The unexpected gesture yanked her attention back to her husband. She'd been trying so hard not to fantasize about her soon-to-be ex during this trip, but right now she welcomed the distraction.

"You remembered." She cradled the warm disposable cup between her hands, a bit of warm marshmallow oozing over the edge. "Thanks."

She flicked her tongue out to capture the sugary goo.

Alex's eyes lingered on her for a heated moment before he said, "You're usually so on top of the meals, I don't cook often. But I do pay attention." He skimmed a finger over her hair. "Speaking of which…I like the feather."

Her hair tingled all the way to the roots. She leaned against the wall, inhaling the scent of chocolate, burning wood and even hotter man.

She forced her hands to stay steady before she spilled her cocoa. "Some of my teenage wild-child still lingers. Better than piercing my eyebrow again. The school board frowns on those."

He touched her eyebrow where she still carried a tiny scar. "You took it out before I met you."

Okay, she was seriously going to melt if he kept that up. She sank into a chair at the end of the long oak table. "I only did it to get a rise out of my dad. He was pretty good at playing it cool, and when I didn't get the reaction I wanted, I took it out. A feather would have hurt a lot less."

"Valid point." He rested a hip against the edge of the table, still standing. "But you must have driven the guys crazy in study hall."

"And in detention when I cut class." On the one hand, the angst of those days seemed so far away, but on the other, how much had she learned about taking drastic action to get attention from the people she loved? For all her obsession with getting him to talk, how much had she actually said? "I was so out of control back then, so angry over my parents' divorce—and hurt by Mom walking out."

"The way I'm walking out now?"

His question rumbled softly between them, stunning her into silence for a second. She'd wanted to have a real discussion with him, and now that it was happening, she didn't know quite what to say.

She sipped her cocoa while she gathered her thoughts, then decided to answer honestly, "I never saw it that way. If anything, I blame myself and worry that I'm…too much like my mother."

"You're nothing like your mother. You remind me more of your stepmom, Julia. You're both the most giving people I've ever met." He reached in his pocket for a dog biscuit and tossed it under the table to Daisy.

"Like Julia? Wow. Thank you." Julia's free spirit and non-judgmental ways had eased something inside teenage Shelby. She'd always looked up to her step-mother. Thanks to Julia, the family had started to heal, to bond again. Shelby had even gotten along better with her father.

Then she'd eloped with Alex and later withdrawn her application to vet school, angering her father and putting distance between them. In the years since, pride had kept those barriers standing between her and her dad, and now she didn't know how she would tell him she'd wrecked her marriage.

Would her father understand, since he'd been through a divorce, too?

Alex scuffed the toe of his hiking boot against the carpet. "Maybe I'm the one that's more like your mother."

What? No way did he share anything in common with her superficial mother. Shelby couldn't bear for him to believe that, for even a second.

She searched for the right words. "When my mom left, she traveled around the world with her new boy-friend. She would send us postcards or local foods, so, rather than use her name, I would call her by the country on the menu that day. If she mailed brie, I called her France. Chocolates, she was Switzerland. Sausage, Germany. Aggie loved the sausage era."

"Ironic—your mother was never there and mine never left the house." He drained his cocoa.

"I wish I'd had the chance to meet your parents."

His mother and father had died in a car accident a few months before she'd met Alex. Maybe she would understand him better if she'd spoken to his parents. He'd told her very little about them other than that his father was an accountant and his mother was a librarian. He only had a few photos of them or even of himself as a child, but she'd always chalked that up to guys not being sentimental.

He crumpled his cup and tossed it in the trash. "No, you don't. Not really. My mother was a very unhappy person."

"You said she suffered from depression." Alex had once revealed that the car wreck had happened as his father was driving his mother to a therapy session. "The holidays must make you think about her more…"

"Actually, no." He met her eyes, full on, no barriers. "Talking about those cats at The Haven did."

"The cats?" She sipped the last of her cocoa.

"My mom had cats…a lot of them." He crossed his arms over his broad chest. "I don't know if today she'd be qualified as a hoarder. We made sure they had veterinary care. They were spayed and neutered. There weren't sixty of them, by any means."

"How many were there?"

"Usually around a dozen. Nineteen at one point."

"Nineteen," she gasped, unable to hide her shock. Barking from the minipack filled the silence between them.

How had she never had this conversation with Alex before? How could she not have known? Probably for the same reason he'd never known details about her teenage years. She'd just pushed him to open up and reveal all while she'd held a piece of herself back. She had failed her husband in a way she'd never suspected.

"It's okay." She touched his arm, his muscles twitching under her fingers even through the open parka he still wore. "She was ill. I understand better now."

He started to turn away under the guise of getting

more cocoa but she gripped his coat. She refused to let this opportunity pass, what could be her last chance at a deeper understanding of the man she'd loved for the last eight years.

"You said your mother's cats got veterinary care. Who took care of that when she was in a depression?"

"There was a vet hospital down the road, within walking distance."

"*You* took the cats to the veterinarian, alone? How old could you have been?"

He glaced around as if searching for an escape, but that would mean walking past Gene and the Swensons, not to mention a family at the other table. "First time I went, I was eleven. Two of the cats got into a fight. One, a calico, was injured with a torn ear and a pretty bad bite in his neck."

Pausing, he returned to the cocoa, his hand steady as he poured, even if his grip on the pot was white knuckled. "I couldn't just let him suffer. I bundled him up in a towel so he wouldn't scratch me and I walked to the vet clinic a few blocks away."

She took the fresh cup of hot chocolate from him. "You had to have been scared."

"I wasn't thinking, really. My feet just moved. The vet called my dad and he gave them his credit card number along with permission to treat and neuter the cat." Alex stared into his steaming cup. "Shortly after that, a gray tabby got sick. I brought her to the clinic and they took care of her and then spayed her, as well. Dad covered the bill again...so the vet and I figured, what the hell? I started smuggling Mom's cats down to get them fixed and the clinic mailed the bills to my dad's office address. I think he was happy to shell out the cash so there wouldn't be any more cats."

Pain and frustration for Alex rose inside her. Her mom may have checked out on her, but her dad had at least tried to pick up the slack. "Why didn't your father just take the cats to the veterinarian himself? Or tell your mom to scale back on the numbers?"

"My dad wasn't what you would call confrontational." He half smiled. "He tolerated the cats. He just wasn't interested in hands-on care."

A cold blast of air swept in as a couple of giggling teenage girls walked inside the clubhouse. An equally chilly blast swept through her as she began to understand why Alex was passive-aggressive in his personal life.

She waited for the two teens to settle in front of the fireplace with their cell phones before asking, "What did your mother say about the cats?"

"Nothing. I always made sure she didn't know when I slipped a cat out of the house."

He'd had to *sneak* the cats out? "Why didn't you ever share any of this with me?"

And why had she never thought to ask, to push harder?

"My parents are dead. It's in the past. And your family's so damn perfect...." He shrugged.

Perfect?

She'd always believed he kept his distance because he disliked her father, and, to be fair, her father hadn't been warm and fuzzy to his son-in-law, either. "My parents are divorced."

"Your dad may have taken a while to figure it out, but he and Julia are rock solid. So I'm sorry if I didn't feel the need to trot out the details of my crazy cat-lady mother and head-in-the-sand father."

She flattened her hand to his chest. "But Alex, we've been married for almost *eight years*."

"Then I guess this is yet more proof of how bad I screwed up." He nodded toward the Swensons and set aside his half-empty cup. "Looks like the dogs have warmed up to each other over there. You've made another match."

She checked over her shoulder at the older couple with their four dogs. Prince was wearing his new sweater and playing tug-of-war with the terrier.

And there it was, her Ghost of Christmas Yet to Come…what could have been. What she and Alex could have had. She'd spent so many years blaming him for being absent. But she'd failed him when they were together. The story about the cats made her realize how very silent his childhood must have been, with a mother secluded in her room and a father escaping at work. Of course he wouldn't know how to communicate.

They'd left a preteen to sneak cats out of the home for sterilization in order to protect himself from being overrun by an out-of-control hoard. He'd been taking care of his mother—and his father—when they should have been looking out for him.

Thinking over their marriage, she suddenly reevaluated the ways he'd taken care of her without words. All those floating marshmallows he'd thoughtfully, silently put in her cocoa made her want to cry.

Her eyes burned and, oh, God, she was seconds away from embarrassing herself in front of her husband, not to mention the cameraman and the Swensons. Alex had seen enough tears and sadness in his life. Her hand slid away from the hard wall of his chest.

She reached inside her parka, pulled out the envelope with the adoption papers and thrust them toward her husband. "Could you go over these with the Swensons? I need to take Daisy outside for a walk."

Before he could argue, she tugged the Labrador puppy from under the table and raced for the door, tears blinding her.

CHAPTER SIX

A FRIGID GUST OF AIR hit Shelby in the face, nearly freezing her tears on her cheeks. She charged down the steps, gasping in each bracing breath, her emotions shaky, her heart breaking all over again...just when she hoped she'd come to grips with divorcing Alex. Daisy yanked on the leash, trying to run toward the little boy and girl still building a lopsided snowman by their RV.

At least she could bring happiness to Daisy

Giving the leggy puppy extra leash, Shelby picked her way across the salted sidewalk toward the kids. Barking, Daisy strained forward, darn near making the walk an ice skating expedition.

"Okay, okay, I'm moving as fast as I can, girl."

Daisy pulled harder, barking louder. Shelby waved at the kids' parents who were sitting under an awning attached to their RV, a portable fire pit crackling. "Is it okay if your kids pet the puppy?"

The mother nodded quickly. "Anything to wear them out before we hit the road again tomorrow."

Shelby let Daisy lead her the rest of the way. "Calm down, girl. We're gonna play. I promise."

Daisy surged forward just as Shelby's boot came down on a patch of ice. Her feet shot out from under her. She landed hard. Pain shot up through her tailbone. Her teeth clacked closed and blood filled her mouth from where she must have bitten her tongue.

Her head cleared and she realized—crap—Daisy had gotten free. The puppy was racing full out *past* the kids and toward the woods, red leash flapping behind her like the tail on a kite. Shelby struggled for breath, panic lancing through her. Sure the puppy was tagged and micro-chipped, but what if she got lost in the woods? Out in the cold?

Shelby pushed to her feet, waving aside the parents and children who'd gathered around to help her. "Puppy," she gasped. "I'll get the puppy."

A gasp from the mother cut the air as she pointed in the direction of the woods. "Oh, my God!"

Shelby tensed, watching apprehensively as Daisy slowed at the tree line. Deeper in the forest, just visible in the late-day fog, a coyote crouched low, growling—directly in Daisy's path.

ALEX PASSED OVER THE last of the papers to the Swensons, wondering when the hell Shelby would come back inside. He could service a multimillion-dollar military aircraft, but completing this road trip without having a breakdown seemed impossible.

What had possessed him to take that morbid journey down memory lane, spilling his guts about his crummy childhood to Shelby? He'd glossed over the worst of it for years. The past was the past, after all. Today, he'd out-Scrooged Scrooge.

A scream from outside split the air.

A familiar voice.

Shelby.

Instantly in combat mode, he plowed across the room, flinging open the door. Shelby was being restrained by some guy—a man seconds away from meeting Alex's fist. A red haze of fury damn near blinded him. His boots pounded snow and ice, and with each stride he got a clearer picture of what was happening.

The older guy wasn't hurting Shelby. He was keeping her from launching forward. A couple of yards away, Daisy was moments away from being attacked by a coyote.

The wild animal growled, fangs glinting. Shards of snow glistened in its silvery fur.

Daisy held her ground between the feral animal and the cluster of onlookers. The mother slowly hustled her two children into the RV.

Alex reached for Shelby, keeping his movements slow, his voice soft. "Shel, move into the RV. I've got this."

"I can't just leave her." Shelby pushed harder against the other man's restraining arm.

Like hell was he letting his wife tangle with a rabid beast. His heart thumping in his ears, he grasped her elbow just as the coyote leaped onto Daisy.

He called to the guy holding Shelby back, "Don't let her go."

On autopilot, Alex sprinted forward, grabbing the two lawn chairs from under the awning. Clanging them together and shouting, he advanced.

Hoping the noise would startle the animal away.

Planning to use the chair as a shield and weapon if it didn't.

Regardless, the coyote couldn't be allowed to stay near a populated RV camp. And Daisy?

The two animals snarled and yelped. Snow sprayed up from the scrabbling paws. Shouting louder, Alex bashed the chairs together again.

The coyote raised his head. The animal made brief,

icy eye contact. Then turned and sprinted away into the woods.

Slowly, the world expanded beyond that patch of snow. He became aware of a screaming, terrified child being soothed by a parent. Doors slammed on RVs and the clubhouse.

Shelby cried, "Let me go! Let me go!"

Daisy whimpered, her blood staining the snow around her.

Alex flung aside the chairs and stumbled the last two steps to the puppy. His earlier detachment was a helluva lot harder to find with his heart in his throat. The coyote had gone for Daisy's neck. The fleshy wound looked bad. Really bad.

"Okay, girl, it's gonna be okay," he said softly as he slid his arms under the puppy. Daisy's chocolate eyes were filled with pain and pleading.

He stood and found his wife already at his side, her teary eyes focused on the dog as she passed him her scarf to staunch the bleeding.

"Shelby, check the GPS. Find an emergency vet clinic."

"Sergeant," Mrs. Swenson called from the clubhouse steps. "Skip's got his fancy phone working on it now."

Skip held his Droid up, racing toward Shelby. "Already got one—thank God for 3G connections. Listing says it's about twenty miles west. They're open on weekends and holidays. Louise is writing down the name and address to put into your GPS. I'll call ahead for you. We've got Prince. You just go."

"Shelby, you drive," he clipped out orders, determined not to lose little Daisy. "I'll hold the dog."

"I'll hold her." She held out her arms, tears streaking down her face.

He cradled the injured puppy carefully, blood already soaking his parka. "She might bite you because she's hurt. Don't waste even a second arguing. Keys are in my front pocket."

"Okay, you're right." She dug for the keys and thumbed the unlock button.

"Gene," he snapped, "do you think you could put the camera down and type the location into the GPS?"

"Oh, right." Gene lowered the camera, his face so pale Alex worried the guy would pass out. The camraman slid toward the SUV and opened the back door for Alex.

Holding the bloody puppy, he couldn't help but remember taking the injured cat to the vet as a kid. Scared as hell the animal wouldn't make it. Frustrated that he couldn't just fix things himself.

The drive to the clinic passed in a blur as he resisted the urge to ask his wife to drive faster on the icy roads. Getting in a wreck would only make things worse for Daisy.

She snuggled into his parka, calm now but occasionally making soft mewling sounds that tore at his gut. He tried to calm the animal—and hell, himself and Shelby, too—with soothing words as they made the endless journey.

Finally they pulled into the parking lot of a pink brick building. Christmas lights blinked in ironic merriment. Shelby drove right up to the covered porch. Gene was already yanking open the back door.

A sports car pulled into the nearest spot a second behind them. A short, wiry man in a tuxedo and long black overcoat stepped out. "I'm Dr. Marcus. The clinic called me in, said we had an emergency surgery patient arriving."

Already the vet's eyes homed in on the puppy.

His attention firmly on Daisy, Dr. Marcus called over his shoulder to the decked-out blonde in an evening gown still in the car. "Babe, you can wait in my office or go back to the party. I'm going to be a while."

SHELBY COULDN'T REMEMBER when she'd been this numb and powerless. She watched the minutes tick by on the waiting room clock until an hour had passed with no word. Alex had taken off his bloody parka while she'd passed over Daisy's vaccination records to the vet with shaking hands. Thank goodness Gene had been able to gather his nerves and park the SUV before he joined them inside. For once, he didn't have the camera shoved in her face. Instead he filmed unobtrusively from a seat in the corner.

She'd replayed that awful, awful moment in her mind at least a hundred times, always coming to the same heartbreaking conclusion. Daisy had been protecting those children, and she'd possibly sacrificed her life to do it.

The wait was horrible, her stomach eaten by an acid worry and her third cup of coffee. A half hour ago, she'd managed to calm down enough to call Tansy, then Daisy's adoptive family, but had only gotten answering machines. In a way, it had been a relief not to have to talk when her nerves were already frayed beyond bearing.

She started to stand, ready to bother the receptionist again for more information, when the clinic door opened and the vet stepped out. His tuxedo was gone, replaced by scrubs stained with the rusty tinge of more blood.

Her throat clogged with fresh tears.

"Daisy made it through surgery," Dr. Marcus announced without delay. "She's still coming out of the anesthesia. Luckily, the injury wasn't as severe as it appeared. And there's no worry about rabies since she's up to date on her vaccinations. We'll keep her on IV antibiotics through the night. She should be ready for you to pick up in the morning."

Before Shelby was able to form a coherent thought and thank him, he slipped back into the clinic area.

The receptionist shot her a wry smile from behind her tinsel-draped counter. "Dr. Marcus likes animals more than people. But I promise, your dog was in good hands during surgery and it will be a long while before he leaves her side. Not even his latest girlfriend and a black-tie dinner could tempt him away."

Alex's arm slid around Shelby, a steadying presence that she desperately needed right now.

Shelby asked, "Can we sit with her?"

"In the morning. She's out for the count now and will be sedated through the night. We have your number if there's any change."

The receptionist's attention was pulled away from them by a family rushing in with their Labradoodle.

"Our dog found all the cooking chocolate and ate a whole bar—"

The staff went into high gear again. Chocolate was especially toxic for dogs.

Stepping away, Shelby sagged against Alex and she couldn't miss the sigh racking his warm, solid body. She remembered other times her husband had been there to hold her, his strong arm fortifying her through one negative pregnancy test after another, supporting her after each miscarriage. Silently, Alex had offered an unconditional love that she'd absorbed through her pores rather than her ears.

She didn't even care that the camera was probably on them as she let her husband guide her to the Explorer. She just wanted to get back to the room and sleep away the night so she could see Daisy again with her own eyes, reassure herself that the fearless pup wouldn't die before she had her chance to live her life loved and treasured in a home of her own.

The ride to the hotel passed in a stream of holiday lights and the occasional group of carolers. She could hardly believe tomorrow would be Christmas Eve. Solemnly, they checked in to their rooms, Gene going his way and Alex leading her to theirs.

Once inside the room, her energy evaporated and she sagged on the end of the bed. It was all she could do to shrug out of her coat and kick off her boots.

Alex peeled his shirt off and threw it in the trash on his way to the shower. His broad shoulders hunched as if they carried the weight of the world. If she hadn't pushed for this trip, right now they would be at their house with all three dogs safe and healthy.

Her heart heavy, she pulled her cell phone out of her purse to check for messages, scrunching her toes in her thick wooly socks. The screen showed four missed calls. She tapped in the code to listen to her messages, staring at the glow of Christmas lights shining outside, even through the thick curtains.

Tansy had called first, concerned, thanking her for getting Daisy help so quickly and telling her to call if she needed anything.

Next, her stepmother, Julia, checking to be sure they were on schedule.

The Bennetts...wishing them Merry Christmas, and reassuring her that their dogs were happy.

And Daisy's new family.

Shelby straightened, listening closely, disbelieving what she heard.

She hit Replay.

Oh, God. Her hand fell to her lap with the phone. Stunned, she sat unmoving until Alex came out of the shower.

One towel wrapped around his waist, he dried his hair with a second. "Everything okay?"

"No," she said simply, still processing and trying not to fall apart.

He peered from under the towel. "What's wrong? Is Daisy—?"

"It wasn't the clinic." She swallowed down the bitter gall of disappointment. "The message was from Daisy's so-called new family. They changed their minds." Her voice cracked with emotion, her composure fracturing right along with it. "Someone was giving away puppies in a box outside their Christmas tree farm and they took one home."

He sat beside her on the edge of the bed and hauled her close. "I am so sorry, Shel. So very sorry."

Giving in to the urge to cry, she let the tears and disappointment rain free. "It sucks, and it's not fair."

"I know, hon." His voice soothed her, along with the warm familiarity of his closeness, his touch. "We'll take care of her until she's well and then your friend Tansy will find another home for her, a better home."

"No—" her voice caught on a hiccup "—I'll just keep her. Daisy is *not* going back to the shelter."

"Okay, you'll foster her until she finds a home. That's a great idea."

"Nuh-uh." She scrubbed a fierce hand over her eyes. "She's mine. I'm adopting her."

"What about Samson and Delilah?" His hand

smoothed over her hair, down to lightly massage her neck. "Are you sure three dogs is a good idea? And what about how much Daisy loves being with kids?"

She jerked away, her hands gripping her knees. "Yes, damn it. Three dogs and no kids. She's staying with me. It's not your problem, anyway, since you'll be gone." Her hands fisted. "All that matters is no one is ever going to reject me again—"

Realizing the massive Freudian slip that had fallen from her mouth, she clapped a hand over her lips in horror. "I mean, *Daisy*. No one is going to reject…Daisy…"

All these years she'd worried about becoming her mother without realizing her deeper, driving fear that someone would reject her again. That she hadn't been perfect enough for her mom so Pamela hadn't even fought for custody. Yet the harder Shelby tried in her marriage, the more she'd pushed Alex away, until it had become some kind of self-fulfilling prophecy. She'd ened up alone and rejected yet again.

Blinking fast, she set more tears free. Alex pulled her to him again and she didn't bother drawing back. She cried harder, his bare skin soaking up her tears.

His hot, muscled chest.

All her raw nerves and emotions collided into one desire—in a day that had made her all too aware of everything she'd lost and the many ways she'd screwed up, she needed something good before she fell apart altogether.

She needed to make love to her husband.

CHAPTER SEVEN

HOLDING SHELBY IN HIS arms was torture. His body throbbed with the urge to recline her onto the bed, to be with her again, to make her feel secure and loved in the only way he knew how. And she'd probably hate him for it, so he held on to his self-control by the skin of his teeth.

But he wouldn't push her away. Shelby's tears were tearing him apart inside. She needed him, needed comfort. So he kept stroking his hands over her hair still damp from snowflakes and icy mist.

The coyote attack and the wait at the vet's had been hellish for him, too. And coming back to the hotel without the grouchy little pup stabbed at him more than he expected. It had to be a nightmare for Shelby.

If it killed him, he would hold her, comfort her, through the night even. He would be there for her now in a way that he hadn't during all those deployments.

Was it his imagination or was she pressing closer to him? He stroked down her spine, clenching his jaw against the temptation of her soft breasts against his chest.

"Alex?"

"Yeah, Shel?"

Her fingers skipped down his chest to his hip, hooking her finger in the edge of the towel.

His heart stuttered. Stopped. Then kicked into high gear. There was no mistaking her sensual message.

Still, he stayed immobile, letting her make the next move. Needing to be sure this was what she wanted as damn much as he did.

Angling to meet his eyes, she plucked at the knotted towel until it eased free.

She slid her hand up his thigh, her cool skin setting his on fire. Then she clasped his erection, wrapping her fingers around him in a slow sweep up.

No mistaking that message, either.

Cupping her head, he kissed her, firmly, fully, no holding back. She met each thrust and sweep of his tongue, their bodies syncing with the familiarity of longtime lovers. The taste of cocoa and marshmallows lingered on her, reminding him of their conversation earlier, of all he'd told her. And she hadn't pushed him away. He'd held so much back from her out of fear. Had that fear been totally baseless?

Right now he didn't want to think, just lose himself in his wife. Savor the hell out of making her as hot and high as she made him. He slid his hand under the waistband of her sweater to the silken skin of her stomach.

"More," she demanded, nipping his shoulder while tugging her sweater up and over her head, shaking her hair free. She struggled to reach behind her to get rid of her bra, but he brushed her hands away.

"Let me," he said simply, unhooking it and sweeping the peach lace down and away.

Words left him altogether. He never tired of looking at her. The cool air pulled her nipples into tight buds that called to his hands and his mouth. He cradled the weight of her in his palms, his thumbs circling both tempting peaks. He couldn't get enough of the feel of her, the taste of her. How the hell had he believed he could ever walk away from this woman?

He kissed his way up her body, along her collarbone to her neck and then her mouth. The warmth of her bare flesh heightened the familiar scent of her raspberry body wash, sending a bolt of desire straight to his shaft.

Her arms looped around his neck, and she threaded her fingers through his hair, tugging urgently. Moaning, she wriggled onto his lap. Her legs wrapped around his waist, the core of her nestled against his erection. The rasp of her jeans reminded him there were still too many clothes between them.

Standing, he turned and settled her on the bed again, silencing her protest with a kiss.

"Trust me," he vowed.

He knelt between her legs and her eyes went wide with pleasure. Rocking back on his heels, he took Shelby's foot in his hands and slipped her sock down, then off. With the perfect pressure, he pressed his thumbs up the arch before shifting his attention to her other foot.

A purr rolled up her throat as she all but melted onto the mattress.

"Every day that I'm away from you, all I think about is being with you again." He opened her jeans and peeled them down her legs. "Ahhh…an emerald belly-button ring."

She smiled, trailing her fingers over his shoulder. "Getting into the holiday spirit."

Would he be around to give her a ruby one for Valentine's Day?

Shoving aside the thought, he sketched his mouth over her stomach, flicking the jewel with his tongue on his way down to the ultimate gem. He tugged her panties off with his teeth then finally nuzzled her, finding the pearled bundle of tight nerves. Her heels dug deeper into his shoulders, her low groan stoking him, encouraging him to tease her close to the edge again and again until—

Her climax came fast and hard, her cries of pleasure filling the room. It had always been intense between them, but even more so after they'd been apart for a while, as if they were saying with their bodies all the things they hadn't—couldn't—put into words.

Before the flush left her creamy skin, he slid over her and settled on top of her, filling her. The urge to finish hammered through him with each urgent throb of his pulse. He pressed his forehead to her shoulder and gritted back the urge to thrust, quick and deep, to completion.

Her fingers feathered down his shoulders and she chanted again and again that it was okay, to let go, but damned if he'd finish without her. Balancing on a razor's edge of restraint, he sealed his mouth to hers, rocking his hips against her. He hooked a hand behind her knee and hitched her leg higher, thrusting deeper, angling her just so to bring her the most pleasure from every roll, every move.

He knew her body, each special spot, and she knew him just as well. The way she used her teeth and nails nudged him closer and closer to the edge.

The scent of raspberry, the taste of cocoa on her tongue—both would indelibly imprint this memory on his brain. Hell, Shelby was imprinted on *him,* she was a part of him, and she always would be. No divorce would end what he felt for her. The power of that tore through him, catapulting him over the edge. Her legs clamped harder around him, drawing him closer, taking him deeper as his orgasm racked through him. He pulsed inside her, claimed her.

Loved her.

Nothing had changed for him. He was still head over ass in love with his wife.

And he didn't have a damn clue how to keep her.

SHELBY RESTED HER FOREHEAD against the SUV window, watching the miles of snow-filled landscape blur by on their way to see her family. It had been a slow-going Christmas Eve trip—picking up Daisy, saying good-bye to Gene, packing everything up…and then getting hit by a blizzard. Their journey had stretched into the night and still Alex drove on while she watched for other cars or hazards.

The silence—other than the low drone of the weather station—left her with too long to think about what happened in that hotel room. Alex had made love to her through the night, until there had been only a couple of hours to sleep before they picked up Daisy.

Thank God, the puppy had been on her feet, tail wagging when they'd walked into the vet's. The clinic tech had given them a list of warning signs to look out for and ten days' worth of antibiotics. But other than that, Daisy was surprisingly spry for a dog that had wrestled with a coyote.

Still, once they'd dropped Gene and his camera at the airport and bought Alex a new parka, she'd insisted on riding in the back with Daisy to be sure she didn't scratch the wound on her neck. And, sure, she was probably avoiding Alex and the emotions he'd stirred in her last night. Like Daisy, she was hiding to avoid being rejected. How damn ironic that she finally had Alex all to herself in the car, could say whatever she wanted, and now she was the one who needed space to sort through her feelings.

What had last night meant for them?

Until she had an answer, she would keep her silence and her distance. God knows she didn't want to start a major confrontation right before arriving at her parents'. Pretending in front of them would be tough enough. She stroked Daisy's satiny black coat, desperate for any peace she could find.

The closer she got to their destination, the more her stomach churned. When they closed the bedroom door tonight, would they silently make love again with no idea where their relationship was going?

Her heart couldn't take that.

But she also wouldn't turn him away.

ALEX UNLOADED THE LAST of the gifts from the car-top carrier, the evening sky starless with thick clouds that created a low ceiling. They'd arrived about fifteen minutes ago, just shy of midnight.

Only her father—the colonel—had been awake. Everyone else was already asleep, since Shelby had called to say they weren't sure how late they would arrive. She was inside now, settling Daisy for the night in their bedroom.

The bedroom he would be sharing with her shortly. And he had no idea how the hell he was supposed to act around her after an entire day of near silence other than bare-necessity exchanges like...

Watch out for that skidding car.

Do you want Taco Bell or Wendy's?

Daisy needs a break.

Alex adjusted his hold on the two sacks of Christmas gifts, none of which had been bought by him—including the gifts *from* him. And now it was too late to buy anything for Shelby.

Her dad stepped out onto the porch of his two-story brick house in a quiet neighborhood. A lanky guy with a full head of steel-gray hair still cut military short, Zach Dawson had retired a colonel after twenty-five years in the air force to spend more time with his family. Now he worked as a consultant for a major aerospace company.

Zach Dawson had never needed to seek out ways to avoid his wife. He knew at least that much about the man…if little else. Last night he had realized he'd been keeping a part of himself from Shelby, afraid that if she knew him completely, she would turn away. Now, with each step closer to Zach, Alex understood that he'd been avoiding her family for the same reason. Not a particularly honorable way to behave.

And regardless of how things turned out with Shelby, he had some fences to mend.

Starting now.

Zach extended a hand for one of the bags. "Need some help?"

"Thank you." Alex handed the older man the lighter bag and followed him into the warm living room, dimly lit with twinkling strings of lights on the mantel and on the tree that stretched up to the cathedral ceiling. A new video game system with a fat red bow rested by the empty plate labeled Santa's Cookies.

Kneeling by the live pine, Alex began unloading the packages. He glanced sideways at Zach. "Sir, I owe you an apology."

His father-in-law paused midstep, an eyebrow shooting upward. "For what?"

A lot of things, but for starters… "I should have come to you before we eloped, or at least right after. Should have shown you the kind of man I was, and reassured you that I loved Shelby and would take care of her."

Except he hadn't. He'd run from her as fast as he'd run from her father.

Alex looked down at the perfectly wrapped gift, with a bow that was damn near a work of art. How many Christmases had Shelby prepped alone, trying to make things perfect for him, working in such a frenzy to prove she wasn't her mother? That she wasn't a failure at marriage and a disappointment to everyone? And rather than telling her how much he loved her, rather than listening to her fears, he'd breezed through her life for a few days, just as quickly on his way back out again the minute the emotions got too intense.

Zach studied the small gift bag in his hand. "Thank you. Apologies are never easy and I appreciate that." He tucked the present under a piney bough. "But to be clear, I wasn't upset with who she married or even that she married so young, just that she'd eloped. My daughter is a competent woman who can take care of herself. But I wanted to walk my daughter down the aisle, wanted to look into the eyes of the man she was marrying and be assured he loved her."

Guilt piled on like a snowdrift sliding off a roof. "I may be eight years late with this, but I do love your daughter, sir. There's nothing I wouldn't do for her."

"Then why the hell are you divorcing her?" Zach said with piercing directness.

Damn. Alex sank back to sit on the rug, the low fire crackling quietly in the fireplace. "You know?"

"I wasn't sure until now." The colonel scrubbed his jaw then sat, as well. "But it's obvious you're both miserable."

Apparently they weren't as good at acting as they'd

thought. Hopefully they'd done better for the camera. "Aren't you going to ask why?"

"No," Zach answered, even though he clearly had an idea in his mind.

"But you have something you want to say."

Late-night silence wrapped around them with only the sound of wind in the trees outside and the occasional pop of a log in the fireplace.

Finally, his father-in-law nodded. "Advice. If you want it. If not, I understand."

"I'm listening."

"I know my daughter worries about being like her mom, but she's more like her old man." Zach smiled in a one-sided grin Shelby had once said resulted from nerve damage to his face after his stint as a POW. "We're both stubborn, driven and convinced if we just work hard enough we can take care of everyone."

"That sounds about right."

Zach picked up a fireplace poker and stabbed at the log, rejuvenating the flame. "Julia and I almost split up once."

Now that surprised him. He'd always believed the colonel and his second wife were rock solid. Their happiness, their success, made it all the tougher to acknowledge his own floundering marriage. "Obviously, you two worked it out."

"We did. But I was all set to give her up because I thought that if walking away made her happy, then hell, I would do it. I would do anything for her…except what she needed most. I was so busy being the damn altruistic hero, I never did the truly heroic thing and fight to win her back."

"What happened to turn that around?"

"*She* fought for *me*." His smile dug deeper into his weathered face. "Thank God."

And if Shelby was like her dad, then the older guy was telling him to get off his ass and fight for his wife. Except he had no idea what she wanted from him anymore. "So I'm supposed to ignore everything she's said and not give her a divorce. Fine, but then nothing's changed. We'll be right back where we started. She deserves better."

"Then figure out how to give her better." Zach pushed to his feet and stowed the fire poker. "See you in the morning, son. Merry Christmas."

Alex stared into the fire long after his father-in-law's footsteps faded. The words of wisdom shifted around in his head. Zach Dawson may have tossed out the phrase *son* offhandedly, but the fatherly advice was real enough.

And a little alien to a guy who hadn't been the recipient of much.

All this time he'd been deluding himself into believing he was giving Shelby what she needed—more money for fertility treatments, then space to deal with her grief. But all the while he'd been like his own father, hiding out at the office rather than facing and fixing his problems. And a little like his mother, bunkering down his fears and insecurities to keep from being exposed, vulnerable. He accepted that now. But he hadn't taken the final step in fixing that problem.

Alex tugged the grate over the fireplace. He might not have the perfect answers. But he was done running and hiding.

Standing, he made his way to the room he shared with Shelby. She lay on her side of the bed, one arm draped over the edge, touching Daisy. Both of them asleep. So he slipped under the covers carefully and slid his arms around his wife, tucking her against him.

His *wife*.

Damn straight, he wasn't giving up.

CHAPTER EIGHT

SHELBY WALKED DAISY off-leash around the fenced-in backyard, leaving fresh footprints in the snow as the sun peeked above the horizon on Christmas morning. The quiet would be short lived once the rest of the house woke. Certainly, her stepbrother, Patrick, would be up to check out his gift from Santa soon—a new video game system.

Last night, she'd tried to stay awake to talk to Alex, but she'd drifted off to the low sounds of his voice and her father's coming from the living room while she'd been upstairs settling Daisy. They so rarely spoke to each other, she hadn't been able to bring herself to intrude, even though she was beyond curious as to what they would have say to each other now, after all these years of polite distance.

She would ask Alex on their way home, when she didn't have to worry about interruption or ruining Christmas. A private conversation would ease her curiosity. Too bad it wouldn't give her the chance to spend another night in her husband's arms. Once they were home, they wouldn't be sharing the same room. The awkwardness of that next phase in their relationship was already making her ill.

At least Daisy was recovering well, exploring the wooden fort. Only the shaved area on her neck served as a reminder of how she'd protected the two children at the RV park.

The back door of the house creaked and her dad walked toward her with a hat in his hand. No doubt for her. She put her gloved hands to her bare ears and smiled in spite of the ever-present ache in her heart.

Her father was always the relentless protector, trying to take care of everyone. It was in his DNA.

"Hey, baby girl." He passed her the green stocking cap. "Merry Christmas."

She tugged it over her ears. "Merry Christmas to you, too. You're up early."

"Julia kicked me out of bed to turn on the coffeepot and move the breakfast casserole from the refrigerator into the oven."

"She didn't make it, did she?" Her stepmom was an amazing person but a horrible cook.

"God, no. Your little sister did."

Her sister was an awesome chef, home from college. "Thank goodness."

Grinning, he stuffed his hands in his coat pockets. "But then I didn't marry Julia for her cooking."

Julia was perfect for her dad in so many other ways, a few burned casseroles didn't matter in the big scheme of things. Shelby rubbed the frown pinching her forehead, remembering all the so-called "perfect" meals she'd put together for Alex, desperately trying to be the model wife. Completely missing the boat on the things that really mattered.

"Hey, Dad? Could you go easy on Alex today? He's just gotten back from overseas and…" She swallowed hard, unable to make excuses anymore. "Things have been tough between us. It doesn't look like we're going to make it."

Her dad glanced over at the house for a couple of heartbeats before saying, "Are you sure about that?"

"Dad, you've spent eight years scowling at Alex and now you're rooting for us?"

"Sure, we all worried that the two of you married too young, too fast, like your mom and I did."

"I've spent my whole marriage working so hard not to be her...Mom. Not to be a failure." The ache swelled inside her, damn near choking her. "And here I sit, on the edge of divorce."

"Whoa, hold on." Her dad slid his arm around her. "I didn't say you were like her. If anything, I've always thought you were more like me."

"I wish." Her laugh was a little watery and wobbly.

"Shelby, Alex is a good man, and I would have considered myself damn lucky to have him on my crew back in the day. I guess there's a part of me that hoped you would marry a civilian and lead a regular life without the stress that comes from being a military spouse."

"You're actually saying you disapprove *because* he's in the air force?"

"I wanted an easier path for you than your mother and I had. And God knows, the military has cost Julia and Patrick too much."

Julia's first husband—Patrick's father—had died in a crash, leaving Julia alone to raise their special-needs infant son. While Patrick was Shelby's stepbrother, she loved him as much as she loved her sister. She'd watched the little guy grow up with Down syndrome, cheered over every milestone he reached—later than other babies, maybe, but all the more hard won.

Her brother had a sunny disposition that was infectious to everyone around him. Things hadn't been easy for him, but his indomitable spirit was an inspiration to her, every day.

"Thank you, Dad, for worrying about me. I love you, you know."

He hugged her tight against his side. "Love you, too."

Emotion clogged her throat as she rested her head on his shoulder, thinking about all Alex had shared about his family. Realizing how lucky she'd been with her own. And most of all, realizing how deeply she wanted a life with Alex.

She still loved him. And the idea of losing him was tearing her apart. She didn't want a divorce. She wanted to fix things with her husband, no matter what the odds.

They fell silent, watching Daisy nose halfheartedly through the snow.

"Shel?"

"Yeah, Dad?"

"That is the saddest-looking puppy I have ever seen—"

The back door swung wide again, the screen smacking the house.

"Merry Christmas!" her eleven-year-old stepbrother shouted, racing out into the yard in his pj's, snow boots and an open parka. "Shelby, I missed you."

He threw his arms around her waist and hugged her hard before he broke away. "And you brought me a puppy for Christmas! You're the coolest."

Patrick took off running toward Daisy.

Her father stared at her with wide, panicked eyes, then looked at Julia standing in the doorway hugging her fluffy red robe closed. Alex was a few steps behind with a mug of coffee.

Shelby opened her mouth to tell Patrick no, but didn't know how. God, this went against everything she'd been taught at the shelter. Pets were never, never to be given as gifts. Everyone in the family had to be on board so an animal didn't end up being taken back to the shelter, an unwanted surprise.

It broke her heart to see Daisy's tail already wagging, her high spirits returning as soon as she spotted a kid to play with.

"Patrick," she began, hating to break up the happy match but certain she couldn't foist a dog on her dad and Julia. "This is a puppy I'm taking care of for my local animal shelter. Her name is Daisy and she's here to spend Christmas with you—"

"Shelby, hold on," Julia interrupted, stepping out into the yard in hastily donned boots. Her nightgown and robe trailed in the snow. She hooked arms with her husband. "I believe Daisy has already claimed Patrick as her own. What do you think, Zach?"

Her father held his arm out to Julia, kissing her on the cheek as he reeled her in close.

"I believe you're right." He looked at his daughter. "Is that okay with you?"

Shelby exchanged a glance with Alex as he came out to join them, coffee mug steaming.

"Absolutely. I have Daisy's adoption papers in my bag."

Patrick squealed, kneeling in the snow with Daisy dancing around him, licking his face. Shelby's eyes met Alex's and she smiled, seeing he understood the Christmas miracle that had played out for them here. Daisy, who innately loved children, would always cherish the little boy within Patrick no matter how tall or old he grew.

A sense of rightness wrapped around her as tangibly as the thick parka she wore. She was exactly where she was supposed to be. Life had brought her—had brought Daisy—here for Christmas.

And as she stared across the yard at her hot, amazing husband with his broad shoulders and quiet strength, anything seemed possible.

AS THE SUN SET ON CHRISTMAS Day, Alex finally found the chance to get his wife alone. He put on his new parka and invited her to take Daisy for a walk to the neighborhood park while Patrick got ready for bed—the first time the boy had let the puppy out of his sight.

Holiday lights glinted in distant windows as they strolled. Boxes stacked by garages were filled with wrapping paper and other debris from the day's celebration.

How ironic that this truly had been his best Christmas ever—spent with Shelby's family. They'd opened gifts in their pj's while eating the breakfast casserole Ivy had made. Their Christmas dinner had been bought from a local caterer, so no one slaved in the kitchen. They'd all feasted and lingered, talking.

Imagine that? Him enjoying talking.

He'd been surprised to get a text from Gene Watts, wishing him and Shelby a Merry Christmas. Gene had also sent some early outtakes of his video footage to Shelby's email for them to enjoy. Julia had plugged her laptop computer into the wide-screen TV and they'd all watched clips from the dog transport unfold…the sentimental and the hilarious.

They'd done a good thing this Christmas.

His boots crunched on the sidewalk, Daisy trotting slowly ahead. "Glad to know I did such a great job shopping for you this year."

"What can I say?" Her arms swung by her side. "I got everything I wanted under the tree."

"I may never live down the ruffled rhinestone collar that *I* supposedly chose for Delilah." But he hadn't minded the good-natured ribbing from her dad.

She tapped his arm. "But you get major kudos for donating new cots for three dog runs at the shelter in my name."

His feet slowed and he grasped her elbow until she stopped to face him. "I owe you a real gift, Shelby, and I haven't forgotten that."

"You gave me one—you agreed to stay here an extra day. Really, this has been a better Christmas than I ever could have expected." Her green eyes sparkled as brightly as the emerald in that sexy belly-button ring of hers ever had. "But I have to confess the whole BFF thing you and my dad have going on is mind blowing, to say the least."

"He and I came to an understanding last night." About damn time. How different things would have been if he'd been capable of that conversation with Zach Dawson earlier. Talking definitely had its perks.

"You did?" She blinked in surprise—and even a hint of wariness. "And what would that understanding be?"

Time to lay it all out there. No more holding back from his wife. She deserved everything he had to give. She probably deserved even more, but damned if he would give her up.

"That I love his daughter. That I'm going to be more open and do everything in my power to win her over and make her feel cherished for the rest of her life. If you agree, of course."

Her exhale blew a long white cloud into the cool air between them. "Alex? Are you serious?"

She searched his eyes and he hated that he'd ever given her cause to be wary. To fear that she'd failed him, of all people. He loved her so damn much it hurt, and he would spend the rest of his life making sure she knew it.

"Completely. I can't promise to be home all the time. No member of the military can. But I won't be volunteering for extra assignments anymore, and when I am home, I will be one hundred percent yours, no more shutting you out."

He couldn't help but smile as her jaw dropped—honest to God *fell open*—before she snapped it shut. "You have no idea how much that means to me."

He did now, thanks to her, and thanks to her father for setting his butt straight.

Alex held up a gloved hand. "Except I'm getting ahead of myself. First, I want to give you your Christmas gift."

"I can't imagine you've got a better present than the one you've just given me." She slid her arm around his waist, her hand dipping into his pocket.

"I'm signing over my G.I. Bill to you so you can go back to school and become a veterinarian."

Watching those video clips, he'd seen a lot more than a dog transport and a couple of adoptions. He'd witnessed his wife's gift with animals. She had a calling to heal, just as he had a calling to serve in uniform.

"Alex…" She shook her head. "Even though spouses can use their husband's G.I. Bill, I couldn't take away your chance at a—"

He silenced her with a tap to her lips. "Shelby, I'm in the job I love. I'm doing what I want to do with my life, serving my country. And if you can accept the sacrifice that comes with that lifestyle, I want you to have your dream, too. I mean it."

Her eyes slid over to Daisy then back to him. "What if we have children?"

"College students can be mothers. Veterinarians can be mothers." Still holding the leash, he cupped both of her elbows. "I'm not saying it will be easy, but Shelby, we can have everything."

"What if we never have children?"

"I've thought about that, a lot, actually." Those miscarriages had hurt him, too, but he'd held it in, wanting to be strong and supportive for her. Now he wondered if they might have been stronger if they had grieved together. "At some point, I would like to look into adoption. Maybe a special-needs child?"

"A child like Patrick." She finished his thought for him.

He nodded, meaning every word. He wanted to share a happy family life with a kid who really needed it.

"God, yes, Alex. Absolutely yes." She hugged him hard, then harder still. "Do you have any idea how much I love you?"

"I think so, but feel free to tell me any time you like." He looped his arms around her, too, creating their own furnace of warmth under the flickering lamppost. "I'm starting to groove on this whole chitchat thing."

Her mittened hands cupped his face and she pressed her cool lips to his. And he kissed her back in the middle of the sidewalk, snow swirling around them. He would have kept right on kissing her, but Daisy barked, tugging the leash.

"Okay, okay, I know you want to get home to Patrick." Except Daisy was pulling him in the wrong direction. He started to guide her around when he heard it—soft mewling sounds coming from a few feet away.

Shelby must have heard it, too, because she frowned,

searching for the source of those soft animal cries. They followed the noise until they reached a nearby bus shelter for students waiting for the school bus. On the bench rested a cardboard box marked with big block letters: FREE TO A GOOD HOME.

Gasping, Shelby rushed to the box, pulling a flap up. Three calico kittens huddled together in a blanket, shivering. Something unfurled inside Alex, a knot he hadn't even known was lodged in his chest. One that had been there as long as he could remember, maybe all the way back to the day he'd carried an injured cat to the vet all by himself.

Already, Shelby was picking up two kittens, slipping them inside her coat and crooning how Miss Tansy was going to help find wonderful homes for all of them.

He scooped up the last kitten and tucked it inside his parka, already knowing this calico would be staying with them. A laugh rumbled in his chest and Shelby stared at him like he'd lost his mind. Maybe he had, because he sure as hell was crazy in love with his wife.

He scratched the top of the kitten's head. "I should have realized those dogs weren't the three wise men. The kings arrived after Christmas. Looks as if we've found the real Melchior, Caspar and Balthazar."

Shelby smiled, her eyes alive with love and the promise of a lifetime more of it to come. "Merry Christmas, Alex."

"Merry Christmas to us both."

* * * * *

This novella is dedicated to my son,
Bryan DeNosky, Techno Nerd Extraordinaire.
Without his technical input this story
wouldn't have been possible.

A PUPPY FOR WILL

USA TODAY Bestselling Author
Kathie DeNosky

CHAPTER ONE

WHEN WILL PARKER STOPPED his SUV in front of The Haven, the no-kill animal shelter in suburban Tacoma where his grandmother volunteered, he noticed a leggy redhead and a man he assumed to be her husband loading three dogs into crates in the back of their Explorer. Nodding a greeting as he walked by, the woman smiled, but he couldn't help noticing that her expression looked forced.

He glanced at the stoic man reaching for the Pekinese she held and realized from his short haircut that the guy was probably in the military. Will didn't know what their story was, but neither seemed all that happy, and Will would bet his next paycheck that if they were married there were big problems in the union.

A feeling of déjà vu swept through him. Three years ago that had been him and his now ex-wife, Suzanne. Will hoped that, whatever their problems were, they had a better outcome than his. Quickly deciding it was best to let some things remain in the past, he shrugged off the memories and climbed the steps of the yellow Victorian that housed the administrative offices of The Haven.

Crossing the porch, Will turned his attention to the matter at hand—the trouble his grandmother had gotten him into. Again. In the past few months, she had solicited sizeable donations from him and convinced him that he was the only software engineer capable of writing a computer program to organize the shelter's adoption records. Now she was trying to coerce him into adopting a pet by getting him to foster one over the holidays.

Of course, he was a pushover when it came to Rose Parker. After his parents had been killed in a car accident, Rose had finished raising him. He owed her more than he could ever repay. She had sacrificed her peace of mind and fretted through more than a few sleepless nights during his rebellious teenage years. But she had seen him through that phase as he dealt with his loss, and she'd still loved him in spite of it.

But he drew the line at a pet. He wouldn't even be taking the animal for the holidays if it weren't for the fact that his grandmother had gotten wind that the company he worked for would be shutting down for two weeks. She hadn't given him a moment's peace until he had agreed to take a puppy named Harley for the entire time he was going to be off work. But fostering a dog temporarily was entirely different than taking on the permanent responsibility of a pet.

He sighed heavily as he opened the door and entered the shelter's reception area. It wasn't that he didn't like pets. He did. But an animal took time, and that was something he hadn't had a lot of since his divorce three years ago. After his ex-wife had walked out on him, Will had thrown himself into his work and taken on as many projects as Snohomish Software Solutions wanted to throw his way. He didn't even have a spare evening for a social life, let alone the time to devote to a dog. And that's the way he liked it.

His grandmother, however, couldn't understand why he chose work over a relationship. But then she had never been in a bad one. He had, and he wasn't about to go down that road again. Once had been more than enough.

"Hi, Will," Faye Barnard, the shelter's receptionist, said, looking up from her work to smile at him. "Rose is in the kennel getting Harley ready for you to take home. I'll call back there and let her know you're here." Once she finished informing his grandmother that he had arrived, the plump, red-haired woman picked up a tin of candy and held it out toward him. "Would you like a piece of peppermint chocolate bark?"

"It looks delicious, Faye, but I think I'll pass this time," he answered, smiling back.

Before he could ask if the software he had developed for them was meeting expectations, Tansy Dexter, The Haven's director, and a lanky teenage girl with a long blond ponytail herded a couple of dogs to the door.

"Hi, Will," Tansy said, struggling to hold on to the feisty shepherd mix she was leading. "Sorry I can't stick around and chat, but Cindy and I have to take Wilber and Trixie to meet the people who are going to drive them to their new forever home in Idaho. I do need to talk to you about the software you developed for us. It's been glitchy, but we may not be using it right. I'll give you a call after Christmas and we can figure out if there's a bug."

"Sure. If there is a glitch in the software, I'll straighten it out." Will stepped over to open the door for the women. "Do you need help getting the dogs into the crates in your car?"

Tansy shook her head as the shepherd hurried her through the door. "Thanks, but I think we can handle it. Enjoy your time with Harley. He's a sweetheart," she called over her shoulder. "And thanks for your generous donation toward the new roof. With your help, we're getting close to our goal."

"You're quite welcome," he said as he closed the door behind the pair.

Will checked his watch. What could be taking his grandmother so long? He had been working since six in the morning to finish up some things before the office closed. He just wanted to get home, get the puppy settled in and start on the new graphics program he intended to develop before he returned to work in a couple of weeks.

A moment later, the door to the kennel area opened and a large black-and-white dog with tan markings pulled Rose Parker into the room. Tail wagging and filled with enough friendly enthusiasm for ten dogs, the animal hurried himself and Will's grandmother over and greeted Will with a swipe of his long wet tongue.

"This is Harley," his grandmother announced proudly. "Sit, Harley." The dog immediately lowered himself to a sitting position.

"That isn't a puppy," Will said, frowning.

His grandmother grinned. "Believe it or not, Harley is only five months old. And the sweetest little guy you'll ever care to meet."

"Little?" Will shook his head in disbelief. "What is he? Part horse?"

"He's a Saint Bernard/Bernese mountain dog mix." She handed him the leash that was attached to Harley's harness. "You two are going to be great friends. His heart is as big as he is. He's only mastered the 'sit' command, but I'm sure you'll be able to teach him a few more in no time."

"Grandma, I can't manage a dog this size. He'll destroy my house and—"

"Nonsense," Rose cut in. "He's very well-mannered and will be a wonderful companion for you while I'm away." She walked over to retrieve a clipboard from the counter. "I would have taken him myself, but as you know my gentleman friend has arranged for us to take a trip to Honolulu for the holidays and I won't be back until the first week in January." She gave him the beseeching look that never failed to get him to go along with whatever she wanted. "I'll feel so much better knowing that Harley will be keeping you company while I'm gone. I worry about you, Will."

"I'm too busy to be lonely," he said, feeling trapped. He had agreed to take the dog, and being a man of his word he saw no way out of the situation.

"You need to stop and smell the roses, enjoy life." She placed her hand on his arm. "If you let him, Harley will help you do that."

Will released a frustrated breath. Resigned to his fate, he took the clipboard from her and signed his name to the foster agreement.

He'd learned long ago that arguing with his grandmother was a study in futility. When Rose Parker set her mind to something, she got what she wanted. Even if it meant playing the guilt card with her only grandson.

"Have a nice time with Mr. Hobson and enjoy the holidays," he said, handing the document back to her.

His grandmother motioned for him to bend down, then she kissed his cheek and smiled. "You and Harley have a Merry Christmas and a Happy New Year. I'll call when Stuart and I return."

WALKING ALONG THE DOCKS of the Crystal Cove Floating Home Community, Macie Fairbanks admired her neighbors' houseboats as she went door to door, invit-

ing them all to her party on Christmas Eve. Each home
was unique in style and had such character that she was
more confident than ever that she had made the right
choice when she decided to buy one and move to the
community. She smiled to herself. Of course, watching
Sleepless in Seattle at least a dozen times hadn't hurt,
either. The movie had only made her fall more in love
with the concept of a floating home.

But as she started to knock on the door of the large
home at the end of the dock, she heard a loud noise
behind her. Turning, she gasped at the sight of a large
black-and-white dog loping toward her. His tail was
wagging and he looked friendly, but she wasn't fool
enough to stick her hand out right away to find out.

Flattening her back against the door, Macie held her
breath as she waited for the dog's next move.

"Harley, sit!"

She and the dog both looked up to see a tall, broad-
shouldered man running toward them holding a leash.
The animal stopped in front of her and, instead of jumping up or making her hand his next meal as she half expected, he sat at her feet and stared up at her adoringly.

When the man reached them, Macie immediately
recognized him as the owner of the houseboat she had
plastered herself to. Her breath caught. Since moving
into Crystal Cove, she had only seen him a few times,
and that had been at a distance as he walked from his
house to his SUV in the parking area. She had thought
he was good-looking then. But now?

Close up he wasn't just handsome, the man was drop-
dead gorgeous. Well over six feet tall with broad shoulders, dark green eyes and light brown hair that was
long enough to be stylish but still short enough not to

appear shaggy, he could easily be the star in her next romantic fantasy.

Macie shook her head. She wasn't sure where that thought had come from. A year ago she had declared a moratorium on men—real *and* imaginary. She had been quite happy with her decision for the past twelve months and hadn't once been tempted to lift the suspension. But as they stood there staring at each other, she was finding it harder to remember why she had come to the conclusion she didn't want or need male companionship.

"Are you all right?" he asked, finally breaking the silence as he snapped the leash to the dog's harness. When he straightened to his full height, he reached up to rub the back of his neck with his hand. "Look, I'm sorry if Harley frightened you. He's just a puppy and I'm afraid he hasn't yet learned all of his manners."

The man's rich baritone sent a shiver of awareness straight up her spine. "I'm…uh, fine." She stopped to clear her suddenly dry throat. "I'm Macie Fairbanks." She pointed down the long row of houseboats. "I'm your neighbor. I just recently bought the house at the far end of the dock."

He stopped rubbing his neck and stuck out his hand to shake hers. "Will Parker."

His name sounded extremely familiar, but the moment she placed her palm against his, a tingling sensation swept up her arm and rendered her incapable of remembering her own name, let alone where she might have heard his. She quickly drew her hand back and tried to think of something—anything—to relieve the uncharacteristic awkwardness she was suddenly feeling. Thankfully the thumping of Harley's tail against the wooden dock drew her attention.

"Did you say Harley's just a puppy?" she asked, eyeing the dog's size.

Will nodded. "When I picked him up at The Haven animal shelter they told me that he's only five months old."

"How big will he be when he's grown?" she asked before she could stop herself.

"Probably the size of a Shetland pony." Will shrugged. "He's a cross between a Saint Bernard and a Bernese mountain dog."

She shook her head. "I'm sorry, I didn't mean to be rude. It's just hard to believe that a dog this big is still so young."

"Believe me, I had the same reaction this afternoon when I went to get him," Will said, smiling.

She tentatively reached down to pat Harley's big head. "You adopted him without even seeing him first?"

"I'm only fostering him for the holidays." Will scratched behind the dog's ear. "It's a long story, but needless to say, I didn't know what I was getting into when I agreed to take him."

"I saw the fund-raising campaign for The Haven the other night on the news." She smiled. "I think it mentioned something about the animals needing fosters over the holidays because the shelter has a leaking roof?"

"The Haven runs on a shoestring budget and finding the funds to replace the roof has been a real challenge for them," he said, nodding. "My grandmother volunteers there and she says even the animals' everyday necessities are sometimes hard to meet."

When they both fell silent, Macie realized she was still pressed against Will's front door, effectively blocking him from entering his house. "I suppose you're wondering why I was about to knock on your door," she said, stepping out of the way.

"It had crossed my mind," he said dryly.

Handing him one of the flyers she had printed for the occasion, she explained, "With all the snow in the Cascade Mountains, I can't make it to my parents' over in Leavenworth for the holidays so I'm throwing a party on Christmas Eve for the residents of Crystal Cove."

He glanced at the paper, then back at her. "Thanks for including me, but I'm going to be pretty busy with Harley and—"

"Oh, I don't mind if you bring him along," she said, smiling. "Most of our neighbors have pets and I'm sure they'll understand your not wanting to leave Harley alone so soon."

Will shifted from one foot to the other and she could tell he was searching for a plausible excuse to decline her invitation. "I hate to commit to anything right now," he finally said. He gestured toward the dog. "I'll have to see how things go with him."

"I understand." Why was she disappointed? She didn't even know the man. Patting Harley's head, she added, "If you change your mind, you're both more than welcome to stop in for a drink and something to eat."

They stared at each other for several long uncomfortable seconds.

"I can't make any promises, but I might drop in for a few minutes," he finally said, retrieving a set of keys from his jacket pocket.

Smiling, she reached down to pet Harley one more time. "I'll see you on Christmas Eve."

As she walked down the dock toward her houseboat, she couldn't help but wonder what had gotten into her.

Why had she practically insisted that Will attend her party? And why was his name so darned familiar?

She was certain they'd never met. She would have definitely remembered him. No woman in her right mind could forget a man who was that good-looking, or who had a voice that smooth and sexy.

Letting herself into her house, Macie shook her head as she removed her coat and headed to her office to work a bit before she turned in.

It didn't matter that with his movie-star looks Will Parker was hot enough to melt the polar ice caps. She'd learned the hard way that men couldn't be trusted, and she wasn't naive enough to believe that he was any different from the rest of them.

When she sneezed, she reached for the bottle of antihistamine. The allergy medication must be clouding her judgment, she decided.

"You're definitely not interested in him or any other man," she muttered as she sat down and booted up her computer. "You're much better off without a man in your life and you'd do well to remember that."

And if she repeated it enough times, she just might start to believe it.

AFTER WALKING HARLEY, then getting the dog settled in for a nap on a blanket beside his desk, Will sat down at his computer and opened the file of the graphics program he intended to write over the next two weeks. He glanced at the latest copy of *Techno Nerd Monthly* lying on top of the file cabinet and smiled sardonically. By the time he finished writing the program code, his nemesis *Ms. Tera Byte,* the magazine's software columnist, would be eating crow. She had given him average to poor reviews for the last four programs he'd written and hinted that Will Parker, Snohomish Software Solutions' head developer, was losing his touch.

Anger burned in his gut just thinking about her and her erroneous opinions. It was true that he hadn't been able to spend as much time perfecting the most recent programs, but consumer feedback had been nothing but positive and other computer magazines had given them good to very good ratings. So why did the opinion of one obviously frustrated wannabe software developer matter to him?

He told himself that it didn't, but deep down he knew the reason behind his irritation. Since his divorce and the put-downs hurled at him by his ex-wife, he had been driven to excel and prove her wrong, developing a short fuse when he received any kind of negative criticism. He probably wouldn't have become so defensive if Suzanne hadn't constantly referred to his job as "playing around."

She had never grasped that the program codes he wrote were important and made a difference to people. From tax preparation schedules to organization of medical records to graphics for websites, the projects he developed made life easier for countless millions. Though no matter how much she'd denigrated what he did, she'd had no problem spending the money he made from his hard work. But eventually even his money hadn't been enough for her and she'd left.

He sighed heavily. He may have failed in his personal life, but he was determined that his reputation as a top-flight software engineer remained impeccable. That was why he'd taken *Ms. Tera Byte's* comments so personally.

Deciding that he'd given more attention to the woman's column than was worth his time, he shrugged off the last traces of his irritation and started to work. But for reasons he couldn't put his finger on, his thoughts kept straying to Macie Fairbanks and her party. He finally gave up trying to work and picked up the flyer she had handed him earlier that evening.

Will grinned as he remembered how she'd flattened herself against his door when Harley had loped up to her. If she hadn't looked so damned pretty it might even have been comical. But with the light evening breeze fluttering her soft strawberry blond curls around her face, and apprehension making her expressive blue eyes go wide, she'd robbed him of breath and the ability to do anything but gape like a teenage boy staring at his first glimpse of a centerfold in a magazine.

He frowned. Maybe he did need to get out a little more. He tried to remember the last time he'd been on a date. Had it been six months or closer to nine? Hell, he couldn't even remember.

Shaking his head, he started to throw the flyer in the wastebasket under his desk, but instead placed it back on his desk. He still couldn't believe he had told her he might drop by her party. Normally he declined all invitations for community gatherings—not because he didn't like his neighbors, but for the simple reason he was too busy working.

But Macie had looked so hopeful he hadn't wanted to hurt her feelings, so he'd told her he might stop by. What he hadn't counted on was that she'd take his noncommittal response as a "yes."

When Harley rose from the blanket to lumber over and rest his head on Will's thigh, he absently petted the dog's head. "You got me into this position by being so friendly. Can I count on you to help me get out of it?"

Harley wagged his tail and stared up at Will with soulful eyes.

"I didn't think so," Will said, resigned to figuring out how to decline Macie's invitation on his own.

CHAPTER TWO

MACIE FINISHED MAKING the filling for her chocolate-raspberry Yule log, then turned her attention to shaping holly leaves from the marzipan she had tinted with dark green food coloring. Her party was only two days away and she needed to get the desserts done before she could move on to finger food. Tomorrow she'd go shopping for the ingredients for the hors d'oeuvres, which she'd make the day of her party.

Popping a piece of the sweet confection into her mouth, she frowned. She still couldn't taste much of anything and only hoped that her allergies cleared up enough for her to enjoy the food she made for her party.

But her concern quickly melted away as she stared down at her first marzipan holly leaf. She loved that her job as a software review columnist allowed her to work from home. It gave her a little more time to pursue her true passion—cooking. Of course, she hadn't realized it was her passion until last Christmas when her then-fiancé had run off with his secretary and she'd needed something to do to keep her mind off his betrayal and the emotional turmoil it caused. That's when she had downloaded a cookbook to her computer and started experimenting with food.

But even though she was fairly new to the culinary arts, she enjoyed cooking and she must be getting better at it. The casserole she had taken to the magazine's

Christmas party last week had disappeared almost as soon as she set it on the food table.

As she sang along with Harry Connick, Jr. and Lee Ann Womack's version of "Baby, It's Cold Outside," she smiled. She had been looking for a reason to try out some recipes from her newest holiday cookbook, and if she couldn't make it home to see her parents for Christmas, throwing a party and making yummy goodies for her new neighbors was the next best thing.

When she had started her search for a home, she had not only fallen in love with the houseboat, she had fallen in love with the Crystal Cove community, as well. The residents she had met so far were all very friendly and shared a closeness that she wanted to be part of. With her family living on the other side of the Cascade Mountains, her neighbors were going to be the nearest thing she had to family in the Seattle area and would hopefully fill her need to belong.

Reaching for a piece of the red tinted marzipan to start rolling into little holly berries, she glanced out the kitchen window. Gasping, she ran for the door, forgetting all about her Yule log and her desire to fit in with the residents of Crystal Cove. Harley was wandering along the edge of the dock and Will was nowhere in sight.

Grabbing her jacket from the coat tree, she hurried out onto the dock, calling to the dog. "Here, Harley. Come here, boy."

What if she couldn't get him to come to her? She hated to think of what might happen if she couldn't. He was dangerously close to the community parking area and the busy street just beyond.

But the moment he heard his name, the puppy turned

and came loping toward her, much the way he had done the night before.

"Sit, Harley," she said, remembering the command that Will had used to keep the dog from running over her. Harley immediately stopped and sat down a few feet from her.

Walking over to him, she took hold of his harness and released the breath she'd been holding since she'd noticed him wandering around alone. At least she was assured he wouldn't run into the street and be hit by a car. Now if she could just get him back to Will's place at the other end of the long dock without him pulling her down, her rescue mission would be a success.

"You're going to be nice and walk beside me like a good puppy, aren't you, Harley?" she asked hopefully.

In answer the dog thumped the side of her leg with his tail and if she hadn't known better, she would have sworn he smiled at her.

She gripped the harness as tightly as she could in case Harley lunged forward and started dragging her along. But to her surprise, he looked up at her as if trying to determine what she wanted him to do, then matched the pace she set.

"Good boy," she praised him as they approached Will's door. Now that there was no danger to Harley, she fully intended to give Will Parker a lecture on the responsibilities of taking care of a dog and the importance of pet safety.

Raising her hand to knock, she frowned at the door standing wide open. "Will?"

When he failed to answer, she called out a second time. Still nothing. Could something have happened to him? What if he had fallen or become ill and was unable to respond? And how had Harley gotten out of the house if Will was incapacitated?

Macie wasn't in the habit of entering someone's home without an invitation, but she didn't think twice about leading Harley into Will's houseboat. Closing the door to keep Harley from wandering back outside, she released the dog and looked around. Will was nowhere in sight.

As she stood in the living room considering whether she should search the house first or call for help immediately, she heard a noise behind her. Turning, she saw Will striding down the hall toward her. He had his head bent, drying his wet hair with a towel and it was obvious that he'd been in the shower. It was just as obvious that the only thing he had on was a loose pair of boxer shorts.

Her heart stalled and she couldn't have looked away if her life depended on it. Never in her wildest dreams would she have imagined that hidden beneath his clothes, Will Parker had such an impressive array of masculine bulges and ripples. A shiver streaked up her spine at the thought of how it would feel to have his strong arms wrapped around her.

When he glanced up to find her staring at him, he stopped dead in his tracks. His eyes narrowed suspiciously. "What are you doing here? Do you need something?"

That was a loaded question if she ever heard one. She forced herself to ignore the double meaning—*and* her wayward musings—and focus on the reason she was standing in Will's living room. "I brought Harley back."

Will looked doubtful. "Where was he?"

"Wandering around outside. By the time I got to him, he was dangerously close to the parking lot," she said, training her eyes on Will's handsome face to keep from being distracted by his broad chest and washboard stomach. He didn't seem the least bit concerned that he wasn't exactly dressed to receive visitors. "When I got to your door it was standing open and I...um, thought something might be wrong."

Darn it all! Her explanation sounded lame, even to her. But it was hard to concentrate. Why did the man have to be the whole package—good-looking, a voice that could charm birds out of the trees and a body that could tempt a saint?

"How did he get out?" Will demanded, oblivious to her disturbing thoughts. "I'm sure I closed the door when we came back from his morning walk. So unless he's able to walk through walls—"

Harley chose that moment to decide that the loose leg of Will's boxers would be perfect for a game of tug of war. Biting the thin cotton fabric, he pulled and began shaking his head. Will grabbed at the waistband, but Harley was too quick and gravity took care of the rest.

As if in slow motion, Marcie watched the boxers drop to the floor a moment before Will cursed and pulled them back up. Realizing that she was blatantly staring at the most beautiful specimen of masculinity she had ever seen, she spun around to face the far wall. "Well, this is a bit awkward," she said, barely able to suppress a nervous giggle.

"Stay right here," Will said from behind her. "I'm going to put some clothes on, then we'll try to figure out how Harley escaped."

He didn't seem bothered by the fact that she had seen him in all his glory, but she sure was. In comparison to Will Parker, Michelangelo's statue of David was rather wimpy.

"God, you've lost every ounce of sense you ever possessed," she muttered.

In an effort to get her mind off Will and his remarkable physique, she looked around his living room. His house was extremely neat and orderly. In fact, the room was *too* neat—as if he never used it. He hadn't even put up a Christmas tree. Why would anyone have a floating home and not enjoy decorating every square inch of it?

As she continued to peruse the room, her gaze landed on a walnut plaque, and curious about the award she moved closer. It was from Snohomish Software Solutions, proclaiming Will the employee of the year for developing a computer program that had revolutionized the organization and storage of hospital medical records.

No wonder his name had sounded familiar to her. She had reviewed that program and several others of his over the past couple of years for *Techno Nerd Monthly*.

"You can turn around," Will said, walking back into the living room. "I'm decent now."

"I was just looking at your award," she said, hoping to avoid a discussion on what had happened with Harley and Will's boxer shorts. "You're a software engineer?"

He nodded. "What do you do for a living?"

"I'm a writer," she said, giving him the practiced answer she always gave whenever someone asked about her career. She had a confidentiality clause in her contract with the magazine that prevented her from revealing her pen name to anyone. Right now she was glad that it did, considering the last couple of reviews *Ms. Tera Byte* had given Will's programs.

"That sounds interesting," he said, smiling. "Do you work from home?"

"Yes, and I love being able to do that. It gives me

more freedom to experiment with new recipes," she said, hoping to steer him away from the subject of what she wrote and for whom.

"So you like to cook?" he asked, sounding as if he had a hard time grasping the concept.

"Absolutely. I've only gotten into it within the past year, but it's quickly become my favorite hobby." Much more comfortable with the change of topic, Macie asked, "What do you enjoy when you aren't working?"

"I don't have free time. I usually have too many projects and deadlines to do anything but work."

"But you're taking time to care for—" She stopped short. "Where did Harley go?"

"Damn! The door's open," Will said, grabbing the leash from a hook beside the door and hurrying outside. "Sit, Harley."

When Macie reached the doorway, she watched Will snap the nylon leash onto the oversized puppy's harness. "How did he do that?"

Leading Harley back into the house, Will closed the door. "I'm not sure, but I'm going to find out. Keep talking."

"Excuse me?"

"Act as if you aren't paying attention to him." Walking over to stand beside Macie, Will positioned himself so he could observe Harley. "To answer your question about taking on the responsibility of a dog, my company is shutting down for the next two weeks, and my grandmother asked me to help The Haven with their Home for the Holidays campaign." He frowned. "But she didn't tell me I was going to be fostering Harley Houdini."

Will's close proximity and the sound of his deep voice were playing havoc with Macie's peace of mind

and making her think of things she had no business remembering. She was done with men and she would do
well to keep that in mind.

"I noticed that you haven't decorated yet," she said,
seizing the first neutral topic that came to her.

"I haven't had time," he answered absently. His full
attention was on the dog.

"If I have a spare moment later today, I'll drop by
again and help you at least get a tree up," she offered.

"Okay," he said, clearly distracted.

"How long do you think this is going to take?" she
finally asked, glancing at her watch. "I really need to
get home. I'm trying to do some of the preparations for
my party ahead of time. That way all I'll have to do the
day of the party is make the hors d'oeuvres."

He nodded, not taking his eyes off of Harley. "I don't
think this will take long. He's already inching toward
the door."

As they watched, the dog slowly walked over and,
laying his chin on the brass lever, pressed down. In the
blink of an eye, he had released the latch and was starting to nose the door open.

"Sit, Harley," Will commanded, walking over to
close the door and secure the lock. "Well, that solves
that mystery. Looks like I'll have to keep the door
locked as long as Harley's here."

"You could change the lever to a doorknob," Macie
suggested.

Will shook his head. "He's only going to be here for
a couple of weeks."

"Do you really think you'll be able to take him back
to the shelter?" she asked as she walked over to pet Har-

ley. "He's such a sweetheart, I'm not sure I would be able to do give him back."

"Why don't you adopt him then?" Will asked, grinning.

"My houseboat is smaller than yours." She disengaged the lock and opened the door. "And if I don't get back to it, I won't have anything to serve my guests."

"Thanks for bringing Harley home." He followed her out onto the dock. "I really appreciate your looking out for him."

"Not a problem." She smiled. "I'll see you at the party."

As Will watched Macie walk back toward her houseboat, he found himself staring at the enticing sway of her slender hips and the length of her shapely legs. Why did he find her so alluring?

There was no doubt that she was attractive. But she wasn't his type at all. He normally preferred tall, willowy brunettes with a quiet, mysterious air about them. Macie was a little below average in height, had lush curves that fascinated the hell out of him and a vivacious, engaging personality.

"I think I'm losing it, Harley," he said, when he walked back into the house where the dog still sat.

Harley thumped his tail, then got up and lumbered to the door. Whining, he looked over his shoulder at Will, then back at the door as if he wanted the man to go after the woman and bring her back.

"That wouldn't be wise," Will said, shaking his head. "I'm not in the market for a relationship. And Macie Fairbanks has permanence written from the top of her head to the bottoms of her feet."

But later that afternoon when he went into his office and sat down at his computer to work, Will found his thoughts straying to Macie once again. Why was she claiming so much of his attention?

And why was he pleased that she apparently found him as appealing as he did her?

When he had discovered her standing in his living room, she had been staring at his chest. And if the wistful expression on her pretty face was any indication, she'd liked what she saw. He chuckled. Thanks to Harley, she'd probably seen more of his assets than she was comfortable with.

Smiling, he started to turn his attention to the program he had been working on when the doorbell rang. Harley immediately jumped up from the blanket beside Will's desk and took off for the door.

Will followed the dog down the hall and across the living room. Who would be visiting him? His grandmother and her friend, Mr. Hobson, had already left on their trip to Hawaii and he couldn't think of anyone else who would be dropping by.

"Hi, Will," Macie said when he opened the door. Her arms were full of a small artificial tree and several large bags of what he could only assume were decorations.

"Here, let me help you with that," he said when some of the sacks she was juggling started to slip. His hand brushed one of her breasts as he took the bags from her and a jolt of electric current zinged straight up his arm. "What is all this for?"

"I told you this morning that if I had time, I'd come back and help you decorate," she said as if nothing had happened.

"I don't usually decorate for the holidays," he said, vaguely remembering her mentioning something about a tree when they were waiting for Harley to pull his escape trick. He watched Harley wiggle and dance around her to show how happy he was to see her. "At least not since I moved here."

"You don't like having a Christmas tree?" she asked, petting the dog.

"'I'll only have to take it down later," he said, shrugging, as he placed the bags on the couch.

"But you used to decorate for the holidays before you moved here?" she asked, frowning.

He nodded. "But after my divorce I didn't see that I had a lot to celebrate."

"I'm sorry, Will." She placed her soft hand on his arm and the contact sent a shaft of longing running the length of him. "How long ago was that?"

"We were together for five years and married for two of those. We've been divorced now for three years." Will laughed, but there was little humor in it. "Not exactly how I dreamed it would go. By now I was supposed to have the wife, at least one of the two-point-two kids and a good start on a menagerie of hamsters, dogs, cats and goldfish."

"Things don't always work out the way we think they will, do they?" she asked, her tone indicating that she might have had a failed relationship of her own in her past.

Before he could ask, Macie turned to set the tree on one of the end tables about the same time Harley bumped the back of her knees in his excitement. Then everything seemed to happen at once. She let loose with a startled cry that frightened the happy pup. The tree went sailing one way, while Harley turned tail and ran the other way. Dropping the bags, Will lunged forward and barely managed to catch Macie to keep her from falling.

"Are you all right?" he asked, holding her to his chest.

"I…uh, think so," she said, sounding delightfully breathless.

Will knew he should make sure she was steady on her feet and then put some distance between them. But her soft feminine body pressed to his felt damned good, and he was reluctant to let her go. Shifting her to face him, Will gazed down at Macie's upturned face for several long seconds. She had the most incredible blue eyes and her perfect coral lips were just made for a man's kiss.

He knew it was insane, but he suddenly felt compelled to taste her and find out if she was as sweet as she looked. Deciding that wouldn't be in either of their best interests, he slowly released her, searching for a distraction.

"I guess if we're going to decorate for Christmas, we should get to it before the holidays are over," he said, smiling.

"That would be advisable," she agreed. "Unless you really don't want to. In that case, I'll take everything back home."

"You went to the trouble of bringing it over, we might as well see what we can do." When neither of them moved apart, he brushed an errant curl from her smooth cheek. "Where should we start?"

"Probably by picking the tree off the floor and re-shaping it," she murmured.

"Do you want me to—"

"Oh, yes," she said, closing her eyes.

Will took a deep breath and used every ounce of strength he possessed to take a step back and reach for the abandoned tree. He knew Macie wanted him to kiss her, and nothing would have pleased him more. But they had only met yesterday, and besides, she wasn't his type. She was definitely a committed relationship girl and he was a casual, strings-free-affair guy. There was no sense in starting something that would inevitably come to a bad end.

"While I shape the tree, why don't you decide where I should put it," he suggested, pulling the bent branches back into place.

From the corner of his eye, he watched her take a deep breath. "Considering Harley isn't all that graceful yet, it might be a good idea to put it on an end table or possibly the snack bar," she said, pointing toward the counter at the far end of the living room.

Hearing his name, the pup slowly ventured out of the office, then timidly put his head under Macie's hand. "It's all right, Harley," Macie said, kneeling down to put her arms around his neck. "I know you didn't mean to knock me over."

If she had thrown her arms around Will's neck like that, he would have kissed her for sure, Will thought as he glared at Harley. He shook his head. He couldn't believe he was jealous of a dog.

Banishing the ridiculous idea from his mind, he placed the small tree on the polished surface of the black granite counter. "The snack bar would probably be safer. Harley might decide one of the ornaments is a chew toy."

"I hadn't thought of that," she said, rising to her feet and grabbing a bag of ornaments.

An hour later, Will stood back and examined the tree. "Well, what's your expert opinion? I'm pretty sure the lights and ornaments are evenly distributed."

"It looks very nice." She reached into one of the

bags to pull out a wreath and hanger, then handed him a string of white twinkle lights. "I think these would reflect very prettily in the water if you string them along the deck railing. Why don't you do that, while I hang the wreath on your front door?"

Grinning, he took the lights and headed for the patio door. "More stuff to take down in a few days."

But somehow he didn't really mind. He had actually found himself enjoying spending the time with Macie, and he discovered that he had missed celebrating the holidays.

"Don't worry. I'll help you take the decorations down and put them away, Mr. Scrooge," she laughed.

Her smile and the delightful sound of her laughter caused an unfamiliar warmth to spread through his chest. "I'm going to hold you to that," he said, looking forward to spending more time with her.

After he had the lights attached to the wooden railing, Will reentered the houseboat to find Macie looking at the ceiling. "Is something wrong?" he asked.

"No, I'm just trying to decide where you should hang this," she said, holding up a small green sprig. "I think maybe the foyer would be best."

Taking one of the chairs from the table in the dining area, he tacked the mistletoe to the ceiling where she indicated.

Though why he was putting up mistletoe he had no idea, he thought as he carried the chair back to the table. He wasn't about to kiss Harley and he had already decided that kissing Macie wouldn't be a good idea.

But as he walked back to where she was standing, looking up at his handiwork, the light scent of her herbal shampoo and the sight of her nibbling on her bottom lip quickly had him realizing he was fighting a losing battle. Where would the harm be in just one kiss? After all, they would only be observing the time-honored Christmas tradition of kissing under the mistletoe.

CHAPTER THREE

"I THINK WE'RE DONE," Macie said, scanning the room. "The tree is decorated, the outside lights are hung—and I need to get home to make one more batch of fudge for the party."

Will nodded. "I have to admit, the place looks pretty good. What do I owe you for the decorations?"

"Nothing. These were all extras from my own decorating."

"Are you sure?"

She nodded. "The tabletop tree is the one I used in my apartment before I moved here and I'm afraid I overbought when I went shopping to decorate for my new tree. My family has always made a big deal out of celebrating the holidays and I may have been trying to assuage my disappointment at not being able to make it to Leavenworth for Christmas this year." She started to get her jacket from the coat rack, but his hand on her shoulder stopped her.

"Where are you going?"

Turning to face him, she caught her breath at the look on his handsome face. "Will?"

Stepping closer, he pointed to the sprig of mistletoe hanging above her head. "If you insist that I observe the holiday decorating tradition, then I suppose we should respect this custom, as well," he said, loosely wrapping his arms around her waist.

Macie couldn't have found her voice if her life depended on it. Earlier, when Harley had bumped into her and Will had caught her to keep her from falling, she had thought he would kiss her. And, heaven help her, that was exactly what she had wanted him to do. But now?

After she had recovered from the embarrassment of practically begging him to kiss her, she'd decided that it was for the best that he hadn't. She was equally glad that they had both ignored the moment as if it hadn't happened. So why now was she even contemplating going along with his suggestion that they adhere to the ritual of kissing under the mistletoe?

"Macie, I'm going to kiss you," he said, his voice so low and sexy, she thought she might melt into a puddle at his feet. "Are you all right with that?"

"I…uh, well…" Why couldn't she seem to form a coherent sentence?

His smile curled her toes inside her cross trainers. "Is that a yes?" he asked.

She started to shake her head, but unable to think of the many reasons it was a bad idea, she found herself nodding that it was what she wanted, too.

Instead of drawing her close as she expected, Will brought his hands up to gently thread his fingers in her hair. As he lowered his head, her eyes drifted shut, and at the first touch of his mouth to hers, the world stood still.

His firm lips moved softly over hers and Macie didn't think she had ever been kissed with such tenderness. When he coaxed her to part her lips for him, the touch of his tongue to hers sent a lazy warmth flowing through her body and her knees felt as if they were made of rubber. Hiding behind the persona of a stoic, workaholic software engineer, was the real Will Parker, world-class kisser and, most likely, consummate lover.

A shiver of desire coursed through her at the thought of making love with him. Swaying, she clutched the front of his shirt to steady herself. He moved his hands to her back to draw her close, and as he explored her with a thoroughness that stole her breath, she delighted in the feel of his solid muscles surrounding her. She knew it wasn't wise to allow the kiss to continue, but it had been a year since she'd been held by a man and she missed the contact, the sense of being cherished.

But the feeling was short lived. Harley pushed against their legs, trying to get between them and claim some of the attention for himself. It effectively ended the kiss and helped restore Macie's sanity.

She hadn't lifted her moratorium on men and didn't intend to. So why on earth had she agreed to kiss Will?

"I…really need to…go," she said, cringing at how breathless she sounded.

Will stared at her for several long seconds before he finally nodded. "I should take Harley out." He took her jacket from the coat rack and held it for her to put on. "We'll walk you home."

"Thanks, but that's not necessary." She had to put some distance between them, had to regain her perspective and ensure her resolve to keep men out of her life was intact. "It's not that far."

"It might be close, but it's dark," he said, bending down to clip the leash to Harley's harness. When he straightened, Will reached up to lightly touch her cheek with his fingertips. "And I want to see that you get home safely."

The intimate tone of his voice and the look in his dark green gaze sent a longing straight to her soul. She couldn't have argued the point any more than she could keep the sun from rising in the east each morning.

Neither had a lot to say, though, as they walked the short distance to her houseboat at the other end of the dock, and by the time they reached her door, Macie breathed a sigh of relief. She needed time and space to analyze what it was about Will that caused her to lose her wits.

"Good night, Harley," she said, bending down to hug the dog's thick neck. "Stay out of trouble and stop trying to be an escape artist." Standing, she smiled at Will. "Thank you for walking me home."

"No, I'm the one who should be thanking you."

"I was happy to help you decorate," she said, her smile broadening.

His intense gaze captured hers. "I wasn't talking about the decorations, Macie."

"Oh." Not her most intelligent response, but staring into his eyes, it was all she could manage.

He grinned, then turned to walk toward the community parking area. "Have a nice evening."

Letting herself inside her house, she headed straight to the refrigerator and opened the freezer. Her cheeks were on fire, but she wasn't sure if the sensation was from embarrassment or the intense longing that still coursed through her. Either way, from now on she fully intended to steer clear of Will Parker. He represented over six feet of pure masculine temptation, and considering her track record with men, an indulgence her sanity just couldn't afford.

THE NEXT DAY, WILL WATCHED Harley romp around the dog park with a border collie and a couple of terriers, but his thoughts kept straying to the night before when he had lost his mind and kissed Macie. What the hell had he been thinking? Hadn't he come to the conclusion that there was nothing even remotely casual about Macie?

He had convinced himself that a simple kiss under the mistletoe was safe and wouldn't harm either of them. He had never been more wrong. He had anticipated that her lips would be soft and sweet, but never in a million years would he have expected the chemistry between them to set a flash fire in his belly that not even a cold shower had been able to quench.

Shifting on the park bench to relieve the growing pressure in his jeans even now, he took a deep breath. Unless he missed his guess, Macie had experienced a similar reaction. And he was certain she was shaken by it, too.

When Harley's new canine buddies and their owners left the dog park, the puppy wandered over to where Will sat and plopped down at his feet.

"Ready to go home and take a nap while I get some work done?" Will asked, reaching down to pet the pup's large head.

Harley looked up at him, then rose to his feet and rested his chin on Will's knee.

"If it hadn't been for you, I wouldn't be in this mess," he said, scratching behind the dog's ear. "I would have been much better off if you hadn't run up and introduced yourself to her the other night when I brought you home."

In answer, the dog whined and licked Will's hand as if to say he needed a woman in his life.

"I'll bet my grandmother told you to say that," Will said, laughing.

Clipping the leash to Harley's harness, Will led

him to the SUV and drove the short distance to Crystal Cove. Maybe now that the pup had run off his excess energy, Will could get some work done. Between taking Harley for walks and Macie deciding his house needed Christmas cheer, he hadn't accomplished nearly as much on the new program as he would have liked.

Speak of the devil. As he got Harley out of the Explorer and started toward the dock, he noticed Macie drive up and emerge from her car, loaded down with bags of groceries. The dog immediately started pulling on the leash to greet her and in good conscience Will couldn't allow her to carry all of that food by herself.

"Let me help you," he said, hurrying over to catch a bag of fresh vegetables that slipped from her hands.

"Thank you, but if you could hook that bag over my wrist, I can make it to the house on my own," she said, struggling to hold on to everything.

Will didn't give her a chance to protest further. Taking the bags she held, he looked inside the car and decided it was going to take him two trips to carry everything. It would have taken her at least three, or maybe four.

"Do you think you can handle Harley while I carry these bags?" he asked, handing her the leash.

"Of course, but—"

"You take the dog, I'll carry these and while you're putting this stuff away, I'll come back and get the—" he looked in the cargo area of her MINI Cooper "—the ham and whatever else is left."

"That probably would save a lot of time," she said, nodding. "You're sure you don't mind?"

Will shook his head. "It's the least I can do."

She looked confused. "What do you mean?"

Because the kiss we shared last night was the begin-

ning and the end of anything between us. "You brought Harley back and helped me figure out how he was escaping."

She visibly relaxed at his words and started leading Harley toward her houseboat. "I wouldn't have thought to do anything else."

As he followed with the groceries, Will considered what Macie had said. He didn't really know her well. Hell, he didn't know her at all. But there wasn't a doubt in his mind that she was the type of person who expected nothing in return for lending a hand when it was needed. His ex-wife had been the exact opposite. Was Macie different from Suzanne in other ways? Would she respect his commitment to his job?

Will set the groceries on the counter and started back out to get the last of the bags from Macie's car while she closed a door off the living room and unsnapped Harley's leash. "Are you sure you want to let him roam around while you're putting things away?" Will asked. "He's been known to clear an end table with one swipe of his tail."

Laughing, she started pulling fruit from one of the bags. "That's why I closed my office door. It's really the only place that he could do any damage."

"As long as you're sure," Will said, heading for her car again. When he'd carried in a huge ham and several more bags of food, he set them on the counter and looked around. "Who are you expecting tomorrow evening? A small army?"

"I sometimes buy more than I need," she admitted as she nibbled on her lower lip.

Will almost groaned out loud as he watched her. Remembering his decision to keep his distance, he reached for the leash and called to Harley, who was lying sound asleep on the rug by her patio doors. "We'll get out of your way and let you find a place to put all of this."

"Please stay for a cup of coffee," she said, motioning toward the coffeemaker. "I just put on a fresh pot and I won't be able to drink it all."

"Thanks, but I should go home and do some work before Harley gets his second wind," Will said, edging his way out of the kitchen. The space was small, and having to stand so close to her was playing havoc with his good intentions.

"Why is he so tired?" she asked when the pup failed to rise at the sound of his name.

"I took him to the dog park to let him run and play off-leash," Will explained.

She grinned. "Those are the words of someone who owns a dog, not just fostering one." Before he could respond, she poured him a cup of coffee and set it on the snack bar. "Cream or sugar?"

"Black is fine," he said, taking off his coat and settling himself onto one of the bar stools. He might have tried declining her hospitality, but if he was completely honest with himself, having a cup of coffee with her was much more appealing than going back to his empty houseboat.

He frowned. Where had that come from? He didn't mind being alone and hadn't had time to be lonely in the three years he'd lived here. So why was he even thinking about it now?

Pondering, he took a sip of the hot, dark liquid. At the awful brew, he took a deep breath and then another to keep from making a face. It was quite possibly the bitterest cup of coffee he had ever tasted.

"Maybe I will take a little sugar," he said, blinking

to keep his eyes from watering. Thankfully she had her back turned to him and was unaware of his reaction.

"I've only made coffee a couple of times," she said, handing him a bowl of sugar and a spoon. "Since I'm by myself, I usually only make individual cups with those instant bags. I hope it's not too weak."

Weak? The damned stuff was strong enough to grow hair on a marble slab.

"No, it isn't weak," he said, hoping the sugar would make it a little more palatable. He noticed that she wasn't drinking from her own cup of the foul tasting brew. "Aren't you having any?"

"I tried," she said, sighing. "But I've been having problems with my allergies and my sense of taste is pretty much nonexistent. I'm hoping it returns in time for me to enjoy the food at my party."

When she moved to stuff the ham into her already full refrigerator, he eyed the planter at the end of the snack bar. He could pour the offensive liquid in the potting soil, but it would most likely kill the plant on contact.

Resigned to drinking it, he added several spoonfuls of sugar. "Seriously, how many people are you expecting?" he asked as she continued to shove food into whatever space she could find.

"Well, the Cravitts next door have gone to visit their daughter's family down in Portland, and Mr. and Mrs. Swenson are away on a charity mission with their church group." She paused to do a quick mental calculation. "I think that takes the number down to about twenty, unless someone brings a friend."

"I'd say you have enough to feed twice that many people." He tentatively took another sip of the sweetened brew and gave up. There wasn't enough sugar in a five-pound bag to take the edge off Macie's coffee.

"Do you need me to warm that up for you?" she asked, reaching for his cup.

He quickly shook his head. "This is fine. I don't usually drink a lot of coffee because it keeps me up at night."

It was an outright lie, but he didn't want to offend her. It wasn't unheard of for him to go through two or three pots a day when he had a deadline looming. But that was coffee he could actually drink.

"I guess it's important for a software engineer to get plenty of rest when he's writing a program," she said, smiling.

Grinning, he nodded. "It doesn't hurt."

"Do you have a lot of projects going at the same time?" she asked, rinsing some fresh vegetables while they talked.

"Unfortunately, yes. In the past year my workload has doubled because of company cutbacks," he said. "I have to juggle being project manager as well as writing most of the code. I would prefer to have more time on the more complicated programs, but I don't have a lot of choice."

"Since you've been working so hard, why aren't you taking these two weeks to rest and relax?" she asked, starting to cut carrots into sticks. "Everyone needs downtime. Otherwise, you'll suffer burnout."

"The powers that be don't see it that way." He shrugged. "My boss told one of our customers that I would have this graphics program ready when we re-open after the first of the year."

In hindsight, he should have insisted on another week

or two. But that was before he met Macie and found something better to do with his time than work.

His heart stalled. What the hell was wrong with him? Why was he thinking about how nice it was to be with Macie? In the past three years, his job had been his life. And that's the way he liked it, wasn't it?

She frowned. "I hope your company appreciates what I would say is going above and beyond what's normally expected of an employee," she said, bringing him out of his disturbing introspection.

"I'm sure they do, to some degree," he said, forcing himself to focus on talking about his work and not on the woman in front of him. "But the reviewers at the tech magazines don't know or care that I'm working my tail off. All they consider is whether it works as advertised or not."

"Have the reviews been all that bad?" she asked, giving him an odd look.

"For the most part they've been acceptable." He shook his head in disgust. "But there's one reviewer who seems to take great pleasure in pointing out any little flaw she can find with my programs."

"Really?" There was a strange tone to her voice. "What makes you say that?"

"There *have* been a couple of minor glitches in some of the programs I've developed over the past year," he admitted. "And if I'd had the luxury of a little more time with them, I'd have caught the bugs before the programs were released. Still, the issues were easily fixed and users have been quite pleased with the programs. That is, everyone except *Ms. Tera Byte*."

As he watched, she quickly turned to place the cut carrots into an airtight bag. "Is that the reviewer's name?"

"Yes—well, her pseudonym, anyway. She writes a column for *Techno Nerd Monthly*. I'd love to know what her real name is so I could confront her and find out what her testing criteria are."

He didn't elaborate further on what he thought of his nemesis and her reviews. For one thing, Macie probably wouldn't have a clue who he was talking about. And for another, he didn't want to think any more about *Ms. Tera Byte*, whose stinging remarks were too close to some of the insults his ex-wife had hurled at him during the last months of their marriage.

"Ready for more coffee?" Macie asked over her shoulder.

Eyeing his mug, he wondered how he was going to pour it down the drain without her questioning why he hadn't taken more than a few sips. "I think I'll pass," he finally said. Just then, Harley got up and stretched, padded to the door and whined. "It seems Harley's ready for another walk," he said, thankful the dog had intervened. Shrugging into his coat, he took the leash and went to the door where Harley stood patiently waiting. "Thanks for the...coffee."

"Thank you for helping me get all this food from the car to the house," she said, giving him a smile that caused his heart to thump against his ribs. "I'll see you tomorrow evening."

"I'll try," he said, hoping his noncommittal answer would let him off the hook.

As he and Harley set off toward the community's designated pet area, across from Macie's houseboat, he was more determined than ever to steer clear of her party tomorrow night. If the engaging smile she had just given him and his reaction to it weren't enough to convince him to stay home and work, there was another fact that should—the more time he spent with Macie, the more he wanted to spend with her.

WHEN MACIE SAW WILL and Harley turn toward the Crystal Cove pet area, she took a deep breath and closed the door. When he had mentioned her column and the pseudonym she used, her heart had stopped beating. She probably should have confessed right then to being *Ms. Tera Byte.* But the confidentiality clause in her contract ensured that if she ever revealed her identity she would lose her job. She also didn't want to put her friendship with Will in jeopardy. And there was no doubt that was exactly what would happen if he discovered that she was his nemesis.

Thinking back on some of her reviews of his programs, she cringed. She had been overly critical of his recent work, but that was only because he had always been known for good, solid programs with few, if any, glitches.

She sighed. When she had written the bad reviews, she had only meant to point out that the quality of his work had slipped a notch or two over the past year. But Will hadn't taken it that way. He had seen her criticism as an attack on his programming skills.

Now that she knew how overworked he was, she understood and actually marveled that he had maintained the quality that he had. Unfortunately, she hadn't been aware of the pressures he was working under when she had evaluated his programs. If she had, she still would have pointed out the issues with the software, but she certainly wouldn't have been as flippant and thoughtless in the wording of her reviews.

Resuming the preparations for her party, Macie decided that it was just as well that she had reaffirmed her moratorium on men. She and Will could be friends, but that was all they could ever be. She just hoped he never found out he had just had an audience with the very woman he had been wanting to confront for the past year.

CHAPTER FOUR

ON CHRISTMAS EVE, the night of her party, Macie surveyed her handiwork. Nearly every flat surface in the living room and kitchen had platters and trays of food. She might have prepared too many different dishes, but as her mother always said, "The secret to being a good hostess is to have too much food rather than not enough." Macie only wished her allergies would let up so she could enjoy it.

When the doorbell rang, she smiled and forgot all about her allergy problems. She walked over to the door to greet her first guest. "I'm so glad you were able to come to the party, Mrs. Baron," she said as her elderly neighbor entered the foyer. Somewhere in her eighties, the woman was the oldest resident in Crystal Cove and got around better than most people half her age.

"It was so nice of you to invite me, dear," Mrs. Baron said, patting Macie's cheek as she took off her coat. "I look forward to these community gatherings and it's a shame that most of our neighbors only think to have them in the summertime."

The holidays had to be lonely for the woman. Mr. Baron had passed away several years ago and their only child had been lost in a tragic fishing accident off the coast of Alaska when he was in his early twenties. But the residents of Crystal Cove were such a close-knit group, they had all come to think of Margaret Baron as the community matriarch. It was one of the many things Macie loved about Crystal Cove and made being so far from her own family a little easier.

"Would you like something to drink?" Macie asked as she hung up Mrs. Baron's coat. "I have coffee, tea, and red and white wine."

Mrs. Baron gave her a conspiratorial wink. "I have been known to indulge in a glass of white wine now and then."

Just as Macie finished pouring Mrs. Baron a glass of wine and helping her fill a plate with hors d'oeuvres, the doorbell rang and she hurried to open the door. As she greeted several more of her neighbors, she felt a bit let down that none of the new arrivals was Will.

"Everything looks delicious, Macie," Tom Harris said, his exuberance obvious as he surveyed the buffet table. The man rubbed his round belly. "I've been looking forward to this all day."

"I have, too," Howard Schultz agreed, smiling. "This was a great idea, Ms. Fairbanks." Always the gentleman, Howard refused to call any of the women in the community by their first names.

"I'm thrilled you could join me," Macie said, smiling. "Please, fill a plate with some hors d'oeuvres and enjoy yourselves."

As she continued to welcome her guests, she told herself it was ridiculous to be disappointed that Will hadn't arrived yet. There was plenty of time for him to drop by, and besides, he was just one of many Crystal Cove residents she had invited. If he chose not to attend her party, it was his loss. She and her other guests would enjoy themselves without him. But as the evening wore on, Macie couldn't help but notice his obvious absence.

WILL SHRUGGED INTO HIS coat and, picking up the end of the leash, let Harley precede him onto the dock. They headed for the community dog area.

He had spent the majority of the day waging an internal battle. He had reminded himself of all the reasons why he shouldn't attend Macie's party. But each time, his reasoning seemed a little less convincing.

And yet, staying away from Macie was the best thing for both of them. He had been in a relationship that had ended badly and he didn't want to set himself up to repeat the experience. Not that he thought Macie was anything like his ex-wife. She seemed to support his career, and had been sympathetic of his recent challenges. But when a man gave a woman his heart, she held the power to bring him to rock bottom.

Macie might be the first woman he felt compelled to get better acquainted with since his disastrous marriage, but that could easily be explained. He was a man with a man's needs and he hadn't been with a woman in quite a while. She was easy to talk to, extremely attractive and kissed with a passion that was staggering. It was only natural that he was drawn to her.

Lost in thought as he passed her house, Will was startled when Macie opened her door to say goodbye to an older couple as they left her party. She saw him and waved.

"How's everything going?" he asked, wondering what excuse he could give for not attending. He certainly couldn't tell her that he had decided not to attend because she made him want more from her than just a neighborly friendship.

"It's been wonderful." Her beaming smile made him feel guilty as hell. "I'm happy you and Harley were able to drop by."

Great! She thought he was just arriving for the bash. Now what was he going to do?

He liked Macie, and he didn't want to put a damper on her enthusiasm. And that was exactly what he would end up doing if he didn't come in for at least a few minutes. Short of being rude, he had no other choice. But why did he have to feel so damned happy about it?

"I need to finish walking Harley, then we'll be back," he promised.

"Great." She glanced over her shoulder. "I have to get back to my guests. I'll see you a bit later." She smiled at the Harrises as they walked out of her house and onto the dock. "Thank you for coming. Have a Merry Christmas."

"Thanks for asking us," Meg Harris called back. "Happy holidays to you, too."

"Let me give you a piece of advice, Parker," Tom Harris said as he got closer to Will, his tone conspiratorial as he glanced over his shoulder to make sure Macie had gone inside. "That girl is as sweet as can be, but she can't cook worth a damn. Whatever you do, don't eat the stuffed mushrooms."

Will frowned at the older gentleman. "Why?"

"I'm pretty sure she used the fertilizer they were grown in to make the filling," Tom said. He shook his head as he placed his hand on his round stomach. "And pass on the onion tarts, as well. They look good, but they'll have you reaching for the antacids in the blink of an eye."

"Thanks for the heads-up, Tom," he said as the couple moved on down the dock.

Will would have expected the man to complain if he'd tried Macie's coffee. But he'd assumed since she enjoyed cooking that she was good at it. Will decided he would reserve judgment until he had tried some of the food himself. Besides, he didn't plan on being at Macie's long enough to eat very much. He hurried Harley on to the pet area. The sooner they were back at Macie's, the sooner he could put in an appearance and then leave.

Fifteen minutes later, Will raised his hand to knock on the door just as Macie opened it to escort more of her guests out. "I'm glad you made it back," she said to him. "But I'm afraid the party is winding down." She thanked Mrs. Baron and Howard Schultz for coming. "Are you sure you won't take some of this food? There's more than enough left."

"Thank you, dear, but I already have a prior engagement at a friend's house for Christmas dinner," Mrs. Baron said, patting Macie's cheek. "But the food was quite…unique, and everything looked so festive."

Howard's smile was a bit forced. "I appreciate the offer, but I have plans as well, Ms. Fairbanks." As he passed Will, he stopped to pet Harley and advised under his breath, "Drink the wine, but stay away from the food unless you have a death wish."

Will nodded as he and Harley walked into Macie's foyer. Looking around he discovered that all of their other neighbors had departed. How did he always manage to find himself alone with her? More importantly, why wasn't he at all that bothered by it?

"I thought the party would last longer," he said, unsnapping Harley's leash and watching the dog walk over and plop down on the rug by the patio door.

"I suppose they all have plans for tomorrow and didn't want to stay out too late," Macie said, sounding let down. She sighed as she surveyed the table still laden with food. "What am I going to do with all this? Most of it was barely touched."

Walking over to the counter where she had set up the beverages, he poured himself a glass of red wine. "You could freeze some of it."

She shook her head. "I only have the freezer compartment in the refrigerator and there isn't enough room."

It took everything he had in him not to groan when she started worrying her lower lip. Why did he have an overwhelming urge to walk over and nibble on it himself?

Swallowing a big gulp of wine, he took a deep breath and reached for a plate instead. "I haven't eaten dinner yet," he lied. "Maybe I can make a small dent in what's leftover."

She brightened visibly. "Please, help yourself. Do you have plans for tomorrow? I would love for you and Harley to be my guests for dinner." Laughing she motioned at the table. "Heaven only knows, there's enough here to feed an army."

Will didn't answer as he put several different types of hors d'oeuvres on his plate, then selected a small slice of ham. No matter what his neighbors said, he was determined to keep an open mind and judge the taste of Macie's culinary efforts for himself.

"Don't forget to try the stuffed mushrooms," she said, putting a couple of them on his plate. "I added extra garlic and pepper to give them a bit more flavor."

"Did you do that with any of the other dishes?" he asked. That would explain their neighbors' strong reactions to Macie's cooking.

"Yes, I always add a little something extra to everything I make," she said. "I read somewhere that it helps make the recipe your own."

"Interesting concept," he said, eyeing his plate. He

suddenly knew what a condemned man must be feeling when he faced his day of reckoning.

"Is something wrong?" she asked, looking worried when he hesitated to pick up his fork.

He gave her a smile that he hoped didn't give away his apprehension. "I'm trying to decide what to taste first."

There was no getting around it; he was going to have to eat something. But that didn't lessen his trepidation. Macie was his friend; what was he going to say to her if the food was as bad as Tom Harris and Howard Schultz had suggested?

Finally deciding the mushrooms were as good a place as any to start, he took a bite of one of the caps and immediately wished he'd tried something else. If anything, Tom Harris had understated how truly bad they tasted. Taking several gulps of wine to wash the offensive food down, Will looked up to find Macie gazing at him expectantly.

"What do you think?" she asked.

He couldn't have destroyed that hopeful look on her face to save his soul. "They have a very…interesting taste," he said, trying for diplomacy over the truth. "I can definitely taste the garlic."

Hell, there was enough of it in the stuffing to chase away a whole herd of vampires. If that wasn't enough to make his eyes water, the extra pepper she had added cauterized his tonsils.

"While you eat, I think I'll start trying to find a place to put all this food," she said, turning to walk into the kitchen.

While Macie carried a tray of empanadas into the other room, Will decided to take a bite of the ham. It wasn't any better than the mushrooms. How had she managed to screw up ham? Even he could bake a decent ham—all you had to do was heat it up.

Calling Harley over, he pinched off a piece of the meat and held it out for the dog's opinion. It was no surprise when the puppy sniffed it, turned up his nose and walked back to stretch out on the rug.

Will abandoned the hope that anything on the plate was palatable and tried to think of a reason to give her for not eating. While he sat there racking his brain, Macie received a phone call. He gathered from her response that it was her parents in Leavenworth calling to wish her a Merry Christmas. She went into her office to finish the conversation, and he seized the opportunity to scrape the contents of his plate into the garbage disposal.

He was also glad their neighbors had been polite enough to keep their negative opinions of her cooking to themselves and instead made a hasty exit. For reasons he didn't want to contemplate, he hated the idea of anyone hurting Macie. If she learned the real reason everyone had left the party early, she would be devastated.

"Do you want more?" she asked when she returned to the kitchen.

"I'm good, thank you," he said, placing his plate in the dishwasher. "Why don't I help you put the food away and clean up? I'm sure you're dead on your feet from making all of this over the past couple of days."

She nodded. "I am pretty tired."

While he carried trays of food into the kitchen, she put the leftovers in containers and shoved them into every available space in her refrigerator. By the time everything was put away and the dishwasher was started, Will had thought up the perfect excuse for not having to spend Christmas with her.

"About dinner tomorrow, I'm at a crucial point in the coding of the program I'm working on and probably won't be able to make it." It wasn't a lie. He was fast approaching the part of the software where he would need several hours of total concentration.

"I understand," she said.

But she looked so dejected he wanted to kick himself. He'd just been thinking how grateful he was that none of their neighbors had hurt her feelings, then he'd gone and done it himself.

Taking a deep breath, he shook his head. "I might be able to make it if we have a late meal."

Her instant smile and the hopeful expression on her pretty face convinced him he was doing the right thing. "How does eight o'clock sound?"

"Eight is good," he said, returning her smile. When she hid a yawn behind her delicate hand, he called to Harley and reached for his coat. "We'll say good-night. You need to get some rest."

He attached Harley's leash and turned to leave, but her hand on his arm stopped him. "Thank you, Will."

"For what?" he asked, confused.

"You've been a good friend these past few days and I really appreciate it."

The sincerity in her voice and in the depths of her blue eyes sent warmth from the pit of his belly straight to the region below his belt buckle. He couldn't have stopped himself from taking her into his arms if he'd tried.

"I just did what any decent neighbor would do," he said, feeling guilty for trying to avoid her earlier.

But the softness of her body pressed to his filled him with a need that quickly replaced his remorse, and when she leaned back to look up at him, he was lost. "I'm going to kiss you again, Macie."

"I…would like that very much, Will," she said softly as she wrapped her arms around his waist.

Without waiting for either one of them to come to their senses, Will covered her mouth with his. He didn't want to think about the foolishness of his actions or that Macie wasn't the woman for him. With her sweet lips clinging to his, no one had ever felt more right in his arms, and that's all he cared about.

He coaxed her to open for him, and when she allowed him entry, Will tasted heaven. To his surprise, she stroked his tongue with hers. He'd never experienced a kiss more erotic or exciting.

His body responded immediately and with an intensity that made him light-headed. Holding her close, he slid one of his hands along her side to the swell of her breast, then, cupping her fullness, teased the hardened tip through the layers of her clothing with the pad of his thumb. A sense of deep satisfaction spread throughout his chest at the sound of her contented sigh and the tightening of her arms around him.

But Harley must have decided that the humans had paid enough attention to each other because he wedged himself between them, much as he'd done the other night when they'd kissed under the mistletoe.

"I think—" Will had to stop and draw in some much-needed air "—he's trying to tell us something."

He gazed down at Macie and the blush of passion on her creamy cheeks and the faraway look in her expressive blue eyes robbed him of breath. She was as turned-on as he was.

"Th-thank you…for coming to my party," she said, sounding delightfully breathless.

"I'll see you tomorrow evening around eight," he said, brushing back a strand of her strawberry blond hair. Deciding it would be best to leave before he took her back into his arms, he kissed her forehead and stepped away. As he picked up Harley's leash and opened the door, he added, "Merry Christmas, Macie."

"Merry Christmas to you, too, Will."

MACIE STARED AT THE closed door for several long moments. What was she doing kissing Will? She was only setting herself up for even more heartache.

He was the first man to tempt her since Stan had left her with a broken promise and a diamond engagement ring that had turned out to be cubic zirconia. She'd found that out when she'd tried to sell it back to the jewelry store. But as she thought more about the man who'd cast her aside for his willowy secretary, Macie had to admit that Will was nothing like her ex. Stan had been the life of the party and had never cared about his career, while Will worked hard and, until she had gotten to know him better, appeared overly serious. And yet, there was the issue of her job....

Sighing, she turned out the lights and headed down the hall to her bedroom. Maybe it would be better if she called Will to tell him that she was donating the leftover food to the nearest homeless shelter and he would need to make other arrangements for Christmas dinner.

But even as the thought occurred to her, she rejected it. She told herself it would be impolite to invite him and then call to cancel. But the truth of the matter was, she liked being with Will. He was easy to talk to, a good listener and, Lord help her, the best kisser in the entire state of Washington.

CHAPTER FIVE

ON CHRISTMAS EVENING, Macie had the table set and her grandmother's china ready when Will and Harley arrived. Greeting the dog with a hug, she smiled and took Will's jacket to hang on the coat tree.

"I'm reheating some of the leftover food for us," she said, leading the way to the dining area of her living room. "After you left last night, I decided I would donate the rest of it to one of the homeless shelters."

He grimaced for some reason and then asked, "Do you want me to open the wine?"

"I decanted it earlier," she said, placing the decanter on the table. "But you could pour each of us a glass."

"I need some wine after the day I've put in," he said, filling their glasses with the regional merlot.

"Did you achieve as much as you'd hoped on the computer program?" she asked, motioning for him to sit at the head of the table.

"Actually, I got more code written than I expected." His grin reflected his sense of accomplishment. "I should have it done with time to spare before I go back to work after the first of the year."

"Congratulations. I'm sure that's a welcome relief." She smiled. "Now you'll be able to relax a bit and enjoy some of your time off."

He nodded as he sat in the chair she indicated. "It will give me the chance to tweak it and make sure all of the bugs are worked out before it's released. It's something I haven't had the opportunity to do since the cutbacks at the beginning of the year."

When the timer on the microwave went off, Macie started toward the kitchen. "I'll only be a minute or two."

"Do you need help with anything?" he asked.

"Thanks, but I think I have everything under control."

When she brought their plates and set them on the table, Will stood up to hold her chair. Stan had never done that when they'd had dinner together—not even when they went out to one of Seattle's fanciest restaurants.

"Oh, I almost forgot," she said, getting up from the table. Walking over she picked up the long brightly wrapped present she had placed under the tree the day before. "I got something for Harley's first Christmas with you. I forgot to give it to him last night."

"I keep telling you it's his *only* Christmas with me."

She noticed that Will didn't sound nearly as adamant as he had the first time he'd told her he was only fostering Harley. "We'll see." She watched Will remove the bright wrapping paper from the rawhide chew bone with a smile. She had bought the bone the day she'd gone shopping for the party. "I predict that by the first of the year, you'll be filling out the papers to give Harley a forever home."

"You're wrong about that," Will said, smiling back. "But Harley and I thank you for his gift anyway."

Macie sliced one of the stuffed mushrooms on her plate and, spearing a piece with her fork, put it into her mouth. She started to tell Will that if it was a matter of someone taking Harley out during the day, she would be more than happy to pitch in, but the words died in her throat as the biting flavor of the mushroom spread throughout her mouth. Her allergy medication had finally started working and her sense of taste had come back, but now she wished it hadn't.

Reaching for her glass she took a big swallow of the merlot. "Oh, dear heavens, that's awful!" She looked at Will. He was cautiously watching her. "Was it this bad yesterday evening?"

"You didn't eat anything at your party?" he asked instead of answering her question.

"I was too excited to eat during the party and I still couldn't taste anything because of my allergies so I didn't bother." She took another sip of wine to try to wash the offensive taste from her mouth. "Is everything as bad as the mushrooms?"

When Will hesitated and then shrugged one shoulder to keep from answering, Macie felt like a complete fool. "That's why my guests left the party early. I served them the worst food in the world. Why didn't you tell me?"

"I didn't want to hurt your feelings," he admitted. "And you had already served it to your other guests, so I didn't see any point in ruining the evening for you."

Tears filled her eyes. She had never felt more humiliated in her entire twenty-eight years. She had wanted so badly to fit in to the community and they had seemed to accept her. But now? Her neighbors would probably never speak to her again.

Getting up from his seat, Will walked around to pick her up, then sat down in her chair and settled her on his lap. His comforting arms surrounded her, and that was all it took to open the floodgates. Laying her head on his shoulder, Macie sobbed.

She had hoped this Christmas would be an improvement over last year when Stan had called her at her parents' on Christmas Eve to tell her he was leaving her for someone else. But this year was even worse. She had just found out that she wasn't any good at the hobby she loved, and now all of her neighbors were convinced she had tried to poison them. She had thought she was getting better at cooking, but the food she'd served at her party was the worst she had ever made.

"It's all right, honey," Will said, holding her close. "It's not the end of the world. I'm sure it was because of your allergies—you couldn't taste anything."

Sitting up to face him, she shook her head as her tears continued to flow. "You don't…understand. Last year, I had a horrible Christmas…and this year has turned out…even worse. I think I'm going to give up… and stop celebrating the holidays."

"What happened last year?"

"My fiancé ran off to Las Vegas…to marry his secretary."

Will gazed at Macie and wondered if the stupid bastard who'd left her had lost his mind. She was everything a man could want in a woman. She was kind, caring and passionate. Any man would be lucky to share his life with her.

His thoughts might have scared him to death if he had given himself a chance to analyze them, but he was too focused on consoling the woman in his arms. Macie's tears caused a knot to form in his gut. He hated watching any woman cry, but seeing Macie so dejected was more than he could bear.

"That's why you started cooking, isn't it?" he guessed. "You were trying to stay busy to keep yourself from dwelling on his betrayal."

"I was so lonely and hurt," she said, staring at her hands.

Will understood exactly how she had felt. He had experienced the same emotions when his ex-wife had left him for another man. The only difference was that he had thrown himself into his work instead of finding a hobby.

"I'm sorry you had to go through that, Macie." He kissed away the remainder of her tears. "But you're lucky he showed his true colors before you married him. I didn't discover how shallow and deceitful my ex-wife was until we were eighteen months into a two-year marriage."

She nodded. "I suppose you're right. But it's the same pain, isn't it? No matter how long the relationship, it hurts to be told that you aren't desirable, to find out that you could be so easily replaced, so easily discarded by the one person you thought loved you unconditionally."

Whether it was the feel of her soft body against his, the sense that she understood or the overwhelming need to assure her that she was very desirable, Will wasn't sure. But he didn't give a second thought to lowering his mouth to cover hers.

The moment their lips met, a spark ignited in the pit of his stomach and, tracing her lips with his tongue, he sought entry to the sweetness that was uniquely Macie. Teasing her with featherlight strokes, he explored her with a thoroughness that sent heat straight to his rapidly tightening groin. Will shifted her slightly on his lap so that she knew exactly how she affected him, how she made him want her.

Easing away from her mouth, he nibbled tiny kisses along her satiny skin to the shell of her ear. "Never doubt that you can make a man want you, Macie," he whispered as he cupped her full breast with his palm. "Just feel what you're doing to me now—what you've done to me since that first kiss under the mistletoe."

He heard her sharp intake of breath a moment before she leaned back to look at him. "Will, I—"

"It's all right, honey," he said, meeting her intense gaze. "I know you don't want this to lead to anything more and I give you my word that it won't."

But to his surprise, she shook her head. "That wasn't what I was going to say."

His heart came to a screeching halt a moment before it started thumping a fast rhythm in his rib cage like a sultry jungle drum. "What were you about to tell me, Macie?" he asked slowly.

"You make me want you, too." Her throaty admission sent another wave of heat surging through his body.

"Before we take this any further, I need you to know that I didn't kiss you with seduction in mind. I'm not trying to take advantage of you or the situation. I'm not that guy."

"I know, Will," she said, touching his jaw with her soft hand.

"Nothing would make me happier right now than carrying you into your bedroom and making love to you for the rest of the night. But I have to be absolutely certain that's what you want, too." He needed her to understand how important lovemaking was to him. "I'd rather stand in a cold shower until I spit ice cubes than have you waking up tomorrow morning regretting what we shared."

She stared at him for what seemed like an eternity, then rose from his lap to take him by the hand. "My only regret will be if we don't make love."

Will glanced over to make sure Harley was still

sound asleep, then followed Macie down the hall. He had tried to keep his distance from her, but why? Because she might hurt him just as his ex-wife had? Macie was nothing like Suzanne. He had wanted Macie from the moment they met. It was past time to stop running from it and see where their explosive attraction took them. Maybe they could even have a future.…

WHEN THEY ENTERED HER bedroom, Macie's hand trembled as she reached to turn on the bedside lamp. She was nervous. Not because she was unsure about making love with Will, but because there hadn't been anyone before or since her fiancé.

What if she was bad in bed? What if that was the real reason Stan had found someone else?

"What's wrong?" Will asked, turning her to face him. "Are you having second thoughts?"

She caught her lower lip between her teeth a moment before she shook her head. "My former fiancé was the only man I ever—"

"You're feeling a little self-conscious." The understanding in his deep voice made her warm all over.

"Yes," she said. "What if the reason Stan left me was because I'm not very good at lovemaking?"

Taking her hands in his, Will sat on the edge of the bed and pulled her down beside him. "You're a passionate, caring woman, Macie. Stan was likely the one with the problem." He gave her a kiss so tender that it sent a shiver of anticipation coursing through her body. "Taking things slow and discovering how to give each other pleasure is one of the most enjoyable aspects of making love."

There was a promise in his green gaze as he reached up to release the top button on her silk blouse, then lifted her hands to do the same with his shirt. By the time the lapels of his shirt and her blouse were free, Macie was quite breathless. She never would have imagined that the simple act of unbuttoning a man's shirt could be so erotic.

Needing to fulfill the fantasy she'd had the day she saw him in boxer shorts, she placed her palms beneath the Oxford cloth and skimmed them over the width of his shoulders, brushing his shirt aside. The warmth of his skin and the light sprinkling of hair on his broad chest thrilled her as she mapped every ripple and bulge, just as she'd imagined doing.

Will closed his eyes as her hands moved over his pectoral muscles and his flat nipples. But when she traced the ridges of his abdomen and the thin line of hair arrowing down to his navel and below, his sharp intake of breath stopped her.

"I'm either doing something wrong or something very right," she teased.

Will opened his eyes and the temperature in the room went up at least ten degrees as he gave her a meaningful smile. "You're doing just fine, honey," he said, his tone slightly rough. He slowly took off her blouse and tossed it on the floor to join his shirt, then reaching behind her, he unfastened her bra. "In fact, you're doing such a good job, I think it's time I treated you to some of the same."

He slid the thin straps of her bra down her arms, and Macie held her breath in anticipation of his touch. When he cupped both of her breasts with his large hands, her heartbeat took off as if she was running a marathon. Her nipples beaded into tight nubs as he caressed and teased, and she had to press her lips together to keep from moaning aloud. But when Will splayed his hands on her back and lowered his head to take one of the tight tips into his mouth, she couldn't stop the sound of her pleasure from escaping. But instead of interrupting the mood, it seemed to encourage him. Kissing his way across the valley between her breasts, he treated her other nipple to the same sweet torture.

Bracing her hands on his shoulders, Macie let her head fall back and reveled in the need that Will was building inside of her. She had never felt as cherished as she did in that moment.

"You're so sweet," he said, raising his head to kiss his way up the slope of her breast to the rapidly beating pulse at the base of her throat.

"You're driving me insane," she said, wondering if that sultry female voice could really be hers.

His dark chuckle sent goose bumps shimmering along her skin. "Honey, we're just getting started. Believe me, it's only going to get better."

Macie wasn't sure how the delicious sensations could possibly intensify. Nothing that she and Stan had shared even came close to the feelings that Will was creating within her.

He stood to remove their shoes, then made quick work of stripping off his jeans and boxer briefs, and she had to remind herself to breathe. The sight of his full erection caused a thrilling need in the most feminine part of her and at the same time she felt slightly intimidated by it.

He must have noticed her fascination with his body because he pulled her to her feet, placing his index finger beneath her chin to raise her head so that their eyes met. "It's going to be all right, Macie. We're going to take things slow and easy."

His words reassured her, and deciding she needed to

concentrate on getting her wobbly legs to support her, she placed her hands at his trim waist to steady herself. He reached behind her to lower the zipper at the back of her tailored black pants, skimming his hands over her sensitized skin. A tremor of need ran the length of her. But when he slid the black linen and her silk panties down her trembling thighs, she yearned to feel his hands on other parts of her body, as well. Stepping out of her clothes, she used her foot to shove them over to join the rest of the mingled pile of clothing on the floor.

Will caught her to him then and the feel of his male flesh against her feminine skin, the strong evidence of his desire for her caused her legs to fail completely. She had never experienced passion so strong or so urgent.

Pulling back the comforter, he eased her onto the bed, then reached into the pocket of his jeans for a small foil packet before joining her. She realized as he tucked the condom under the pillow that she'd been so caught up in the moment, she hadn't given a second thought to protection. Thank goodness he had.

"You're so beautiful, Macie," he said, drawing her to him. He pressed his lower body to hers, causing her to shiver with longing. "I'm going to love you so completely that by the time I'm finished there won't be a doubt left in your mind about how desirable you are."

He lowered his head and as their lips met, Will moved his hand from her waist to her hip, then down her thigh. The anticipation of his gentle touch was driving her crazy and when he found her, then parted her to stroke and tease, Macie thought she might ignite from the heat flowing through her veins.

Needing to touch him as well, she caressed the strong muscles along his side, then down his lean flank. When she took him into her hand to measure his length and girth, she was rewarded with a low groan rumbling up from deep in his chest.

"Honey, your hands on my body feel damned good," he said through gritted teeth. "But you're going to destroy my best intentions if you keep that up." Capturing her hands in his he shook his head. "I don't want to rush this."

It was her turn to shake her head. "Will, I can't take much more. If you don't make love to me soon, I'll burn to a cinder."

He smiled and reached beneath the pillow for the foil packet. "Tell me if you need to slow down," he said, kissing her until they both gasped for breath.

"I promise," she said, needing him inside her. "Please make love to me, now."

Rising over her, he nudged her knees apart then guided himself to her. At the first touch of his blunt tip, she closed her eyes and waited for him to make their bodies one.

"Open your eyes and look at me, honey," he said.

When she did as he commanded, Macie lost herself in his heated green gaze as he pressed his hips forward and slowly, carefully entered her. He filled her completely then gently began to rock against her.

His tender lovemaking was the most beautiful thing she had ever experienced, and she soon dissolved in the haze of passion surrounding them. All too soon his rhythmic thrusts began to work their magic and her tiny feminine muscles began to tighten as she raced toward the pinnacle they both sought.

Will deepened his strokes and Macie suddenly felt the tight coil of need deep inside set her free. As wave upon wave of pleasure flowed through her, she felt his body go still a moment before he surged into her one final time. Locked in each other's arms, together they rode out the storm of mutual release.

CHAPTER SIX

THE FOLLOWING MORNING just before dawn, Will eased out of bed and began separating his clothes from Macie's. Glancing over at her, he smiled. She was still sleeping peacefully and he was tempted to get back in bed and make love to her again. Her responsiveness to his touch was mind blowing, and if he had anything to do with it, they would be making love again. The sooner the better.

But Harley was waiting in the other room to go out and Will needed to take care of him before he went back to his place for a shower and a change of clothes. Then he intended to return and make breakfast for Macie. He told himself the reason he wanted to make coffee and cook breakfast was to avoid having to tell her that her coffee tasted worse than swamp water. That was much easier to admit to than his need to make her feel special by serving her breakfast in bed. That sounded too much like a man who was on the brink of entering into a full-fledged relationship.

An hour later, as he let himself and Harley back into Macie's house with the key he'd found hanging by the door, Will was pleased to see she was still asleep. Quickly cleaning up the remnants of their dinner the night before, he located a tray in one of the cabinets and, placing the donuts and coffee on it, carried it to the bedroom. He'd had to revise the breakfast-in-bed plan when Tansy called him a few minutes ago.

Setting the tray on the dresser, he walked over, kicked off his shoes and lay down beside her, taking her in his arms. "Wake up, honey."

"Are we going to make love again?" she asked, snuggling against his chest.

He kissed the top of her head as he held her close. "I wish we could, but I had to get up to exercise Harley and I got a call from Tansy Dexter, the director at The Haven. They're having an issue with the software I wrote for their adoption records and they need me to come over and check it out."

"How long do you think it will take to fix?" she asked, leaning back to give him a quick kiss.

Macie's spontaneous affection caused a warmth deep in his chest. His ex-wife had never bothered kissing him unless they were going to make love. In hindsight, he realized she had viewed it as more of an obligatory gesture than a show of desire or affection for him.

"I don't think I'll be gone more than an hour or two." He sat up and, getting out of bed, walked over to get the tray. "I intended to make breakfast, but after the call from the shelter, I went to the coffee shop a couple of blocks from here. I hope you don't mind coffee and donuts to start your day."

"You're so thoughtful. I didn't…expect…"

He set the tray across her lap and noticed a tear in her eye. Will reached up and wiped it away, then tilted her chin up until their gazes met. "What's wrong, honey? Why are you crying?"

"This is the nicest…thing anyone's ever done…for me," she said haltingly. "The only other time anyone served me breakfast in bed…was when I was ten and my mother brought my meals to me when I had the chicken pox." She sniffed back her tears and gave him a watery smile. "Thank you."

"After last night, it's the least I could do," he said, taking a sip from one of the cups of coffee. "I'm afraid I didn't let you get a lot of sleep," he said, grinning.

She blushed, her cheeks coloring a rosy pink. She had never looked prettier.

"Did you hear me complaining?" she asked, smiling.

As they ate the donuts and drank the coffee, Will asked, "What do you have planned for today?"

"I have some writing that I need to get done and then I'm going to clean out the refrigerator and throw away all of that horrible food from the party." The rose on her cheeks deepened. "I still can't believe what a disaster my cooking turned out to be. I'll never do it again."

"Don't beat yourself up over it," he said, kissing her forehead. He couldn't seem to stop himself from finding every possible excuse to kiss and touch her. "I'm sure you'll get better."

She shook her head. "If I do attempt to make something, I'm following the recipe and forgetting about making the recipe my own." She grinned. "And I'll only cook when I'm sure I'll be able to taste what I've made before subjecting others to it."

"That might be a good place to start," he agreed.

She stared thoughtfully at her half-eaten donut. "But I should probably get another hobby. Maybe I'll buy a book and some yarn and try my hand at crochet or knitting." She laughed. "If I screw that up, at least I won't be making anyone sick."

"Nope. Instead, you can make sweaters with three arms or socks with no toes," he teased.

Laughing harder, she picked up a donut and stuffed it into his mouth. "Hush or I'll make my first pair of toeless socks for you."

He swallowed the donut and chuckled. "And I'll wear them, even if my toes get frostbitten."

Her expression turned serious as she took a drink of coffee. "You would, wouldn't you?"

"Since you haven't made them yet, I don't think it's an issue," he said, wondering where she was going with the question.

"But you *would* wear them." She placed her cup back on the tray. "You were going to eat more of that horrible food last night, just to prevent my feelings being hurt, weren't you?"

He nodded.

"And you wouldn't have complained."

"No."

She set the tray aside and threw her arms around his neck. "You are, without question, the sweetest, most caring man I've ever met, Will Parker."

"I didn't say I was looking *forward* to eating the food," he said, hugging her back.

"It doesn't matter." She touched his cheek, sending a wave of heat straight to his groin. "If I had thought it tasted all right, you would have suffered through it for me and not said a word."

His cell phone chirped, intruding. He glanced at the screen. "It's a text from Tansy at The Haven."

"While you answer that, I'm going to take a quick shower," she said, getting out of bed to enter the adjoining bathroom. "I'll only be a minute."

He sent a message back to Tansy to tell her what time he'd be there to fix the glitch in the adoption records program. Then Will carried the tray back into the kitchen.

Looking over to see how Harley was doing on the rug he had claimed as a suitable place to snooze, Will panicked. The puppy was nowhere in sight. Checking the entrance door and finding it securely locked, Will couldn't imagine where the dog could be. Macie's houseboat wasn't *that* big.

As he tried to figure out where Harley had wandered off to, Will noticed that the door to Macie's office was ajar. Breathing a sigh of relief, he walked in to discover the puppy lying on some scattered papers, happily chewing on the rawhide bone Macie had given him for Christmas.

"Harley, you're about to get us both in a lot of trouble with Macie," Will said, kneeling down to scratch behind the dog's ear. "You'd better go back to your rug in the living room while I pick up these papers you've knocked off her desk."

In answer, Harley got up and, taking the chew bone with him, ambled out of the room, leaving Will to deal with collecting the sheets of paper.

As Will picked up after Harley, he noticed some of the words were crossed out and others added in red ink—probably Macie proofing her work and making corrections.

He picked up the last sheet of paper and read the byline that leaped off the page at him.

He was a fool.

Macie was the columnist who had ripped his programs to shreds in *Techno Nerd Monthly.* The very woman he had spent the most incredible night of his life making love to was *Ms. Tera Byte.*

"WILL?" MACIE CALLED as she walked down hall.

Where was he? She had only been in the shower a few minutes. Surely he hadn't left without telling her.

"I'm in your office, *Ms. Byte*."

A terrifying chill slithered down her spine. *He knows who I am,* she thought, her world crashing down around her.

"Will, I can explain," she said, hurrying into the room. "I couldn't—"

"I don't want to hear it, Macie," he said, his voice bitter. He was standing by her desk holding the rough draft of her latest column. He was furious. "The time for your confession has come and gone. You should have told me who you were several days ago when I complained to you about your columns." He shook his head as he tossed the papers onto her desk and turned to face her. "You must have laughed your ass off at me after I left."

"No, Will. It wasn't like that," she said, shaking her head. She had to get him to listen to her. "I was going to tell you—"

"Save it, honey," he said as he walked out of her office. "Come here, Harley."

He snapped the leash to the dog's harness, then reached for his coat.

"Please, Will, if you'll just listen—"

"I'm not interested," he said, opening the door. "I thought you were honest, I thought you respected me and my work. I was wrong. Goodbye, Macie." The quiet click of the latch sounded more final than if he had slammed the door behind him.

Tears spilled down her cheeks as Macie stood in her living room, wondering how everything could have gone so very wrong, so fast.

The confidentiality clause had prevented her from

revealing who she was to him that day. The threat of losing her job had been powerful motivation to keep the secret.

But she knew that wasn't the whole truth. She could have made the time, should have told him she was his nemesis before they slept together, even if she risked being fired. Maybe they could have talked about it, resolved the issues he had with her reviews and made love without her deception coming between them.

About to collapse, she sank down onto the couch, covered her face with her hands and sobbed.

What was wrong with her? Was she destined to be rejected by every man she fell in love with?

She stopped crying and sat up straight. She loved Will? When had that happened? How had it happened?

She had only intended to be his friend. But she should have realized after that first kiss under the mistletoe that they were destined to be more than friendly neighbors.

Initially she had been attracted to him because of his good looks and impressive physique. But the more she got to know him, the more she realized what a special man he was—how kind and caring. He had eaten the worst food ever to grace a table without a word of complaint just so she wouldn't feel bad. And nothing had ever felt as right or as natural as making love with him. He had filled her body and become part of her soul.

Then, after the most incredible night of making love to her, he had treated her like a queen by bringing her breakfast in bed. He had even apologized that it was only coffee and donuts.

Who wouldn't love a man like that?

Her heart felt as if it had been shattered into a million pieces. Will Parker was the type of man who came along once in a lifetime. The type a woman could search for all of her days and never find. And she had just ruined any chance that he would ever love her in return.

WILL WASN'T IN THE MOOD to deal with a computer glitch in The Haven's adoption records program, but he had promised to fix it, and never broke his word. Besides, it beat the hell out of sitting at home, wondering how he could have let Macie play him for such a fool.

"You're lucky, Harley," Will said, glancing in the rearview mirror at the dog crate in the back of his SUV. "You've been fixed, you never have to worry about some cute little collie or poodle tying you in knots."

Even as the words left his mouth, he winced. He sure as hell wasn't going to get "fixed," but he definitely wasn't going to let a woman get under his skin again. He had loved two women in his life and they had both laughed at him and deceived him.

His heart stalled, then started beating at his rib cage like an out-of-control jackhammer. He didn't love Macie. Nobody fell in love that fast, did they?

But as he thought about his family's marital history, he had the sinking feeling that it was indeed possible. His grandparents had gotten married less than two weeks after being introduced, and his parents had tied the knot within a month of their first date.

Parking his Jeep in front of The Haven, Will got Harley out of the back and led him up the steps of the picturesque Victorian. He suddenly wanted to get to the bottom of the problem with the program, slap a fix on it and get back home. He needed time and solitude to analyze his feelings for Macie and decide how to rid himself of them.

"Good morning, Will," the receptionist said as he entered the reception area.

"Hi, Faye, I hear the adoption software is acting up." He looked around, but didn't see the director. "Is Tansy in her office?"

"Go on. She's expecting you," Faye said, waving him toward the back as she reached to answer the ringing phone.

Harley hesitated and Will wondered if the dog was afraid he was being returned to the shelter. "It's all right, buddy," he said, patting the pup's wide head. "You're stuck with me for another week."

When they reached the director's open door, Will knocked on the frame. "Are you ready for me to check out the program?" he asked.

Tansy Dexter stood up and motioned for him to sit in the chair behind her desk. "We've noticed it duplicates entries, though it doesn't happen every time. I'm afraid I won't be able to catch all of the duplications and correct them manually, and as a non-profit our records have to be impeccable."

Will nodded. "Otherwise it looks as if you're padding your success rate of finding homes for the animals."

"Exactly," Tansy said. "We could lose our funding."

"I understand," he said, sitting down in front of her computer and loading the program. He wasn't surprised that Harley got as close to the chair as he could and lay down. It had become a ritual for the dog to lie at Will's feet when he was working.

Going into the log files, he scanned for errors and checked his code to confirm that his algorithms were correct. Finding the bug, he quickly implemented the fix, then ran a unit test to insure he had repaired the problem.

How could he have missed something so simple? He had tested the program at home before turning it over to The Haven and it had run perfectly. But he'd been short on time and had only run the program once or twice. With extended use, it had failed to perform correctly.

"That should take care of it," he said, looking up at Tansy. "Is there anything else the program's been doing that it shouldn't?"

"No, other than the duplications, it's worked beautifully. We can't thank you enough for developing it for us," she said, beaming. "Now, if we could get donations for the new roof just as easily, I might be able to sleep at night."

"Are you getting close to your goal?" he asked, hoping they were. With the amount of rain that fell on Seattle, it was imperative to have a roof that didn't leak.

"Let's just say we're closer than we were, but we can't call the contractor just yet." She sighed. "But I can't do anything about it until after the first of the year, so the top priority on today's 'worry list' is ensuring we have enough money to meet the day-to-day expenses of The Haven."

"It sounds like a headache," Will said, meaning it. He didn't want to think what might happen to the animals if The Haven ran out of money.

"So, how are you and Harley getting along?" she asked as she bent down to pet the dog.

Telling her about Harley's ability to open doors with lever handles, Will laughed. "I've nicknamed him Harley Houdini."

"Oh, my, I'll have to make a note of that," Tansy said, grinning. "That's something his adoptive parents will need to know when we find him a forever home." She gave him a beseeching smile. "You wouldn't be interested in sharing your life with a big teddy bear of a dog, would you?"

"'I *am* tempted to keep him," Will said, realizing it was true as he reached down to stroke Harley. He hadn't intended to become attached to the pup, but Harley was easy to bond with and Will had a hard time imagining his life without the dog. "But it wouldn't be fair to him," he said, regretting that he couldn't keep Harley. "I'm gone all day and there wouldn't be anyone to take him for walks until I got home."

She nodded. "I understand, but had to ask."

Rising to his feet, Will picked up Harley's leash and started toward the door. "I'll let you get back to it. If you run into any more problems, don't hesitate to call me."

"I will, and thanks, Will," Tansy said, already sitting down behind the desk to get back to work.

Making a mental note to donate more to the roof fund when he brought Harley back after the New Year, Will left The Haven and drove the forty-five minutes home to Crystal Cove.

He had a lot of thinking to do and the sooner he got started sorting out his feelings for Macie, the better.

CHAPTER SEVEN

FOR SEVERAL DAYS, Will agonized over Macie and her reviews of his software. He hated to admit it, but most of her comments had been right on the money. He *had* been making mistakes, and whether they were minor bugs or not, they were stupid errors that he should have caught. The bottom line was, he had been rushing jobs in order to take up the slack at Snohomish Software Solutions, and the quality of his work had suffered.

He also couldn't seem to stop missing Macie. He felt empty without seeing her every day. Somehow she had managed to get past his defenses with little effort. All she'd had to do was flash that cute little smile of hers and the battle had been lost. He might have tried telling himself that he wanted nothing to do with her, but he had known from the beginning that she was special. That what they shared was special. Otherwise, he would have thrown away her invitation to the Christmas party without a second thought and forgotten all about her.

But Macie Fairbanks was hard to forget. She was everything a woman should be—soft, curvy and so damned responsive to his touch. His body hardened at the memory of what they had shared on Christmas night. In their entire five-year relationship, he had never experienced even a fraction of the passion with his ex-wife that he had shared in that one night with Macie. But what's more, she respected him. She'd been the one person to believe in him so much that she had told him the truth.

But could he have fallen for her so hard, so fast?

It certainly hadn't been that way with Suzanne. He had taken two years to propose, and if he was completely honest with himself, he wouldn't have been all that upset if she had turned him down. When he thought of asking Macie to marry him, a painful knot twisted his gut at the idea that she might say no.

Damn! He had to be losing what little sense he had left if he was fantasizing about proposing to a woman he had only known for a week.

Will took a deep breath, then another. Even if he was in love with Macie, he wasn't sure he could get past that she'd intentionally hidden her identity from him. They'd talked about her alter ego's negative reviews of his software and she hadn't said a word about her pseudonym. So how could he ever trust her to be completely honest with him?

He had already been in one marriage that ended because of his wife's lies. He'd be damned before he repeated that mistake.

Will sighed heavily and turned his attention back to the computer screen. Even if Macie had a reasonable explanation for not revealing who she was, it was all water under the bridge now. He hadn't seen her since the day after Christmas, and if he had, she probably wouldn't have talked to him.

"It's probably for the best, Harley," he said, glancing down to where the dog was normally curled up at the side of his desk on a blanket. Except the space was empty.

Calling the puppy, Will went to see where he was

and what he had gotten into. But panic began to grip him when he couldn't find the dog.

A sinking feeling formed in the pit of his stomach as Will walked into the living room. The door was standing wide open. Harley had let himself out of the house again.

Not bothering to put on a jacket, Will grabbed the leash and ran down the dock calling the puppy. Nothing. As he approached Macie's house at the end of the dock, he hoped the furry traitor had decided to pay her a visit. Every time they had gone to the pet area across from her place, Harley had tried to pull Will over to her door as they passed by.

Ringing the doorbell, he waited impatiently for Macie to answer. When she did, he didn't bother with pleasantries. "Is Harley with you?"

"No, I haven't seen him," she said, her tone cautious.

He rubbed the tension building at the back of his neck as he looked up and down the dock for any sign of the puppy. "I must have failed to set the lock properly when we came back from our last walk."

"Have you checked the parking lot and the pet-friendly section?" she asked, shrugging into her coat and joining him outside.

"Not yet, I was hoping he was here with you," Will said, his trepidation growing with each passing second.

"While you check the parking lot, I'll see if he's in the pet area," she said, pointing across the dock.

As she hurried one way, Will took off at a run in the other. When he found no sign of the dog, he was filled with a mixture of relief and dread. He was glad the dog wasn't in the parking lot, but still concerned that he might have wandered off down the street or worse yet, been run down by a car on the busy street beyond.

Retracing his steps to the dock, he spotted Macie running toward him. Her worried expression told him that she hadn't found Harley, either.

"No luck?" she asked.

"No."

"Where could he be, Will?"

He shook his head. "I don't know, but I can't just stand here, I have to find him. It's going to be dark soon."

Macie scanned the perimeter of the floating home community. *Wait,* she thought when she spotted a black-and-white dog at the far end of the small cove. "Is that him?"

"Thank God." Will sprinted in the direction she had pointed. "Thanks for the help," he yelled over his shoulder.

"Thanks for the help, Macie," she repeated, making a face. "I'll accept your assistance to find the dog I let get out of my house, but I won't listen to anything you have to say."

She quickly looked around to see if any of her neighbors had witnessed her little display of temper. If they had, they probably thought that she had lost her mind after eating too much of her own cooking.

As she waited for Will to bring Harley back from the woods, she wondered how she was going to be able to live in the same community with him. Seeing him come and go every day, running into him occasionally in the parking lot, or passing him on the dock was going to be sheer torture.

She'd come to terms with the fact that she had fallen in love with Will, and that nothing would ever come of it. How could it?

Relationships couldn't be built when there was a huge

lack of faith. It was clear that Will had trust issues and combined with a good amount of male stubbornness, it made for an insurmountable obstacle between them.

Macie sighed. It would be easy to place all of the blame on him. But she couldn't. She had her fears, as well. The other morning when Will had left, it had reminded her that she wanted a man she could count on to be there for her, not one who walked away at the first sign of a problem or disagreement.

When Will finally returned with a wet, muddy Harley in tow, she was waiting for them. "You're going to need help giving him a bath," she said, falling into step beside them.

"Thanks, but I can handle it," he insisted.

She huffed at his stubbornness. "Really? As big as he is, you're going to be able to hold him in the shower and shampoo the mud out of his coat at the same time?"

"I'm going to try," he said, opening his door.

Macie laughed when he dropped the leash and Harley immediately made a beeline for the carpet in the living room. Lying on his back, the dog began to roll, then stood up and shook. Mud flew everywhere.

"Oh, yes. You're doing a fine job on your own, Mr. Parker," Macie said, not even making a halfhearted attempt to mask her sarcasm.

Will looked fit to be tied as he caught Harley and hauled him down the hall. "Don't just stand there. Close and lock the door, then come into the bathroom to hold his leash while I get the water going."

"I thought you didn't need my help." She couldn't help but grin as she secured the door then followed him into the guest bathroom.

"Just hold on to him and keep him from slinging any more mud," he said, turning on the shower.

When he had the water adjusted to the right temperature, Macie handed him the leash and turned to leave. "Have fun."

"Where are you going?" he asked, frowning.

"I assumed I had fulfilled your command and am no longer needed," she said, enjoying the chagrin on his handsome face.

"Look, I'm sorry," he said, struggling to get a reluctant Harley under the spray of water. "You were right." He took a deep breath as he hefted fifty pounds of squirming puppy into the shower stall. "There, I've said it. Now will you please grab the dog shampoo from the cabinet and start scrubbing the mud out of his coat? I'm drowning here."

Laughing at the sight of Will's hair plastered to his head and the water dripping off of his chin, Macie grabbed the bottle and squirted it over the dog. "Were you anticipating something like this?"

He frowned. "No. Why do you ask?"

"You're only supposed to be fostering Harley for a couple of weeks," she said, squeezing in beside him to work the shampoo through the dog's coat. "Why do you have dog shampoo?"

"My grandmother gave it to me about six months ago when she started needling me about getting a dog to keep me company," he answered.

And why did you keep it, Will?

A half hour later, she, Will and Harley emerged from the bathroom, wet from head to toe. "Do you have stain remover?" she asked. "While you dry him off, I'll see if I can get the mud out of your carpet."

"On the shelf above the sink, along with some disposable rags," he said, briskly rubbing down Harley's coat.

Once she had cleaned up the carpet and wiped off

the spots on the walls where mud had landed, she put on her coat and turned to go, but with her hand on the door handle, she stopped. She was going to have her say, whether Will liked it or not.

"Not that it makes a difference," she said, facing him. "But there's a confidentiality clause in my contract with *Techno Nerd Monthly* prohibiting me from revealing that I'm *Ms. Tera Byte*. That's why I didn't admit that I was the reviewer you despise that day. I like to eat and pay my mortgage. And I didn't tell you before we had sex because all I could think about was how much I cared for the man holding me. The last thing on my mind was the magazine or the reviews of your programs."

Without waiting for him to respond, she opened the door and stepped out onto the dock. As she walked home, she felt better that he knew everything, but extremely saddened by the fact that he hadn't tried to stop her when she left.

Pulling her coat around her, Macie took a deep breath to keep from sobbing. She was renewing her moratorium on men. And this time, it would be permanent.

On the evening of New Year's Eve, Will took a shower, put on his suit and tie, then checked his watch. An hour before midnight and he had plans. If everything worked out the way he hoped, he would have good reason to celebrate the New Year. But only if the woman he loved was able to find it in her heart to forgive him.

Tucking an envelope into the inside pocket of his suit jacket and a small velvet box in his trouser pocket, he picked up the bottle of champagne he had chilled earlier and called to Harley. "Let's hope she'll forgive me and doesn't throw us both off the end of the dock," he told the dog as they left the house and started walking toward Macie's.

A few minutes later, waiting for Macie to answer the door, Will took a deep breath. He had some serious apologizing to do and he just hoped Macie would listen to him. He hadn't been willing to listen to her the morning he discovered she had been the one reviewing his software. He deeply regretted that, and if she gave him the chance, he would spend the rest of his life listening to every word she had to say.

When she opened the door, Macie looked confused. "What are you doing here, Will? It's almost midnight. Is everything all right?"

"I hope so." He smiled. "Do you mind if Harley and I come in?"

"I wasn't expecting company," she said, clearly reluctant to let him in.

"We need to talk," he said, allowing Harley to nose his way past her.

"Well, I suppose it's all right," she said, standing back for him to follow the dog inside. "What's this all about?" She was dressed in a fuzzy pink robe, matching fuzzy slippers and a flannel nightgown, and he had never seen her look prettier. "Why are you wearing a suit and tie?" she asked, frowning. "Are you drunk?"

"No, I'm as sober as a judge, but I was hoping you would help me and Harley bring in the New Year," he said, walking into her kitchen to put the champagne in the refrigerator. He noticed the inside compartment was practically empty with no signs of any food prepared by Macie.

"You dressed up to walk fifty yards to my house in order to ask me if I would help you celebrate the

New Year?" she asked, staring at him as if he had lost his mind.

"Yup." He stuffed his hands in his pockets to keep from reaching for her as he watched Harley amble over to stretch out on the rug by the patio door. "And I also wanted to talk about my refusal to listen to your explanation."

She closed her eyes a moment, then she looked directly at him and shook her head. "Will, there isn't anything left to say. I told you why I couldn't reveal my identity as the reviewer and why I had to adhere to my contract. Accept it or don't. It's the truth and I'm not going to apologize for protecting the only income I have."

"I'm not asking you to apologize to me, Macie." He stepped closer. "After you left yesterday evening, I had a lot of things to think about, and there isn't a doubt in my mind that if I had been the one under a confidentiality clause, I would have done the same as you."

She wrapped her arms protectively around her waist. "When you condemned me without hearing what I had to say, you hurt me deeply, Will." The emotional pain he heard in her voice just about tore him apart.

"Honey, I'm sorry for being such an ass, and I'm sorry for causing you even a second of emotional pain." Unable to keep from touching her, he reached out and drew her into his arms. "Like most people who've gone through a divorce, I have some baggage."

"I understand that," she said quietly against his chest. "As you learned the other night, I have some of my own."

"But I think we overcame yours," he said, kissing the top of her head. "We never got around to discussing mine."

She leaned back to look up at him. "I assume by your reaction that she didn't have faith in you, that she betrayed you."

He nodded. "My wife lied about everything—the money she spent, the men she had affairs with after we got married. The only thing she didn't lie about was how little she thought of my job. She called me a hack and a drone and a bunch of other things I won't repeat. That's why those reviews were so cutting to me."

"I'm sorry," Macie said, her tone reflecting her sincerity. "But first, I didn't lie to you. There's a difference between being dishonest and omitting information. And contrary to what you might believe, I wasn't keeping my secret to laugh at you behind your back. You are good at what you do, Will, that's why I was hard on you."

"I know that, honey." He raised his hands to cup her face. "I guess she made me overly sensitive to any kind of criticism."

"In other words, I added another bruise or two to your ego," she said, looking thoughtful.

"I'm afraid so," he agreed. "And after busting my rear end, day in and day out, to take up the slack at Snohomish, your reviews pointing out the flaws in the software I developed irritated an already raw nerve."

She nibbled on her lower lip, trying to digest what he had told her, and he almost groaned. He loved kissing her and wanted to nibble on her perfect lips himself.

"I understand, and I have to take some of the responsibility for aggravating that nerve," she finally said, surprising him. "I could have phrased some of my comments differently and been less frivolous with my remarks about you losing your edge. I took a cheap shot to boost the popularity of my column. I'm truly sorry for doing that, Will."

He shook his head. "No, you were right the first time. I've been on the verge of burnout for a while and I've been making mistakes you would expect from an entry-level programmer, not a senior project manager."

"But I shouldn't have—"

"Hush, Macie," he said, lowering his mouth to hers. They could debate the issue later about which one of them was more at fault.

Kissing her with everything he had been trying to suppress for almost a week, he let her taste his need and the desire he had for her alone. By the time he raised his head, she looked a bit dazed and he was harder than the Rock of Gibraltar.

"Can you forgive me and overlook my stubborn male pride, honey?"

"Yes, but only if we promise…never to keep secrets and…to always be honest with each other," she said, sounding more than a little breathless.

"Honey, you have my word that I'll keep my end of that bargain," he said.

Her forgiveness was a rare and precious gift. A gift that he didn't deserve, but one that he intended to spend the rest of his life cherishing.

"There's something else we need to talk about," he said, smiling at the woman who had broken down his carefully constructed walls and claimed his heart.

She looked a bit cautious. "What's that?"

He tucked an errant strand of her strawberry blond hair behind her ear. "You'll probably think I'm crazy, but I love you, Macie Fairbanks."

"Oh, Will!" She threw her arms around his neck. "I love you, too." He had suspected as much, but hearing her say the words was a balm to his soul.

Checking his watch, he grinned. It was five minutes

till midnight. Time for him to seal the deal and start the New Year with a new beginning for both of them.

As he held her with one arm, he reached into his pants pocket to retrieve the little black velvet box. Then dropping down on one knee, he opened the top. "I love you with every breath I take, Macie. Will you marry me?"

He knew a moment's panic when she remained silent. Then she lightly touched the solitaire diamond with trembling fingers. "It's so beautiful, Will."

"Is that a yes?" he asked, needing to hear her say the word.

"Absolutely," she said, starting to nod. Tears began to stream down her cheeks. "I love you so very much. Yes, I'll marry you."

Taking the ring from the box, he slipped it on the third finger of her left hand, and rising to his feet, he took her into his arms. "The ring is a little big, but we can have it sized to fit," he said, beaming at the woman he was going to spend the rest of his life with. "And now that you're officially going to be mine, I've got an engagement present for you."

"Will, I didn't expect—"

"Don't thank me just yet," he said, laughing as he reached into the inside pocket of his suit jacket. "You might decide to throw me overboard."

"I doubt that," she said, her smile filled with a love that humbled him.

He handed her the envelope. "You haven't seen what I've got here, honey."

"I'm sure I'll love whatever it is." She opened it and her laughter sounded like a beautiful melody. "I can't believe you've signed me up for cooking lessons at the community college."

"I want to support the pursuit of your passion," he said, grinning.

She gave him a quick kiss. "No, you just want to be assured that what I cook is edible."

"Well, there is that," he said, happier than he had ever been in his life. "I've also decided to quit my job at Snohomish Software and open my own company."

"Really?"

He nodded. "I have a good reputation in the software industry and enough connections that I should have no trouble finding work." Kissing her, he added, "And it will give me more time to spend with you."

"Oh, Will, I love that you're going to be taking it easier," she said, giving him a kiss that just about sent him into orbit.

Harley chose that moment to nudge between them, then looked up as if to ask, "What about me?"

Will gazed at Macie. "What do you think?"

She bent down to hug the big puppy's neck. "Do you really have to ask?"

EPILOGUE

WILL PARKED IN FRONT of The Haven and Macie turned to smile at him. "Do you have the check?"

He nodded and patted his jacket pocket. "If my calculations are right, this should put them over the top of their goal for the new roof."

"If it doesn't, I'll see if I can get the magazine to make a donation," she said, smiling.

She got out of Will's SUV, then waited as he released Harley from his newly purchased canine seat belt in the backseat. Together they walked up the steps of the shelter with the dog and entered the reception area.

"This is my fiancée, Macie Fairbanks," Will said, introducing her to Tansy Dexter, The Haven's director, and Faye Barnard, the receptionist.

Once they had all exchanged pleasantries, Will gave Macie a smile filled with such love that she had to blink back tears of happiness. "We've got two things we need to do, Tansy," Will said.

"You're going to adopt Harley, aren't you?" the woman guessed, her grin one of delight.

"Yup, give me the paperwork," he said.

"Your grandmother is going to be thrilled when she returns from Hawaii and finds out you're giving him a forever home," Faye said as she started keying in information into the computer.

"We would also like to make a donation," Macie

said when Will handed her the check from his pocket. "If this isn't enough to meet your goal for the new roof, please let me know and I'll see what I can do about soliciting a donation from the magazine I work for."

Tansy's eyes widened a moment before she grabbed both Macie and Will to give them huge hugs. "The Home for the Holidays campaign was a huge success and now we've got more than enough to repair the roof and build the second Kitty Condo. Thank you so much." She sniffed, fighting tears. "We'll be able to help so many animals with this."

"We're happy to help," Will said, as he signed the papers to make Harley theirs. "We wouldn't have this big teddy bear of a dog if not for this shelter."

Pointing to the Christmas tree in the corner with paper angel ornaments, Macie added, "Maybe you can use the extra to meet the special needs of this year's angel tree."

Tansy nodded. "Believe me, it won't go to waste. We use every spare dime we get on the animals."

Will handed Macie the pen for her to sign the adoption papers. "Is there anything else we need to do?" he asked.

Tansy shook her head as she bent down to hug Harley. "Just love him and bring him by every now and then so we can see how much he's grown."

While Will took Harley back to his SUV to strap him into the special seat belt, Macie waited for Faye to hand her their copy of the adoption papers. "Harley was the one who brought Will and me together," she said, smiling at Tansy.

"Really?" Tansy laughed. "That seems to have been the order of the day this holiday season. Just before

Christmas, my fiancé, Ben, and I were brought together by a cat with health problems."

"And don't forget one of our transport volunteers, Shelby Conrad and her husband, Alex. They were having some serious marital problems that they worked out while taking some of our dogs to their new forever homes," Faye added, winking as she handed Macie the papers making Harley her and Will's dog.

"I'm glad things worked out for all of us." Turning to go, she added, "I hope you run the fostering campaign again next Christmas."

"It's been such a success this year, I'm sure we will," Tansy said, waving.

As Macie walked out to Will's SUV, she looked up to find the man she loved more than life itself watching her with an adoring smile. Smiling back, she hoped The Haven did make their Home for the Holidays fostering campaign a yearly tradition. Then maybe more couples would find what she and Will had found through the love and companionship of a shelter pet—a forever home.

* * * * *

The Humane Society of the United States (HSUS—www.humanesociety.org/) estimates that between six and eight million cats and dogs enter U.S. shelters every year. Happily, three to four million of those pets are adopted. But that still leaves two to four million animals waiting for their forever home.

For more information on adopting a new friend from a shelter, visit HSUS's The Shelter Project at theshelterpetproject.org.

Alternatively, both of the following rescue and adoption websites allow you to type in your zip code, and even specify species, breed and age of pet you would like to adopt:

Petfinder.com: www.petfinder.com

Adopt-A-Pet: www.adoptapet.com

Also according to HSUS, less than two percent of lost cats and between 15 to 30 percent of lost dogs are reunited with their owner. Here are some tips to help reunite you with your lost pet:

- Collars and tags are the fastest way to reunite you with a lost pet. But if your dog slips its collar...
- Microchip your pet and keep information up to date, including a cell phone number. If you lose your pet while traveling, a cell phone number can be particularly helpful if the dog is found.
- Make flyers and include a current photo—and don't forget to post the flyers online, as well.
- Check pet lost-and-found networks such as:

Missing Pet Network: www.missingpet.net

Lost Pet USA: www.lostpetusa.net

Lost Dog Finder—Find Fido: www.fidofinder.com

And lastly, check your area shelters for your missing pet—and check again. Sometimes weeks can pass before a stray animal is brought into a shelter. Check with neighboring county shelters, too.

"Saving one dog won't change the world, but it will change the world for that one dog." ~Anon

Happy holidays,
Vicki, Cathy and Kathie

REQUEST YOUR FREE BOOKS!
2 FREE NOVELS PLUS 2 FREE GIFTS!

ALWAYS POWERFUL, PASSIONATE AND PROVOCATIVE

YES! Please send me 2 FREE Harlequin Desire® novels and my 2 FREE gifts (gifts are worth about $10). After receiving them, if I don't wish to receive any more books, I can return the shipping statement marked "cancel." If I don't cancel, I will receive 6 brand-new novels every month and be billed just $4.30 per book in the U.S. or $4.99 per book in Canada. That's a saving of at least 14% off the cover price! It's quite a bargain! Shipping and handling is just 50¢ per book in the U.S. and 75¢ per book in Canada.* I understand that accepting the 2 free books and gifts places me under no obligation to buy anything. I can always return a shipment and cancel at any time. Even if I never buy another book, the two free books and gifts are mine to keep forever.

225/326 HDN FEF3

Name	(PLEASE PRINT)	
Address		Apt. #
City	State/Prov.	Zip/Postal Code

Signature (if under 18, a parent or guardian must sign)

Mail to the **Reader Service:**
IN U.S.A.: P.O. Box 1867, Buffalo, NY 14240-1867
IN CANADA: P.O. Box 609, Fort Erie, Ontario L2A 5X3

Not valid for current subscribers to Harlequin Desire books.

Want to try two free books from another line?
Call 1-800-873-8635 or visit www.ReaderService.com.

* Terms and prices subject to change without notice. Prices do not include applicable taxes. Sales tax applicable in N.Y. Canadian residents will be charged applicable taxes. Offer not valid in Quebec. This offer is limited to one order per household. All orders subject to credit approval. Credit or debit balances in a customer's account(s) may be offset by any other outstanding balance owed by or to the customer. Please allow 4 to 6 weeks for delivery. Offer available while quantities last.

Your Privacy—The Reader Service is committed to protecting your privacy. Our Privacy Policy is available online at www.ReaderService.com or upon request from the Reader Service.

We make a portion of our mailing list available to reputable third parties that offer products we believe may interest you. If you prefer that we not exchange your name with third parties, or if you wish to clarify or modify your communication preferences, please visit us at www.ReaderService.com/consumerschoice or write to us at Reader Service Preference Service, P.O. Box 9062, Buffalo, NY 14269. Include your complete name and address.

HDES11B

SPECIAL EDITION

Life, Love and Family

NEW YORK TIMES BESTSELLING AUTHOR

DIANA PALMER

brings you a brand-new Western romance
featuring characters that readers have come to
love—the Brannt family from Harlequin HQN's
bestselling book *WYOMING TOUGH*.

Cort Brannt, Texas rancher through and through,
is about to unexpectedly get lassoed by love!

THE RANCHER

Available November 13 wherever books are sold!

Also available as a 2-in-1
THE RANCHER & HEART OF STONE

HARLEQUIN *Presents*

When legacy commands, these Greek royals must obey!

Discover a page-turning new Harlequin Presents®
duet from *USA TODAY* bestselling author

Maisey Yates

A ROYAL WORLD APART

Desperate to escape an arranged marriage, Princess
Evangelina has tried every trick in her little black book
to dodge her security guards. But where everyone else
has failed, will her new bodyguard bend her to his
will…and steal her heart?

Available November 13, 2012.

AT HIS MAJESTY'S REQUEST

Prince Stavros Drakos rules his country like his
business—with a will of iron! And when duty demands
an heir, this resolute bachelor will turn his sole
focus to the task….

But will he finally have met his match in a world-
renowned matchmaker?

**Coming December 18, 2012,
wherever books are sold.**

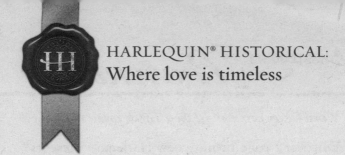

HARLEQUIN® HISTORICAL:
Where love is timeless

Fill your Christmas with three tales of warriors,
Vikings and passion with author

MICHELLE WILLINGHAM

IN THE BLEAK MIDWINTER

It's a year since Brianna MacEgan's husband was killed, and she
remains coldly obsessed with avenging his death. But Arturo de
Manzano is intent on distracting her with his muscled fighter's body.

THE HOLLY AND THE VIKING

Lost in a snowstorm, Rhiannon MacEgan is rescued by a fierce
Viking. Her lonely soul instantly finds its mate in Kaall,
but can they ever be together?

A SEASON TO FORGIVE

Adriana de Manzano is betrothed to Liam MacEgan, a man she
absolutely adores. But she's hiding a terrible secret.

Look for

Warriors in Winter

available November 13 wherever books are sold.